My Woman His Wife:

20 Year Anniversary Edition

My Woman His Wife:

20 Year Anniversary Edition

Anna J.

www.urbanbooks.net

Urban Books, LLC
300 Farmingdale Road, N.Y.-Route 109
Farmingdale, NY 11735

My Woman His Wife: 20 Year Anniversary Edition
Copyright © 2004 Anna J.

ISBN 13: 978-1-64556-669-4

First Trade Paperback Printing December 2024
Printed in the United States of America

10 9 8 7 6 5 4 3 2 1

This is a work of fiction. Any references or similarities to actual events, real people, living or dead, or to real locales are intended to give the novel a sense of reality. Any similarity in other names, characters, places, and incidents is entirely coincidental.

Distributed by Kensington Publishing Corp.
Submit Orders to:
Customer Service
400 Hahn Road
Westminster, MD 21157-4627
Phone: 1-800-733-3000
Fax: 1-800-659-2436

This special reedition is a celebration of Urban Books Publishing's twentieth anniversary. We are bringing back into the fold some of our earliest novels, as well as other favorites of street literature. This reissue of *My Woman His Wife* is a classic by Anna J, the first in a beloved series about the complexities of marriage. When couple Jasmine and James invite another woman into their bedroom, the story that follows is lusty, dramatic, and riveting from start to finish.

In the two decades that have passed since the origin of Urban Books, we have played a hand in launching the careers of *Essence Magazine-* and *New York Times-* bestsellers and continue to bring the hottest up-and-comers into the fold. A lot has changed in those twenty years in the landscape of publishing, for better or worse. From the bottom of my heart, I want to extend a thank you to all of our loyal readers, old and new. Whether you have been rocking with Urban since 2003, or you picked this book up by chance at your local bookstore, we couldn't do this without you.

As we celebrate our twenty-year anniversary, you can expect to find new editions of your favorite Urban Books originals by beloved authors like Ashley & JaQuavis, Roy Glenn, La Jill Hunt, Chunichi, and more. Be on the lookout for these hot new covers to add to your collection.

Sincerely,

Carl Weber
Founder and Publisher, Urban Books LLC

Also By Anna J

Novels

The Aftermath
Get Money Chicks
My Little Secret
Snow White: A Survival Story
Hell's Diva: Mecca's Mission
Hell's Diva: Mecca's Return
My Woman His Wife 3: Playing for Keeps
Exposed: When Good Wives Go Bad
The Double Cross
The Double Cross 2: Shot's Fired
The Serial Wife

Anthologies

Stories To Excite You: Menage Quad
Morning Noon and Night: Can't Get Enough
Fetish
Fantasy
Flexin' and Sexin: Sext Street Tales Vol. 1
The Cat House
Full Figured 4
Full Figured 15
Bedroom Chronicles

Independent Projects

Lies Told in the Bedroom
Motives 1& 2
Erotic Snapshots Volumes 1-6

Acknowledgments

I've always been an avid reader. My love affair with books began from the time I could comprehend words. I can vaguely remember writing my first short stories in elementary school, and *Love Jones* sparked the poet in me right after I graduated from high school. My infatuation for stories has been a lifelong thing. It's like breathing to me.

I remember reading books by Sister Souljah, E. Lynn Harris, Zane, and James Earl Hardy, amazed at their skill set. I also remember constantly saying to myself that there was a story that I wanted to read, but no one had written it yet. I decided to take on the task, and while working my night job I wrote *My Woman His Wife*. I was 22 years old, not really knowing what I was going to do with my life, and an avid reader who wanted a story that wasn't yet in publication. It took me six months to write the story, and I sat on it for two years before I showed it to Mark Anthony, the owner of Q-Boro books, whom I had met at my twenty-fourth birthday party. I recall emailing him when I got to work on Monday because the story was saved on my work computer. I had only sent him the first three chapters to see if he even wanted to read it in entirety. When I got to work on Wednesday I got a call from Mark asking me if the book was done. On Friday I had a book deal and became the first lady of Q-Boro Books. On January 6, 2004, *My Woman His Wife* hit the shelves, and it was on and popping ever since.

Acknowledgments

I still can't believe that was twenty years ago! Twenty years ago I felt a void in the book industry and was brave (or foolish) enough to think I could fill it. With the encouragement of my family and peers in the industry, we got out there and moved major units, traveled the globe, and put *My Woman His Wife* on the map. Every Black Friday, I along with authors like Treasure E. Blue, K'Wan, and Eric S. Gray would go down to Norfolk and do book signings all weekend. Those were the days! Back when we used to be hype about the Harlem Book Fair. I'm so happy to be here twenty years later to celebrate it.

I want to thank all of you for embracing my crazy and welcoming Monica into your hearts and homes. Her character is so wild, I was able to take her story and write her into other books that you all have loved over the years. Some of y'all are still asking for more Monica! My heart is so full knowing that people are still enjoying my baby, this being one of my greatest accomplishments. Thank you to all of the people that only need to see my name on the book, and don't hesitate to pick it up. That's major! Thank you to all the author friends I have made over the years, and I am very appreciative for everyone that gave me the courage to embark on celebrating Monica, James, and Jasmine again!

If this is your first time reading this story, I truly hope you enjoy it. It's continued in *The Aftermath,* and *My Woman His Wife 3.* Monica's shenanigans continue in *The Serial Wife.* If this is a reread for you, welcome back. I took some time to go back through the story and fill in some things that I felt were missing the first time I wrote it. I hope you enjoy the additions I've made to the story, and that you are pulled in the same as you were before.

Thank you to everyone that has ever held me up, picked me up, and carried me throughout the years in the industry and beyond. It gets wild in these book streets, and it's not for the weak. I haven't always felt my strongest, but I've always had the love of many to keep me together.

Mrs. Dynita Maddox, you get me. I know it doesn't seem like you do because I'm super difficult to deal with, but I promise you through it all you've made it all make sense. I haven't always been the best spouse to you, but you've always stood beside me. Even when I blatantly told you that you didn't. Thank you for staying. Thank you for sticking it out. Thank you for dealing with my crazy. I love you more than I can ever tell you, and you might see some Sponge Bob Legos (insider, LOL) in your future as a thank you for tolerating my shenanigans. After you get that car situation handled, but we not going to talk about that here. LOL.

Heather Butler, I know I don't even have to say it, but you know I love me some you. You've been rocking with me since day one, and I appreciate you more than I can ever show you. People don't even know that most times before I post anything, I'm in your inbox or texting you like, "Sis, how this look?" Thanks for always being solid, and I appreciate you.

Atoiya Williams . . . sis. You came at a time when I was at my lowest and vulnerable, and you showed me who I was again because I forgot along the way. Thank you for picking me up and not telling everybody that you had to. Wednesday mornings at 7 a.m. hit different because of you. I love me some you, babe! I really can't thank you enough, but overall I thank you for being kind and not being judgmental. I was just Anna to you. Not an author, not a creative, just a regular person that needed to empty my brain out so that I could start living again. You're truly a lifesaver.

Diane Rembert, you already know what it is with me and you. It was you who brought me back to the literary world because I was done with it. We had a simple conversation, and you was really like, "But don't you want to write another book?" Thank you for always being there literally just a phone call away no matter the hour. You hold me down in ways no one would ever be able to understand, and they don't need to. Thanks for being your authentic self, which allows me to easily be who I am with no pretense. You are the bomb! I love you, sis!

Kevin Dwyer, you came through with the edits! Thank you so much for helping me out with this. When I originally wrote this book, I had no clue what I was doing, and I wrote it in first and third person. Transitioning it all to read as a first-person narrative had me stressed out, but you came through and saved the day. I really can't thank you enough, and I will be requesting to work with you on future projects.

Now before I start getting all emotional and shit (because I'm a damn crybaby), I'm going to let y'all go ahead and get into these pages. Thank you, God, for the gift! Thank you all for your support, and be sure to leave a review!

In the Beginning . . .

Chapter One

Jasmine

Imagine that, imagine that, imagine that, imagine . . .
At five foot two, 136 pounds, dark chocolate skin, and almond eyes, sexy Monica was standing over me topless in a red thong, giving me one hell of a show. My girl was popping it like she was trying to get rent money and she only had two days left to scrape it up. You would think there was a pole in the center of the bed the way she was rotating and grinding her body to the beat of the music. Heavy on the guitar, the sound making her body contort in ways that shouldn't be possible. She was a professional and knew how to reel me in. It was more than her body though, but we'll get into that later.

My eyes were fixed on hers as she did a sensual butterfly all the way down until the lips of her vagina kissed my stomach, leaving a wet spot where they landed. She bent over, and a tattoo spelling her name in neat cursive peeked out over the band of her thong. She took her right nipple into her mouth and caressed the other as she continued to move to the beat of the music. Her body seemed to shimmer as light from outside landed on her skin, making her almost glow. She worked up a light sweat, making her glisten a little in the sparsely lit room.

Stepping off the bed, she bent over to remove her thong, afterward hooking it onto my foot. A double-headed dildo magically appeared as she crawled toward me. My legs spread invitingly when her lips made contact with the space behind my right knee. I heard R. Kelly hyping it up with the guitar, making the love of my life sweat just a little more, and my body was shaking in anticipation for what was to come. She had yet to disappoint me, and I'd bet my last dollar that today would be no different.

Well, the second love of my life. While I was lying here, legs spread-eagle, playing with my clit, I couldn't even fully get into it because I should have been at home with my husband and two kids. Yeah, you heard that right. A bitch was married, but I was out in these streets acting single. I could have just gotten up and gone, but I didn't feel like the drama and tears I had to see every time I was ready to leave. Monica was so damn dramatic sometimes, and today I just didn't have the energy to do it with her. I knew in my heart that I had no damn business being here in the first place, but I was thinking with my pussy in anticipation of all the wonderful orgasms I would have. Shit at home died down a long time ago, but it wasn't until I found myself lying here looking up at another woman's breasts that the guilt set in. I'd been here many times, but today it just hit different, and I felt like crap about it.

It wasn't supposed to be like this. I knew I should be at home making love to my husband, but he wasn't producing multiple orgasms like Monica. She did things with her tongue no one has written about yet. She had ways of making me have blinding explosions that left my brain scattered. My husband had no idea on how to even find the spot, and I could forget about him lasting all night. The five minutes he gave me I could do myself with just a flick of my middle finger in the right spot. I needed satisfaction that my own hands didn't produce, and Monica gave me what I needed without any questions. Well, maybe some questions, but that's beside the point. Stay focused.

I didn't want to have to tell my partner what I wanted. After all these years, he should already know what made me cum. *If you're going to hit it from the back, put a finger in my asshole or leave a handprint on my ass cheek. Take it with one of my legs on your shoulder while you use your thumb to play with my clit. While I'm riding, take both of my nipples into your mouth at the same time. Hell, I like it a little rough sometimes. Toss me around a little bit. Choke me out. Do something besides pound me all hard for five minutes then roll over and fall asleep.*

Then if that weren't enough, this fool wanted to invite company into our bedroom! The blackassity of a minute man killed me every time. He could barely handle me alone and he wanted company? He was very bold for that move, but I agreed to those shenanigans, and that was why I was in this mess now. If nothing else, know for sure that once a person *shenans* once, they will *shenan*-again!

It all started about two months before the twins' fourth birthday. It had already been eight months since my husband and I had so much as fondled each other, let alone had any actual sexual contact. We were literally passing each other like ships in the night, merely escaping colliding into an iceberg. I tried to pretend like I was unfazed by it, moving along with raising our children like our lack of bedroom action didn't matter, but the truth is I wanted to get fucked. Good at that. Not this mediocre shit I was getting from James's tired ass. He had been on my last nerve about having a threesome with some chick he'd met from God knows where, and I was about tired of hearing it. All I got was five minutes. What was he gonna do? Break it down to two and a half minutes between the both of us? He must have been suffering from hallucinations from sitting up in that news station all day or something. And what the hell were this girl and

I supposed to do? She could eat all the cat she wanted to, but I didn't get down like that! Never did. Never would. Wasn't about to start.

Back in the day, my husband and I made love constantly. It was nothing to be bent over the kitchen counter getting served from behind. He would be stroking me from the back with one finger playing with my clit, and the other in my asshole while kissing me on my neck and talking dirty to me all at the same time. I loved a man who talked dirty, and he had the gift for real. Talking me through an orgasm was probably the best thing you could do for me in life. I would ride him in the dining room chair until my legs hurt, and he would then pick me up and lay me on the table, devouring me from feet to head, and not necessarily in that order. He liked for me to hold my lips open so that my clit stood right out as he simultaneously sucked on it and fingered me with three fingers the way I liked it. I would lean up, and watch his tongue go to work, sopping me up sloppily until I squirted in his face. He didn't mind it at all and would just lick the mess up while still teasing my overly sensitive clit. My body would feel like it was on fire, and I loved every minute of it.

All of that stopped for one reason or another, and I didn't feel like fucking him or this girl he was trying to sell me on. It got to the point where this fool started leaving notes around the house, practically begging me to jump on board. One night he tried to show me a picture of the girl, and I just snapped the hell out. What part of no didn't he understand, the "n" or the "o"?

"Babe, just hear me out," he said, pleading on his knees at my side of the bed. "You won't even listen to what I have to say."

I remembered the days when he would be on his knees on my side of the bed, only my legs would be thrown over his shoulders as his lips and tongue would have me squirming and begging for mercy. Right then, the sight of him was contributing to my already-pounding headache.

"James, I done told you fifty thousand damn times that I'm not doing it, so why do you keep asking me?" I almost reached up and throat punched his ass. He was working the little bit of nerve I had left, and I just wasn't in the mood for this. He didn't even realize that I was ready to bust him in the head with the alarm clock. Why wouldn't he just go to sleep?

"Because you're not keeping an open mind."

"Would you want me to bring another dick into the bedroom? A little friendly competition?" I asked and waited for a reply. It was always some double standard with men. They wanted what they wanted, but when you flipped the script, all of a sudden they were mute. He looked at me like I was crazy and got up to go on his side of the bed.

That shut his ass right up, if only for a second. I was so damn tired of hearing about this Monica chick. I was ready to just go ahead and get it over with so he would just shut the fuck up about it. This entire scenario was making me sick to my stomach. What his dumb ass didn't realize was I might have gone along with it just to please him, but I'd be damned if I would be pressured into doing anything I wasn't down for. *We aren't teenagers. We are grown, and I will not be bullied by my spouse to have sex with strangers because essentially that's what this is.*

"So, is doing it in the bedroom the problem?" he asked in a desperate voice.

"What? Didn't I just tell you I didn't want to talk about it?"

"I'm just saying that if your concern is bringing her into our home, I could easily get us a room over at the Hyatt or the Marriott."

"James, how do you even know this girl? What kind of shit are y'all into over at TUNN?"

I was guessing this fool couldn't see the big-ass pile of salt on my shoulders. *If this were a cartoon, steam would be coming out of my ears right about now.*

"My buddy Damon hooked it up for me. It's his wife's sister or something like that. They do it all the time."

"He fucking on his sister-in-law, too? What kind of shit they into over there?" I asked, my face showing the disgust of what I just heard.

That only made me wonder what kind of freaky shit her family was into. I didn't know too many people just putting their own flesh and blood out there like that. Was Damon doing both the wife and the sister and just passing her off to us? Or as a collective, this was just some shit they were all into. My head was swimming just thinking about the many scenarios, and none of it made me feel better about it. It all sounded absolutely ridiculous to me, but James's slow ass was game for anything apparently.

"No," he said, just as irritated, putting his head in his hands. "Not with his sister, with other women."

"What do you know about her, James? This chick could be HIV positive for all we know. There is no cure for that!"

"We would all be using protection," he said as if he was offended. *Shit, I'm offended he won't let it go.*

"Will she be putting a condom around her mouth?" I asked. "Semen and saliva can carry the same shit."

"Here you go taking the conversation to another level. Why can't you just relax and enjoy life for once? It's only this one time."

"What I'm about to do is enjoy this six hours of sleep. Good night!" And with that said, I turned my behind over and went to sleep. Enjoy life? Was this man serious? I was five seconds from enjoying bashing his damn skull in, but I digress. The headache I was trying to avoid was slowly creeping in, and I did my best to fight it off so that I could get some sleep.

Of course it wasn't over. When I woke up, James was in the shower. As much as I hated to go in the bathroom while he was in there, I figured if I could at least brush my teeth, I could shower real quick and be out of the house before he had a chance to come at me with some bullshit. I was hoping he wouldn't bring this Monica shit up at 6:37 in the morning because I would hurt him.

By the time I was done brushing my teeth and cleansing my face, James was stepping out of the shower. Through the mirror I peeked at his toned body and semi-erect penis. At the age of 32, standing at least six feet three inches, he still had the body of a college football player. He was definitely well endowed, but what difference did it make if he was only good for five minutes? He caught my eye as he was drying off, and a sly smile spread across his face as he covered his midsection with the towel and went into the bedroom. I hopped in the shower and lingered a little longer because it was his morning to get the kids ready.

We used to fuck in the shower all the time. Many mornings I woke up early just to ensure we had time to get it in. I closed my eyes as my soapy hands started to roam my body as memories of James banging me against the wall infiltrated my brain. I'd be hanging on to the showerhead for dear life as our bodies would collide under the spray of the water. Many mornings I ended up with my hair brushed into a bun because the water ruined it. When he told me to grab my ankles, I obliged, enjoying the water running over my shoulders and head. The grip he had on my hips was the only thing keeping me standing as he brought me one climax after the next. Those were the good old days, and I briefly wondered what happened to them. I couldn't keep my fingers off my clit as I rubbed one out while I leaned against the back of the shower wall. These days I had to take what I could get, even if that meant me doing it myself.

When I stepped out of the steamy water and into our room, I could still smell his One Million by Paco Rabanne cologne. That made me wet instantly, but he'd never know. I'd just as soon please myself than waste my shower on a few minutes with him. After putting my outfit together and plugging in the flat iron, I was finally able to sit on the bed and moisturize my skin. Out of the corner of my eye I noticed a single yellow rose on my pillow and a piece of heart-shaped chocolate with "I Love You" printed on the foil resting next to it. I smiled but continued to rub my Coach Floral body lotion into my skin.

I loved my husband, and maybe we could talk about this entire Monica thing later. I mean, I wanted spon-taneity, right? I couldn't keep complaining about what I wasn't getting if I wasn't at least trying to get something. Right? All of this shit was exhausting, and I just wanted to be left alone for the moment.

Surprisingly he had nothing to say at breakfast. He smiled a lot, and that just pissed me off. Not that I had any conversation for him, but his being quiet made me nervous. At least if he were talking, I'd know how to vibe off him. He just sat there smiling the entire time, and that just made me suspicious.

When I started gathering my stuff up to leave for work, he already had my briefcase and files along with my lunch stacked all nice and neat in the passenger seat of my 2003 Blazer. I got a kiss on the cheek, and he even offered to take the kids to childcare for me. Something was definitely up, and I wasn't at work for five minutes before I figured it out. I was looking through the files that I was supposed to be working on over the weekend when a hot pink folder that I didn't remember having before caught my eye. When I opened it, a five-by-seven photo of Monica was pasted to the left, and a three-page printout about her was on the opposite side. I was too shocked to be offended.

The pages included her date of birth, zodiac sign, likes and dislikes, a copy of her dental records, last HIV test results, and the results of her gynecologist exam, which I was glad to see were all negative. Her being a Virgo might have piqued my curiosity because I heard they were some undercover freaks and all that shy shit was just a game. Her address and phone number were also included, along with directions on how to get to her house from my job off Google Maps. I had to laugh to keep from being pissed because I was sure my husband was going crazy.

As if that weren't enough, further inspection produced a key card from the Hyatt and an invite to meet him and Monica at the hotel restaurant for dinner. A note, handwritten by James, said the kids would be at his mother's house and I should be at the hotel by 7:00 p.m. I put everything back in the folder and went to my first meeting of the day. I didn't even want to think about that right now, and I would have a few choice words for James later on.

When I returned to my office for lunch, I opened my door to ten bouquets of yellow tulips crowding my space. On my desk sat a bouquet of tulips and white roses mixed in a beautiful Waterford crystal vase. My secretary informed me that they were delivered only ten minutes before I got there, and the card could be found next to the vase on my desk. I was too overwhelmed to think clearly and mechanically walked over to my desk to retrieve the card. It was in a cute yellow and white striped envelope to match the flowers and was written with a gold pen. It read:

> *Jasmine,*
> *You must know that you're the love of my life, and there is nothing in this world I wouldn't do to make you happy. This one time I want us to be happy together. Please reconsider . . .*
> *Love Forever,*
> *James*

In that instant, I knew I would be at the hotel later. If I'm being totally honest, I'd been considering it all day. When I saw her picture and put a face to the name it stayed on my mind during my entire meeting. I figured this one time wouldn't kill me, and it might spice up our love life so that it would be like it used to be. I hoped I wasn't making the biggest mistake of my life by doing this. After gathering my thoughts, I went on with the rest of my day trying not to think about what I would be getting into later. I had a trial at two o'clock that I had to go to, and on my way there I mentally checked my schedule to make sure I would be out of the office by five and chillin' in the suite by five thirty. That way I could freshen up and put on something sexy for dinner.

I got out of court at four thirty, having had my client's charges dismissed. That made me feel great, and I planned to take the next two days off to celebrate. When I got back to the office, my secretary was smiling at me and holding a vase with what looked like two dozen powder pink roses accompanied with another card. She gave them to me and offered to open my office door because my arms were full. When I walked in I almost dropped the bouquet I was holding because I was totally surprised. As if all the yellow tulips weren't enough, my office was now crowded with just as many powder pink and white roses and seemed to triple as I got farther inside.

"Someone is either madly in love with you or is apologizing. Whatever it is, let me know your secret," my secretary replied as if she really wanted an answer. I just turned to her with a smile on my face, stepped to the side, and closed my door. We were not cool like that, and now wasn't the time to start.

I set the bouquet on my desk next to the one I received earlier. There was nowhere for me to sit, so I walked over to the picture window so that I could gather my thoughts while I looked down on the city from the twenty-third floor. The envelope holding the card smelled like Pleasures by Estée Lauder. I loved that scent and was pleased to find out someone else did as well. When I opened the envelope and pulled the card out, little gold hearts and stars fell from it. The card was from Monica, requesting my presence at the hotel later. I was flattered and speechless. Maybe she wasn't that bad after all.

"Sheila, have the ladies on this floor come take a bouquet. If there are any left over once they are done, extend the invitation to the other floors. I want everything out before I'm back in the office. You can just leave these two to decorate my office," I instructed as I prepared to leave for the day.

"Absolutely. I'll get on it right now," Sheila replied, getting up to gather the ladies on our floor. A line quickly formed with smiling faces as each lady took a bouquet out. I left before they were done, knowing Sheila would lock my door once the flower parade was over.

I counted fifty flower arrangements. I didn't need that many. No one wanted to come back to a bunch of dead flowers. All of these flowers were taking up way too much space, and I really didn't have anywhere to put them all. On my way to my Jeep I called to check up on the kids before stopping at Victoria's Secret for something sexy. I wanted this to be a night to remember since it was a one-time thing. I wanted it to be perfect and was prepared to pull out all the tricks.

I decided on a cranberry spaghetti-strapped one piece with matching thong. The gown was ankle length with thigh-high splits on both sides, and the front dipped down all the way to my navel. The back opened to the middle of my back, showing off my curvaceous size ten, even after a set of twins. I purchased a bottle of Breathless perfume and a pair of sandals to match, then made my way to the hotel.

When I got to the suite a little flustered from sitting in traffic longer than I expected, I was taken aback by the decor. I didn't think that I would make it in time and started getting a little antsy. As I rushed up to the room, I was making a plan to get ready quicker than I originally anticipated, and it added to the already-nervous energy that I had about the evening ahead. Pink and white rose petals decorated every inch of every room and floated in the Jacuzzi on top of rose-colored water. Yellow tulips sat in crystal vases around the living room and bedrooms, and Maxwell's *Urban Hang Suite* played softly in the background from invisible surround-sound speakers. A mixture of pink and white rose petals and yellow tulip petals covered the California king–sized bed. A bottle of Passion Alize sat in a crystal ice bucket accompanied by three long-stem wineglasses on the end table closest to the bathroom door. On the other a glass bowl was filled with condoms of different textures and colors.

A note was tucked into the mirror in the bathroom with instructions to meet my dinner guests in the dining room at seven o'clock sharp. It was already six thirty, judging by the clock on the bedroom wall, so I stepped up the game as I showered, dressed, and did my hair in record time all while not disturbing the romantic setup.

I was walking into the dining room at five of seven. The waiter sat me in a cozy booth away from the other guests with a glass of Moët and a yellow tulip and a powder pink rose courtesy of my husband and Monica. At seven sharp my dinner guests walked in. I briefly wondered where they were all this time since I had the suite all to myself to get ready. Did Monica have a room here too? Were they engaged in anything sexual before getting here? It was taking everything I had to stay seated, and before I could bail out, I just took a sip of my drink and held my breath, releasing it calmly. Tonight was going to be a good night. It had to be.

James was sharp, dressed in cream linen slacks with dark chocolate gator shoes that matched perfectly with the button-down shirt with different shades of browns and tans swirled through it, compliments of Sean John fashions. His wedding band glistened and shined from the door, and the light bounced off it all the way across the room. I could smell his cologne way before he reached the table.

Monica was equally impressive in a short, champagne-colored one piece that showed off perky breasts and fell just above her knee. The bottom of her dress had that tattered look that people are wearing nowadays, and it accented her long chocolate legs. Her toes peeked out of champagne stiletto sandals, and her soft jet-black curls framed her face. Her makeup was flawless, and she smelled sweet.

I stood up as they made their way to the booth, and I couldn't stop staring at them. When my husband and Monica reached the table, he gave me a soft, lingering kiss on my lips that made me wet instantly. He hadn't kissed me like that in months. Monica gave me a soft kiss on my cheek, and James made sure we were both seated before he took his.

Before we could start conversing, the waiter was at our table with appetizers. We were served seafood-stuffed mushrooms and Caesar salad with glasses of Moët to wash it down. I glanced over at my husband periodically and couldn't believe the thoughts I was having. For the first time in months, I wanted my husband the way a woman wants her man, and I couldn't wait to get upstairs.

"Did you get the roses I sent you?" Monica asked between small bites of the crab-stuffed mushroom she was eating. She had the cutest heart-shaped mouth that made you want to kiss her. Her tongue darted out every so often to the corners of her mouth to remove whatever food or drink was there. That turned me on and made me wonder how her tongue would feel on my skin.

"Yes, thank you. They were nice."

"Did you enjoy the tulips?" my husband asked, his eyes never leaving me. "I know yellow is your favorite color."

Tonight, he looked different. Kind of like he was in love with me all over again. His eyes twinkled with mischief, and his lips begged for me to kiss him. I wanted to so badly.

"Yes, baby, I did. Thank you."

"You're welcome, baby. How'd your day go?"

Monica, James, and I made conversation over the smoked salmon, wild rice, and mixed vegetables we were served for dinner. Before dessert was served, James and I slow danced to "Reunion" by Maxwell as I watched Monica from the dance floor. She swayed from side to side in her seat, never taking her eyes off me. I didn't know what she did when I wasn't facing her, but when I did, she looked me right in the eye, her facial expressions telling me what I had to look forward to.

As we danced, my husband held me close, his mouth on my ear, singing the words to the song. His warm hands felt good on my bare back as he made small circles, massaging me. I truly felt like this was indeed our reunion because it had been a long time since we'd been like this. I closed my eyes, and I tightened my arms around his neck, enjoying the feel of him in my arms, and me in his.

Slices of double chocolate cake waited for us when we got back to the table. I couldn't touch mine because I was ready to go upstairs. James fed me and Monica his cake off the same fork, and that only made me more excited. I wanted to get this party started, but I went with the flow because I didn't know what they had planned.

"Are you ready for ecstasy, baby?" my husband asked me after we finished dessert. Instead of answering, I grabbed both of them by the hand and led them upstairs.

Chapter Two

Jasmine

Once we got into the elevator, James pulled us into a group hug with my and Monica's heads resting on his shoulders. We looked at each other curiously, probably thinking about how far the other would go. Before I could react, Monica leaned over and kissed me, and it wasn't a peck on the lips, either. She slid her tongue into my mouth, allowing my taste buds to sample the chocolate cake left on it from dessert. Her lips felt soft as she sucked on my bottom lip, then my top, causing a tingling sensation to shoot down my back straight to my toes, and finally resting warmly on my clitoris. My body was buzzing with nervous energy, and I willed the elevator to move a little faster. I wasn't ready just yet, but from the way Monica was moving, I didn't have a choice but to get ready.

I could taste a hint of her cherry lip gloss when my tongue touched the corner of her mouth. A moan escaped my lips when her hand made contact with the left side of my neck, pulling my face closer to hers. I opened my eyes to look at her facial expressions while she kissed me, and to my surprise, she was already watching me. I blushed, a little embarrassed at being caught, but she let me know it was cool by kissing my eyelids. She kissed the tip of my nose and went back to my lips while my husband made small circles on my back with his fingertips. Her kiss was slow and sensual and thankfully not wet and sloppy like most men do. She allowed me to lead, and then I allowed her to teach me what she knew.

My right hand found my husband's erect penis just as we were approaching the fourteenth floor. When I stepped back to adjust my hand around his shaft, the elevator suddenly stopped and the lights went out. We were all stuck on stupid for about thirty seconds before either of us moved. We were on our way to erotica beyond our wildest dreams and the damn elevator stopped! You talking about pissed? I finally got up the nerve to go through with this wild night and here I was stuck in a hot-ass elevator. Oh, how I was *so* not in the mood for this.

"James, do something," I said while slightly hyperventilating. We were stuck between the thirteenth and fourteenth floors, and I wanted out.

"Baby, just calm down. I'll call the service desk to see what they can do," he replied as he stepped from between us to get help.

While James was on the phone, I sat down in the corner to slow my heart rate and collect my thoughts. I didn't know how long we were going to be stuck, and this was not the place to pass out from lack of oxygen. I was hoping to still be in the mood when we got out because at this moment, I wanted to be off this elevator and in my bed.

Just as I leaned my head back against the wall, I felt a pair of warm hands parting my legs. I still heard James on the phone, and my body tensed up because I couldn't believe Monica was trying to sex me at a time like this. Having an orgasm was the last thing on my mind at the moment, and I was almost certain everyone felt the same way. Before I could protest, Monica had my thong pulled to the side and her tongue stroking my clit. Her tongue felt hot on my panic button, and the way she used her fingers made my knees touch the elevator walls instantly. She sucked my clit up into her mouth softly, sliding her tongue back and forth across it, making my breath come in shallow pants. My hips involuntarily ground into her mouth, and she pushed back, snaking her tongue from my opening up to my clit and back down again.

She took her time moving two fingers in and out of me in a "come here" motion that was playing havoc on my G-spot while she sucked, licked, kissed, and played mercilessly with my clit trapped between her lips. My body shook involuntarily because I was trying not to explode. I didn't want to moan aloud while James was on the phone, but it was killing me trying to hold it in. She held the lips of my cave open and her tongue twisted around inside me, my walls depositing my sweet honey on her tongue. For a second, it felt like we were the only two people trapped in that hot box.

"Okay, ladies, the attendant said we'd only be in here for a . . . damn."

When James hung up the phone and looked over at our silhouettes in the dark, he was speechless. I guess the sight of his wife being pleased by another woman shocked him. It wasn't completely dark. The little track lights they had around the edges gave very little light to the room. We couldn't see clearly, but we could see enough to know what was going on.

His back was to us the entire time, so it had to have been a pleasant surprise to see Monica and me the way we were. James never could do more than one thing at a time, so it didn't surprise me that he didn't pay us any mind until he was done with his call.

He stood back and watched for a while, taking in the sights and sounds of what was happening. With the little bit of light coming from the call box, I could see James massaging his strength through his pants. He squatted down behind Monica, lifting her dress up over her hips, exposing her plump ass. My eyes were now adjusted to the dark, and even though I couldn't clearly see what was happening, his outline said it all. I could make out in the mirror on the ceiling of the elevator what was happening right in front of me. Monica was in the doggie-style position with her head buried between my legs. James had inserted his fingers into her walls just as Monica did to me only moments earlier. I could see James maneuvering his body so that he could taste her. In the meantime, Monica was pulling another orgasm out of me.

She moaned against my clit from my husband pleasing her. The more James pushed and pulled on her, the more intense her pleasing me became. I scooted forward so that I could lie flat on the floor. Monica stood up and positioned herself over me. She pulled her French-cut panties to the side and placed her lips on mine. I just imitated what she did to me, switching from kissing and sucking her clit and sticking my tongue inside her. James was inside of me, stretching my walls to fit him.

He stroked me slowly, teasing me with just the head before sliding it all in. His thumb created friction on my clit and before we could stop it, I exploded on his length and Monica exploded in my mouth. We were about to switch positions when the lights came on and the elevator started moving. James pulled out of me still rock hard, making it a little difficult to pull up the zipper on his pants.

When the elevator door opened, the attendant and the security guard were waiting on the other side. They tried to apologize but we just rushed past them and scrambled down the hall to our suite so that we could finish what we started. We didn't think about the fact that they could probably smell sex in the air, and I don't think we really cared.

Upon entry to the room, Monica went to run hot water into the Jacuzzi because the water that was in there got cold. I sat on the side of the bed, anxiety covering me like a blanket. I couldn't believe what I'd just done and what I was about to do. I was excited and scared at the same time. Excited because I was finally letting go of my inhibitions and stepping outside the box. Scared because I didn't want to disappoint my husband.

I'll never do this again, I thought, but I did want him to enjoy this night of pleasure.

Monica came out of the bathroom in her bra and panties. I was hesitant about looking her in the eye because I knew my cheeks were red from blushing. We were all silent, not wanting to be the one to say something first. James changed the CD in the stereo to a slow-jams mix he put together. When R. Kelly started crooning, "Come to Daddy," Monica started doing an erotic dance in front of the full-length mirror. James leaned back on the dresser to watch the show, and I just sat there with a shocked expression on my face. She danced like she had ballet lessons but with just enough eroticism to make you think she might have been wrapped around a pole in a strip club once or twice.

As she got closer to me, I scooted back on the bed to keep her at arm's length. What we did in the dark elevator was cool because I couldn't see it, but now we were in a well-lit room with my husband able to see everything. I wasn't sure if I wanted to go through with it, but when I looked over at James stroking his length and gazing at us, I couldn't stop. Just the fact that he had been hard for more than five minutes was amazing.

The look on my face screamed, "Help," as I looked from James to Monica. Monica advanced toward me slowly, and James smiled as he watched us work. I was now up against the headboard with my legs up to my chest. When Monica reached me, she took my feet into her hands and started to massage them one at a time. I was as stiff as a virgin on her first night, and Monica did her thing to help me relax.

She took my toes into her mouth one at a time. My moans escaped involuntarily. Her soft lips traveled up my thighs until they rested against my pelvis. Her tongue dipped in and out of my honey pot. She held my lips open with both hands, exposing my now-wet pearl to my husband.

"James, can I taste it?" Monica asked my husband in a husky voice. I looked over at him to read his face. It showed nothing but excitement.

"Go ahead and make her cum," he responded in a deep, passion-filled voice. His hand moved at a slow, lazy pace, up and down his erect shaft. A hint of pre-cum rested on the tip of his penis, and I motioned him over to the bed so that I could taste it.

He disrobed on his way over, his body looking like he should be on the cover of *GQ* magazine. Monica had her full lips pressed against my clit, causing me to squirm and breathe heavily. James stood beside the bed with his chocolate penis standing straight out. I didn't hesitate to wrap my lips around him, taking as much in as I could without choking.

James fondled our breasts simultaneously while trying to maintain his balance as I gave him head. Monica held my legs up, and kept her face buried in my treasure chest. Our moans were bouncing off the walls, tuning out the music that was playing. If there were people in the suite next to us, I was sure they heard everything. Monica moved back off the bed and pulled me with her. James lay down in the middle of the bed on his back, his erection pointing at the ceiling. I straddled his thickness like a pro, dipping all the way down until my clit touched his pelvis, then coming back up until just the head was in. James leaned up on his elbows and took my nipples into his mouth one at a time. Monica had my ass cheeks spread so that her tongue could make acquaintance with my asshole. I was having orgasms back-to-back like I used to when me and James first met. I was damn near about to pass out from exploding so much.

We switched positions in order to relax a little more. Monica put on a strap-on vibrator with clitoral stimulators around the base. I looked at her like, *who does she think she is using that on?* She took James's place in the center of the bed and motioned for me to get on top of her. I looked at her and my husband like they were crazy.

"James, I am not getting on her like that. She done . . ." The mood was changing quickly, and Monica was looking frustrated. Ask me did I give a damn. Some shit just ain't meant to be tried, and she was one of them.

"Baby, it's okay. It'll feel just like the real thing. Trust me on this one," James said to me in a calm, soothing voice. I wasn't buying it.

"And what are you going to do with that?" I asked, referring to his erect penis.

"You'll see, and you'll enjoy it. Just trust me."

He gave me a reassuring look as he led me to the bed. I closed my eyes and got on top of Monica, doing to her what I did to my husband. It was feeling good, and I really got into it. When I bent over to kiss Monica, I felt a warm liquid oozing down the crack of my ass. My husband held my back so that I couldn't move, and I could feel him inserting a finger into my forbidden place. I tensed up automatically, and he whispered to me to try to relax.

I didn't do back shots often, and my husband knew that. Literally I'd never taken anything more than a finger from him, so anything bigger than that had me nervous. I wanted to get an attitude, but what they were doing felt so damn good. I reminded myself that it was only one night, and I tried to relax myself so that my husband could join in the fun. I wondered how he was going to fit it in because my husband was definitely blessed in the dick department. He was long and thick, with a big mushroom-shaped head that I knew was way bigger than the hole he would try to get it into. It would be like trying to put a block into a round hole. A finger in the ass was one thing. He could do that all day, but ten inches in the ass was something to scream about.

"James, I don't think I'll be able to take it back there, baby," I whispered. "You're too big."

I was hoping he would have second thoughts when he heard how scared I was, but that wasn't the case.

"Jasmine, I won't hurt you, baby. I'll take my time, and I'm using this so you'll be okay." He held out a bottle of KY Warming Liquid for me to view.

"Won't it get too hot back there?"

"You'll be fine, just relax," Monica responded before taking my nipples into her mouth. A moan escaped from my lips, totally catching me off guard.

I tried to relax as James eased himself into my back door. Lord knows it was killing me, but I stuck in there. He slowly pushed the head in, which was the most painful part. It felt like he was ripping me a new asshole, and tears gathered at the corners of my eyes, threatening to fall and land on Monica's forehead. Once he got in as much as he could comfortably, he began pleasing me with long, slow strokes. In combination with Monica pushing and pulling on the bottom, I was going crazy from the new feelings I was having. When James pulled out, Monica pushed in, causing me to lose my breath on more than one occasion. James reached around my waist and teased my clit while Monica held my lips open for him. His other hand fondled my right nipple while Monica's mouth warmed the other one.

I didn't know whether I was coming or going. Sometime during the mix, the pace quickened and we were going at it like animals. Monica sat on the lounge chair with the vibrator in hand, watching me and James become one. He held me by my ankles, pushing my legs all the way back, my knees touching my ears easily. He was driving his dick deep in me with slow strokes, and I never wanted him to stop.

"I'm cumming, baby," I said to my husband between inhaling and exhaling. "Cum with me."

James slowed it down, and we looked at each other as our orgasms played out. My legs wrapped around him tightly until our rapture subsided. Monica looked spent as she, too, was exploding along with us. James pulled out of me and rested with his head between my breasts while we caught our breath. The session we just had was the best thing since sliced bread.

"I'll meet y'all in the Jacuzzi," Monica replied as we reluctantly untangled ourselves from each other. At that moment, I wanted Monica to leave so that James and I could enjoy our weekend alone, but I didn't want to be rude. I later found out that was mistake number one. The red light was practically blinking right in front of my face, but for reasons beyond even me, I went with the flow instead of stating my wishes. She served her purpose, and now it was time for her ass to go.

We joined Monica in the Jacuzzi a little while later. James popped open one of the Alize bottles, and we sat back and chilled. *Friday After Next* was playing in the DVD player, but I paid it no mind. I wanted some more of my husband, but with Monica there I knew it would be a group thing. We relaxed a little longer, and before the movie was over, we scrubbed each other clean and dried ourselves off.

James had another movie playing in the room while we fell back on the huge bed. He told us of our plans for the next day. Monica would only be with us for tonight. After breakfast, she would be heading home, leaving me and James to enjoy the rest of our mini vacation, which was cool with me because I was ready for her to leave anyway. I didn't see why she had to stay the entire night. I mean, he could have easily put her in a cab and sent her on her merry way. I started to suggest that to James, but I didn't want to spoil the mood. He also made mention of a shopping spree and a couple's spa treatment we would be attending here at the hotel.

I half watched the movie and half played back what went down earlier. Out of the corner of my eye, I took in Monica. She was definitely gorgeous, and I could see why James thought her to be the perfect candidate for our evening of adventure. She had skills and knew what she was doing, but I couldn't help but wonder how much it took for her to be here. Had she and James hooked up before? I tried not to entertain the thought, but it was bugging me. Then on top of all that, I was wondering if I could maybe hook up with her on the low at a later date. She was phenomenal, and I wanted to see exactly what she could do. Maybe it was just the liquor talking, but I was definitely thinking about meeting up with her soon.

We gave each other full body massages and orally pleased each other until we drifted off to sleep. The next morning, we showered together and had breakfast over conversation of our activities the previous evening. When James got up to use the restroom, Monica just kind of stared at me. I wanted to ask her if I had a boogey in my nose or something. For some reason I felt a little uncomfortable.

"So, Jasmine, did you really enjoy yourself last night?" she asked as if she really wanted to know. I answered after watching her tie the stem of a cherry into a knot with her tongue.

"Yeah, it was different. I had fun," I said nonchalantly. I did not want to have this conversation with her. I was still thinking about having her one on one, but I wouldn't dare approach the subject. I was a heterosexual woman. Surely this one event did not change that aspect, or did it? Monica got dirty in the bedroom, and although my mind was telling me to leave it alone, my body was buzzing just being in her presence.

"Well, if you want us to hook up under more private circumstances, you know how to contact me."

"I'll do that," I said coyly, not wanting to show my hand just yet. Just that quickly, I had made up my mind that Monica would get to have me again. I just had to figure out how to go about it without damaging my marriage. Keeping us together was the most important thing to me, and I couldn't let Monica fuck this up for us. We were barely hanging on by a thread as it was.

Just then James joined us at the table. He thanked Monica for a wonderful evening and put her in a cab to go home. I saw the envelope he slipped her, but I decided not to comment on it. I might need that bit of information later on. We went back to our suite to change, and then we went on the shopping spree. We only had three hours to shop because James scheduled our spa time for early afternoon.

We made it back to the hotel with ten minutes to spare before we had to go and get pampered. Instead of shopping, we ended up going to a miniature golf course. We had a ball as we missed hole after hole because neither of us could hit the ball straight. After that we had lunch at the Hibachi, a five-star Asian cuisine bar located on

Delaware Avenue. It felt like we were dating again, and I didn't want the day to end. I did pick up a pair of sexy stiletto sandals from Charles David before we went back. I had a thong to match them perfectly, and that's all I planned to wear with them later that night.

Thoughts of Monica kept trying to infiltrate my mind, but I was determined to concentrate on the moment I was having with my husband. That entire threesome thing was cute, but that was supposed to be the gateway to bringing us back together. With that being said, she definitely came in and rocked my damn butt, and now my silly ass was feeling confused. I didn't like girls like that, but I really liked Monica, at least on a sexual level. Maybe if I had her just one more time, I'd be good. You know, just to flush her all the way out of my system. That way I could give James my full attention, and we could start to build again.

All too soon our weekend was over and it was time to go back to work. We had a good time just hanging out and being stress free, and we got into some hellified sex sessions that left me speechless and smiling every time. No more of the five-minute poundings were going on. We made love for hours. Sometimes it was slow, sometimes it was heart-pounding fast, but it was more than five minutes and that's what mattered. We took pictures on the strip and some nude ones in the room. We also climbed into the big champagne glass–shaped Jacuzzi and had our picture taken, and once the picture guy was gone, we got it on something fierce, splashing bubbles all over the place.

Before we left, I made sure everything was packed and we weren't forgetting anything. I sat on the lounge chair to catch my breath and enjoy the room for a second longer. James was in the restroom making sure he packed all of our toiletries. When he came back in the room, he kneeled in front of me and put his head in my lap.

"Jasmine, I am so happy you are my wife. This weekend was wonderful, and I appreciate you going through with our plans. You have made me very happy," James said while rubbing the backs of my legs.

"I'm glad you enjoyed yourself. We needed to get away for a second," I responded while fondling the wavy texture of his hair.

Instead of responding, he reached under my skirt and pulled my panties to the side. I couldn't protest because he was already tasting me. We went at it for another hour and were late checking out. We had to pay a fee, but it was well worth it. Hopefully this was the start to how our lives would be moving forward. This, minus Monica's contribution, was all I ever wanted from James. For us to connect again on a level beyond just surface. To be in love like we used to be. To turn the heat up so high we would both feel the burn and wouldn't care. This was the man I married. This was who we were. Unfortunately, there was a nagging feeling in the back of my mind telling me I played myself, and I couldn't let the feeling go.

Chapter Three

Jasmine

Once James and I got home, things were better than ever. For the first time in months, we made love on a daily basis, and sometimes three or four times a day. In the past two months, we'd met up for quick sessions during lunch, and we'd sneak off into the garage late at night while the kids were sleeping to add a little spice to our lovemaking. James sent me tulips at least twice a week, and we made it a must-do to have dinner out on Saturday nights just so we could have our time together. We made acquaintance with the kitchen table on more occasions than I can remember, and for once life was good.

I didn't think much about Monica, and for me that night was a distant memory. A thing we never spoke about once we left the hotel. I never let on to how much I really enjoyed myself and that I was seriously contemplating doing it again. Monica made my skin feel like it was on fire. I love a nice stiff one, but her soft lips could be a wonderful replacement. The contrast between James's rugged exterior and her softness was a serious turn-on. I wanted more, but I didn't want more. Just pay attention. You'll get what I mean later.

The only thing that kept me from going through with it was my job. I didn't want anyone at the firm thinking I was a "swinger" or anything like that, and a scandal of that caliber could ruin everything James and I worked so hard for. We had our children to think about and these high-priced vehicles that we were pushing around town. We were used to living ghetto fabulous, and I couldn't see anything that petty taking it all away no matter how wet my pussy got thinking about her. I didn't know for sure if we could trust Monica to hold the secret, but we had already done the dirty deed. It made me a little nervous not knowing if she was a conniving bitch. James didn't seem bothered at all, and I was taking my cue from him to just chill the hell out. If she were going to flex, it would have already happened, right? I was tripping for nothing, and I tucked those thoughts neatly in a box in the back of my mind where they were less bothersome. For all I knew she had just as much to lose, so I was probably tripping for nothing.

I pushed that thought out of my head almost as soon as I thought of it and tried to refocus on my most troublesome client, Bryan Campbell. He was a petty thief who just couldn't seem to stay clean. I personally thought he liked jail more than his freedom. He told me once that at least in the pen he was guaranteed three free meals a day and that there were more drugs on the inside than in his neighborhood.

It was sad because he could make some woman a good husband. The drugs had him torn down, but you can tell that if he cleaned himself up, he could be fly. I was working his case now because the last number he pulled landed him almost six years. He and his cronies decided they wanted to be like the girls in *Set It Off* and rob a bank. Never mind they ain't have any guns. Well, he didn't. This fool was holding the guard hostage with a sausage in his pocket. I wanted to bust him in his head myself.

One of the guys he was with shot the guard in the chest, and everyone got away but him. He was sitting in jail because he didn't want to tell who did what, and on top of that he was a repeat offender, so the judge just threw a stack of books at him. I wanted to leave him in there for being stupid, but you know you have to work each case to the best of your ability.

So I was in my office trying to wrap up my long, tiring day when my secretary buzzed me to let me know I had a delivery. I didn't think anything of it as I circled around my desk to pick up what I assumed to be a package. I often had items shipped directly to my office since neither I nor James were at home during the day to receive them. We lived in a very nice neighborhood that porch pirates loved to visit, and I learned my lesson after my kids' laptops were swiped from our steps just minutes before James pulled up from work. When I opened my office door, a beautiful bouquet of powder pink roses was waiting for me.

Speaking of the devil.

I thanked my secretary and picked up the bouquet to take it to my office. Before I could close the door, my secretary called out to me.

"Mrs. Cinque, I have to say I admire you," she commented with a straight face. I was puzzled as to what brought that about.

"Why is that?"

"Because you bust your behind around here day in and day out, and to me it seems to go unnoticed. Then your husband does little things like send flowers to let you know he's thinking about you, and it all seems to be okay. My son's father would never do that."

I didn't know what to say, and my face must have said it all. The funny thing was she'd been my secretary for the past two years, and I couldn't even think of her name at this moment. I wanted to say something positive, but my mind drew a blank. I could smell Monica's perfume coming from the card in the bouquet, and I wanted to hurry and open it.

"You'll know when you've found the right one. Believe me." With that said, I closed my door and went to inspect my card.

Monica had beautiful curvy handwriting that matched her perfectly. The way you write says a lot about you, and her script was just as sassy as she. She wrote a short paragraph inviting me to have dinner with her in her home without my husband. She said that the night we spent together had been on her mind, and she wanted to show me pleasures I could only dream about. I was shocked but pleased at the same time. That night we shared was nice, but I really wanted her to leave because my husband did things to me he hadn't done in a good long while, but what she did was hardly overlooked. The girl had skills. I had to give it to her.

Now my dilemma was this: we shared that one night on some threesome-type shit, but wouldn't me and her one-on-one make me bisexual? I mean, let's be real. The first time was just experimentation, the second time is just being greedy, and any time after that it's curtains. Don't get me wrong, I was very comfortable with my sexuality, but Monica was the bomb with a capital B. If she could make me feel like I felt that night, I may just have to see her again.

At the end of the note she included her address and phone number and asked that I confirm our meeting by five thirty this evening. I looked at my watch, and it was already five twenty. I didn't know what to do, but curiosity got the best of me, and I decided to go for it. We were only having dinner, but my walls were already contracting. *Monica can turn you into Spiderwoman in no time, and I am ready to go there. Now, what do I tell James?*

Before I had my story together, I was already dialing the number to the studio and hoping I could come up with something by the time he answered the phone. I already decided to call my brother so that he could watch the kids until James got home, and I promised myself that I would not stay over there too late. As soon as I exploded, I would leave.

"Thank you for calling the Urban News Network. This is Cindy. How may I direct your call?"

Cindy was the overly polite receptionist over at the station. If it weren't for her looking to be well past 100 years old, it would be cool. Her voice and her appearance clashed. Nothing matched about it. Her voice was very youthful, but her face was decades ahead.

"Hi, Cindy, can you connect me to James, please?"

"Sure, Mrs. Cinque. Hold for a second." She put me on hold, and Anita Baker crooning about being in sweet love flowed through my receiver. I felt bad for a second because I loved James, and even though Monica was the same sex as me, it was still cheating. I started to back out and just go make love to him until he answered the phone.

"Thanks for calling the Urban News Network. Who am I speaking with?" James answered with his deep voice. It sounded like things were a little hectic over there, and he was a little agitated.

"Hey, sweetheart. How's your day going?"

"Hey, baby. I was just about to call you. Our system shut down unexpectedly and we've been trying to get it together for the past hour. I might be here all night."

"Baby, just relax. You're the best they have over there, and whatever the problem is, you can fix it. That's why you're the director of engineering."

"Thanks, babe, but I know we had plans to dip off later, and I don't want to disappoint you."

"Sweetie, it's okay. I was calling to tell you I would be running late because I'm trying to finish up with the paperwork from the Campbell case, and Trish just made partner, so we were going to get a few drinks afterward to celebrate."

I felt like shit.

Those lies rolled off too easily. Well, they weren't total lies. Trish did make partner, but that was like last week, and technically I was working on a case, but I was putting it to the side to go bump coochies with Monica. If James even thought I was still seeing Monica, he'd probably die. I knew I would be pissed if he were stepping out on me.

"Tell Trish I said congrats. I'm sorry about tonight, and I'll make it up to you tomorrow, okay?"

"Okay, baby. Don't stress too much. It'll be fine."

"I know, baby, I know. I love you. Be safe."

"I will, and I love you too. Talk to you later."

We blew each other a kiss, then hung up. I called Monica next to confirm, and she told me that dinner was almost done and that I could come on through. I straightened up my desk and put everything in order so that I could bust it out when I came in tomorrow morning. I hated clutter and never left my desk a mess. Afterward,

I freshened up in my private bathroom and made my way down to Monica's to enjoy dinner . . . and whatever dessert came with it.

I was having all kinds of doubts on my drive over to Monica's house. I knew we would sleep together. That went without saying. My only problem was if James ever found out, there would be some serious explaining to do. He would have questions, and I knew I couldn't possibly give him an honest answer. How do you tell your husband his sex is the bomb but you prefer the feel of another woman's lips to his? That wouldn't go over too nicely.

When I pulled up to her house, I wasn't the least bit surprised. She lived in a cute two-story Victorian-style single home that sat way back off the street. Her house had a beautiful wraparound porch set off by a well-manicured lawn. There was a wood swing off to the left that was perfect for cool summer nights. Her windows sported pastel pink shutters to match the trim on her white house. She had several rosebushes sprinkled around her yard, and her address hung from a powder pink mailbox on a black address hanger. It was written in script with little roses around the border. Monica definitely loved pink flowers.

By the time I parked my car and began to walk up the path to her door, she was already standing there. Monica was a lot shorter than I remembered. A cute little petite something. She had on a one-piece halter dress that stopped just under her ass and showed off her perfect legs. Her hair was cut short in one of those spiky styles like Halle Berry would wear that showed more of her pretty face and bright eyes. It was cute and different from the full curls she had when we met on that night. Both styles looked good on her.

She greeted me with a tight hug like she really missed me and invited me into her home. The inside was just as breathtaking. She had a sunken living room decorated in pastel yellows, pinks, and blues. Her walls had splashes of all three colors to match the designs in her furniture. The fireplace was to die for, and I could almost picture us lying in front of it on a cold winter night, touching and tasting each other.

There was a spiral staircase with steps made of clear marble with rose petals embedded in them. The railing was gold plated with a vine design wrapped around it with crystal roses appearing to bud from it. She had pictures of couples making love in various positions on top of pink rose petals with gold leaves. The flowers really stood out because the couples were sketched in black and white. It wasn't until I took a closer look that I realized that Monica was the woman in the pictures. That left me speechless in a confusing kind of way. Like, were these done purposely? I wanted to get a closer look and really inspect them because I felt like I had seen some of these people before.

"So, you sketch?" I asked as I stopped in front of the one picture that had a man who kind of looked like our mayor. Let me rephrase that—he looked exactly like our mayor, but I didn't want to just assume. "Are these live models or memory sketches?" I quizzed as I moved along.

"A little bit of both," she answered slyly. A slight smirk was on her pretty face. She didn't confirm or deny what I was thinking, but that just added to the mystery that was Monica, and I decided not to press the issue.

Her dining room was nothing but candlelight. An intimate placement for two was set on her pure ivory dining table. Candles burned in ivory candleholders, and pastel pink silk dinner napkins sat beside patterned china. Lasagna and buttered crescent rolls shaped like hearts were presented on crystal dishes. A bottle of Passion Alize and two slightly chilled crystal flutes made up the decor. I was still speechless.

Her kitchen housed every kitchen gadget you could think of. Her subzero refrigerator encased in chrome was absolutely beautiful. Pink and white found its home here also in the shape of window curtains, potholders, and countertops. A little dinette set made of wood took up space in one corner of her huge kitchen. I thought my house was saying something until I walked up in here.

Through the back door I could see her swimming pool, and I had to get a closer look. When I looked in, a portrait of Monica in a pink teddy could be seen painted on the bottom. I wanted to hate, but I was living good, so there was no reason to complain. I just wanted to know what she did for a living to be able to afford all of this. I wanted to see the upstairs, but she suggested we eat dinner before it got cold. I mean, hell, we would be up there later anyway.

"So, tell me who the real Monica is," I suggested as we had polite conversation while we enjoyed our meal. I was a little nervous and resisted the urge to jet several times. I felt so bad about being there while James was stressing at work, and the fact that I lied to him about where I was made me feel even worse.

"I am what you see," she said nonchalantly. A flash of sadness crossed her face that I almost missed, but she quickly masked it with her smile. "I paint, I'm a photographer, I draw little M's on small chocolate candies." She smiled, causing me to laugh at her M&M reference. "What about you? I know your husband told me you were a lawyer. What's your concentration in?"

"Criminal law. I used to love it, but not so much any-more," I replied, not even wanting to go down that road. Lately my job had been feeling more like work than it used to, and I was over it.

"Really? Why?" she quizzed as she got up from the table, removing our now-empty dishes from in front of us and setting them in the dishwasher.

"My clients keep making the same mistakes. There are only so many times I can save you from going to jail when you keep getting out and doing the same thing repeatedly." I sighed.

"Now, that I can understand."

Monica picked up on my mood and suggested we con-tinue our conversation on the couch. I was sure she was thinking it was something she did, but that was far from the case. This wasn't the time to get into the woes of work life. That wasn't the reason I was here. She motioned for me to follow her to the living area, and I jumped up without hesitation. Once we got comfortable on her sofa, we resumed the conversation while she rubbed my feet. It felt so good I could hardly talk. Before I knew it my head was resting on the arm of the sofa, and I was asleep. For a second I thought I was at home. I felt James massaging my feet turn into him moving his soft hands up my leg. Then I was like, *how did his hands get so soft all of a sudden*? When I opened my eyes, Monica's hands were high on my thighs, my prize not far away. Surprisingly I didn't flinch or pull back. I almost wanted her to hurry up and get there because I knew it was going to be good.

She stood up, I assumed, to take her clothes off. She walked toward the stairs, leaving pieces of clothing along the way, which wasn't a lot because she didn't have much on. By the time she got to the third step, she was standing in nothing but a thong, and I was like, *damn*. She looked even better than the last time. Her chocolate skin made you want to kiss her all over, and her nipples were just a shade darker than the rest of her body, putting you in mind of a Hershey's Kiss. I was hesitant at first, but I followed her up the stairs and into the master bedroom.

Totally different from the downstairs, her bedroom was decked out in neutral colors. Dark browns, honey, tans, hunter green, and maroon made this room look very sexy. Her sleigh bed sat up off the floor, and you had to walk up about four steps to climb into it. The furnishings were made out of heavy cherrywood that she definitely paid some money for. I stood just inside the doorway taking it all in.

Monica turned on the stereo, and I felt like I was listening to a late-night smooth grooves session on the radio. She walked over to me and took my hand, leading me to the steps that led up to her bed. No words were needed as she slowly undressed me, kissing the body parts that she revealed on the way down. My head was screaming, *get the hell out of here,* but the rest of my body was whispering, *girl, you about to cum a zillion times, so chill.*

She walked me up to her bed and told me to lie flat on my stomach. I did what I was told and closed my eyes, listening to the melody in the background. She straddled me, her warmth and wetness seeping into my pores and causing a puddle of my own nectar to form under me. The oil she poured onto my back was cool on my already-hot skin, but her hands warmed it up in no time. The room smelled like citrus instantly. Monica was good at what she did, causing all of the tension in my body to leave almost instantly. James became a distant memory as I moaned under the hands of this woman.

She kissed the center of my back as she massaged me, her juices caressing my skin from her pressing her clit against me. She ran her hands down between my thighs, her thumb entering my tunnel then pulling out quickly. She traced the outside of my lips with her well-oiled finger, and I moaned like she put something in me. I didn't even remember turning over, but Monica was kneeling on my right side massaging the front of me, her tongue feeling hot on my sensitive nipples. I tried to stay cool, but my back arched to meet her lips. I was about to cum, and we hadn't done anything yet.

Monica tied a silk scarf around both of my wrists and attached both arms to the headboard. Now, I was like, *hold the hell up.* I didn't even let James tie me down, but Monica didn't give me room to protest. She was between my legs and on my clit before I could say anything. It was a good thing my hands were tied because otherwise they would have been holding her head while I glazed her face completely.

She took her time "inspecting" me. Monica held both lips open, leaving room for her tongue to explore all of me. My legs were spread into a perfect V while she sucked and licked on me. She put her tongue so far up in me you couldn't have told me she didn't touch my cervix. I moaned like crazy and tried to catch my breath because she was pulling orgasms out of me left and right.

I felt something cold slide up inside of me, and I almost lost it completely. On the side of the bed, I noticed among the bottles of oils and body butters sat two long and thick dildos made of ice. She must have had three, because one was inside of me driving me crazy. I was exploding all over it, almost ashamed at the way I was messing up her bedspreads. She sucked on my clit and worked the ice in and out of me until there was only a small piece left. Silly me, I thought she would just toss it out. Monica put the ice in her mouth and pushed it into my cave using her tongue. She would push it up and suck it out, causing a whole other explosion until it was gone.

The fact that my thighs had her in a serious headlock didn't seem to bother her or mess up her rhythm. She continued to push and pull on my clit until I was screaming for mercy, opening my legs wide so that she could move her head. She leaned up to look at me, her wild hairstyle still in place. She licked my essence off her lips seductively while her middle and forefinger still played around my insides. My walls were gripping her like she had a penis, and soon I found myself exploding again.

"Now, I'm going to let you go," Monica said in a soft, sexy voice, "but only if you're ready to go there."

"Go where?" I asked already knowing the answer. She just gave me one of those "stop playing with me" looks before leaning over to the table next to the bed.

"If you don't know, I guess I need to use another one of these," she said, referring to the ice-shaped penises she had sitting on the side. I knew for sure I couldn't take any more of that.

"No, I got you. You can untie me now."

She motioned for me to scoot down to the middle of the bed. I did as I was told with my arms still stretched out. She stood over me with her legs on either side of my head. Slowly she bent her knees until her lips rested on mine. My tongue found her opening instantly. She untied one hand and undid the other once I captured her clit between my lips. I could see Monica's hands on the wall helping her keep her balance over me.

I was barely able to reach the table but was able to snag one of the ice pieces without missing a beat. I continued to stimulate her clit while teasing her with the ice just at the opening of her tunnel. She moaned in appreciation as I teased her with just the head before sliding it all in. Positioning the ice-cold sculpture on my chin, she rode my face like she was riding a real dick, with me capturing her clit in my mouth when she came down and her pulling it out on the way up. The ice melted quickly from her warmth. Her juices flowed effortlessly. I stuck my index finger in her asshole for good measure, and my girl went wild.

She stood up off my face and placed herself softly on my stomach, her explosion running down my sides and forming puddles on both sides of me. She rotated on me with her eyes closed, moaning until it was over. I rubbed her clit with my thumb until her shaking subsided and she was able to open her eyes and look at me. I blushed a little at what just went down, partly because I didn't think I had it in me to please another woman. Besides the bullshit orgies I had in college, it never got this intense and I never had to use as much of my imagination. I never wanted to. I was always on the receiving end and never had to put much into a performance, so this was something new.

Don't ask what made me do it, but for some reason I looked across the room toward the dresser and the clock caught my eye. I thought my eyes were playing tricks on me until I sat up in the bed.

"Does that clock say ten thirty?" I needed her to tell me because I didn't want to believe it.

"Yes. Why, are you in a rush?"

"Hell yeah! I didn't tell James I would be out this long. He's going to kill me."

"It's still early. Don't you want to finish up in the shower? I have some treats in there waiting, and—"

"Did I not just tell you I had to roll? I ain't got no business being here in the first place. My husband is going to kill me!"

In the midst of me running around the room trying to find the damn light switch and a washrag, I thought I heard Monica sniffling. In the middle of my panic performance, I stopped to look at her. She was curled up in the middle of the bed, crying. Even though the room was barely lit, I could see her shoulders move up and down with every sob. I started to just leave her like that, but my heart wouldn't let me do it. I guess, for some odd reason, I cared about her. Dropping my head in defeat, I walked over to the bed to see what was wrong with her. Sis was tripping, and now was not the time.

"Monica," I called out to her softly as I made my way up the steps to her bed, "sweetie, what's wrong?" I sat and listened to her, but on the real I wanted her to hurry the hell up. I had to get to the west side in twenty-three minutes and four seconds.

"Nothing. I don't want you to go."

"I have to go, sweetie, but I'm sure there will be other times," I said, trying to console her. Honestly, this behavior made me question if there would be. *Who does this? We barely know each other.* What type of time was she on?

"You promise?" she asked as she sat up on the bed and wiped her nose with the sheet.

"I promise, but right now I need to get washed so I can go home and tend to my family. Can you help me do that?" I asked, hoping my gentleness would get her ass out of the bed and some light in this room.

She got out of the bed looking like a helpless little girl, and I tried not to give a damn. I just wanted to hurry up and get home. She finally turned the light on and allowed me to see what was what. While she ran the shower, I gathered my clothes from the floor and tried to press the wrinkles out the best I could with my hands.

Without saying anything, she pulled me into the bathroom and into the shower, washing me quickly but thoroughly. She tried to go down on me in the shower, but I gently reminded her I didn't have time. I already told her I had to go, but she was acting crazy, and I didn't want to end up knocked out and somehow finding myself chained to a pole with a lump on my head hours later. I could see I had to be careful with her, but to keep it totally one hundred, she was scaring me. Once we were done, she dried me off and gave me the cotton sweat suit that she purchased for me to put on along with a new pair of sneakers to match.

"I figured you would need them since your clothes are a mess now," she said, answering the question I never asked out loud.

I thanked her as I got dressed in record time. I practically ran to the door after I put my belongings into the bag my new outfit came in, but for some reason I couldn't find my panties. I told her if she found them to hold them for me, and I dipped. When I got in my car, I could see Monica standing in the window, waiting for me to pull off.

I got home before James and was showered and in the bed a half hour before he came in. I tried to play like I was just waking up when he came into the room.

"Hey, babe," he said to me after kissing my cheek, "how was the celebration?"

"It was cool. I only had a few wine coolers, and then I came on home," I lied to my husband with a straight face. I felt horrible because he looked like he had a rough day at work, and I was out busting nuts with Monica across town.

"That's good, baby. Can we talk in the morning? Right now I need to close my eyes for a second and get some sleep."

I turned over on my side so that he could lie in my arms. He was asleep almost instantly. I was up thinking about what happened with Monica for hours. The sex was off the chain, but the entire scene at the end threw me off completely. What grown adult cries after sex? I mean, I'm sure its a thing, don't get me wrong, but it's a little off-putting if I do say so myself. Still, I low-key wanted to go back to get some more. I wished I could've stayed to see what we were going to do in the shower. If it was anything like how that bedroom session went down, there was nowhere else to go but up. I didn't really know what to make of it and decided it wasn't worth the effort as I finally drifted off to sleep.

Chapter Four

Jasmine

For the next two months, I tried to avoid Monica. I felt absolutely horrible about how things went down on that night and even worse when James woke up the next morning wanting to make love. I felt like he was getting sloppy seconds, and the night before did indeed get sloppy. The entire time James was in me I kept thinking about the ice sculptures and Monica's warm hands. A few times I almost slipped up and called her name out when James thought he was making me cum. I mean, I came, but it was because I was thinking about Monica's tongue roaming all over me. Not because he was banging my back out. The two of them were as different as night and day, and I craved the danger that came with the night.

I received flowers and "Thinking of You" cards constantly from Monica and James, and it began to get a bit overwhelming. James would just pop up at the office unexpectedly, and I would have to hide the numerous cards Monica sent me and make up excuses as to where I was getting all the roses from. He hinted that maybe he knew Monica was sending them to me, but he never came right out and said it. The two of them competing for my time was exhausting, and I needed to get away from both of them for a while. I was seriously considering packing up my and my kids' stuff and going to Mexico. The two of them together were nerve-racking.

One day at the office, Monica and James must have been playing tag team on the phones because as soon as I hung up from one, the other would call, and vice versa. I was like, *what the hell?* And they were calling for stupid shit. *Like, leave me the fuck alone for five seconds! I'm trying to get some work done, and these two are acting like fools.* It was like they knew what was up and were trying to outdo each other. But in actuality all they were doing was giving me a damn headache. During one conversation with Monica, shit got tense real quick, and I had to hang up on her.

"Why don't you ever tell me you love me back? I show affection toward you twenty-four seven, even when you're at home playing house with James and the crew. Are you saying you don't care about me?" Monica asked like she honestly expected me to give her an answer.

Monica had been crying in my ear for the past twenty minutes about my so-called "lack of affection." How much affection did she want? *I go down on her more than I do the person I'm married to. I've seriously licked more clit than dick in the last few months, and that isn't even my twist. She doesn't even have to ask for it. It's a given.* James had to damn near beg me to suck his dick, and even then it was only until he got it up enough to slide it in me. He was getting the short end of the stick and not even complaining about it. *The blackassity of some people is unnerving.*

"Monica, we have been over this so many times already. I don't love you, I'm not in love with you, and 'James and the crew' are my family. They come first, and you act like you don't know that," I said after taking a deep breath. *I hate when she gets like this.*

"That's stuff I already know, but—"

"Then why do you keep asking me do I love you if you already know the answer?"

"Because I know you have to care about me a little bit or else you wouldn't keep coming here," she said through her tears. I hated to hear her cry, and I was trying my best to console her so that I could get off the phone. I had a court date in a half hour, and I did not have time to be dealing with this emotional-ass Virgo. By far they were the most unstable creatures on the planet.

"Monica, look," I said through clenched teeth as calmly as possible, "I care about you, baby, okay? You know that already! I just don't understand why I have to constantly remind you of my feelings. It's too much at one time to deal with, and honestly you're starting to push me away."

I tried to sound stern as if I were talking to one of my kids. She needed to understand the situation she was in. She was the sidekick in this play, no more, no less. On no table in America has a side replaced the main course. People really needed to learn how to play their positions. Especially when you already know what you're getting into.

"Jazz, I'm not trying to push you away. I just need to know that you care about me. I need to hear you say it every once in a while," she tried to reason with me as she sniffled. I was completely over this shit.

"I care about you, Monica, I really do. Do you believe me?"

"Yes, I believe you," she said between sniffles as she tried to get herself together.

"Okay, now dry those tears and straighten up that pretty face. I'll make it up to you later on tonight," I promised as I tried to devise a way to get away from James for a little bit without him questioning my where-abouts. I figured if I knocked her off real quick, she would chill for a bit.

"Will you stay the entire night?"

"Monica . . ."

"Okay, okay. I'm sorry, I know you can't stay. Can you at least stay until eight?"

"Sure, I'll leave work at six and come chill with you until eight, okay?"

"Eight thirty," she pleaded from the other end.

"I'm about to change my mind," I warned her over the phone line.

"Okay, eight it is. I love you."

Instead of replying, I just hung up. This girl was going to drive me into a white jacket by the time all of this was finished. I gathered up my documents for court and threw on my leather jacket so I could head out. Just as I was reaching my hand out to turn the knob, the phone rang again. I thought about not answering because I thought it was Monica again, but I went on and took the call anyway. My secretary was on lunch, so I had no way of intercepting it.

"Jasmine Cinque's office," I said into the phone, praying it wasn't some bullshit on the other end.

"Hey, baby, how's your day going?" my husband inquired as if he didn't already know. He too called more times today than he should have, but I digress. I wanted to tell him I had a love-sick stalker calling me every five minutes to make sure I didn't stop caring about her, and the reason why she was acting that way was because I was face-to-face with her clit damn near every night. Then I'd come home and tongue kiss him after giving my children a kiss on the cheek. Instead, I opted for the logical answer.

"It's going okay. Right now I'm on my way out the door to the Campbell trial. What's good?"

"Me and you, dinner at the Hibachi at six tonight."

"Tonight? Can we do it tomorrow?" I panicked a little because I just told Monica I would chill with her, and I knew if I didn't go, I would be on the phone another three hours tomorrow trying to explain to her that my husband came first no matter how much sex we had.

"Baby, I already made the reservations," James responded, sounding kind of down.

"Okay, baby. I'll meet you there," I agreed, remembering that home came first. That gave me enough time to talk to Monica after I got out of court because I knew I would need at least an hour to calm her down.

"Well, actually you're scheduled to take the rest of the day off. Your boss cleared your schedule for the rest of the afternoon after your trial. I have a couple's spa set up for us also, so I will be at the courthouse waiting for you. See you there. I love you."

He hung up before I could say anything. I didn't have time to call Monica because I would be late for my trial for sure messing around with her. I ran out to my Jeep, and once I got into the flow of traffic, I tried to call her. Her answering machine kept picking up, and I didn't want to be inconsiderate and just leave a message. I tried calling all the way until I got into the courthouse, and once I walked into the courtroom to represent my client, I had to turn my cell phone off.

I tried to get my client out on the strength that I would shorten his probation, but the judge denied him bail because he had gotten into several fights since he'd been incarcerated and had been sent to the hole numerous times. I didn't even feel like the fight today, and I called it a day as the judge gave him a year on top of the six he already had with a chance of making bail after three years and good behavior. That was unlikely to happen, so I promised my client I would be upstate to see him, and I left out to meet James. Normally I cared more about losing, but today I had other shit to deal with.

I was not prepared to see what I saw when I walked out of the courthouse. Upon leaving the building and trying to find my cell phone, I looked up to see Monica and James talking by his car. I knew why James was there, but why did Monica show up? I approached them cautiously because I didn't know who would cut the hell up first.

"Baby, you remember Monica, don't you?" he asked me after he embraced me in a bear hug. Monica was shooting me dirty looks over his shoulder, and I pleaded with my eyes for her to keep cool.

"Yeah, how have you been?" I asked, reaching out to shake her hand.

"I've been good. Thanks for asking," she offered, leaving my hand dangling in midair. I pulled my hand back, a little hurt by her actions.

"Baby, she was just telling me about a young lady she's been dealing with who has her head over heels. I ran into her out here on my way to get you. She was on her way to buy her flowers for their date tonight."

"Really," I replied with a dry throat. I didn't know what type of shit Monica was trying to pull, but today I swear she would get her ass whipped.

"Yeah, she's a lawyer too. You might know her," she replied, trying to sound innocent. I wanted to black her eye on the spot.

"I might," I replied, trying to change the subject. "James, don't we have reservations?"

"Yeah, we do. Monica, it was nice running into you. Be safe, and I hope to see you soon."

"Yeah, both of you do the same," she replied after shaking James's hand again, still leaving me hanging in the process. Maybe it was just me, but that sounded a little like a threat. I wanted to call her on it, but I didn't want to draw attention to our situation.

James walked around the car to open the door for me, and I moved to put my belongings in the back before I got in. When I looked up at her, I could see a single tear drop down her cheek before she turned and walked away. I felt like shit, but what could I do? She was the side dish on this plate. No more, no less. I was married when she met me. It was up to her to keep her feelings in check, not me. Or at least that's what I told myself to help get a good sleep at night.

I was distracted during dinner and couldn't really enjoy the massage treatment at the spa because thoughts of Monica were weighing heavily on my brain. Every time James asked me what was on my mind, I told him I was thinking about the Campbell case so that he wouldn't have too many questions.

Monica was just wearing me down. It's not like I was in a relationship with her, and I tried to reason with myself for treating her the way I did. Who thought a couple hundred orgasms would turn into stalker mania? I should have known she had a screw loose when she cried that first night, but my dumb ass kept going back. I promise I was a sucker for punishment.

The girl was like a drug, though. She had a warm bath ready most evenings when I got there. Whether I got in or not depended on how she acted when I walked in. Yes, I said "walked in" because she gave me a key to her place. I knew I shouldn't have taken it, but she started crying then, too. She would often have a meal cooked or would feed me grapes or strawberries. She treated me like a queen, something James didn't do.

Now, don't get it twisted. James was doing well in the "dick Jasmine down" department. He was keeping up his stamina, and it seemed as though the day of the five-minute brother never existed. He was good to me. We went out often, and he surprised me with little gifts here and there. James gave me all the material possessions I could hold and more. He was affectionate and attentive, all the things a wife wanted from her husband.

Monica, on the other hand, spoiled me. She catered to my every sexual need without me having to instruct her on what I wanted done. She always had a different way of pleasing me that amazed me every time. She gave me back rubs after my many long work hours and made sure I was fresh and clean before I left her home. All of that came with a price, of course. Some days she would cry and holler at the top of her lungs because she wanted me to stay. I guess going with her to Vegas for the weekend that one time made her think I could stay like that on a regular basis.

A few times she got on the floor and wrapped herself around my legs so that I wouldn't go. I had to practically drag her across the floor before she let go, and when she did she would lie right where I left her and cry. The next day I would go over and kiss her rug burns from me having to drag her across the carpet the day before, and we would be right back to square one. Emotionally, she was way too much for me to handle. I wanted out, but I also wanted to stay in. It's hard to explain, and every time I thought she would act right, she would start to cut up again.

I thought her seeing me with James that time might have made her snap. She was truly in love with me, and it was a shame because I wouldn't allow myself to love her back. It wasn't fair to my husband or our children, and I just wasn't having it. I just hoped she wouldn't start leaving dead rabbits on my doorstep or playing on my phone or whatever it was stalkers did to get back at their mates. I wasn't in the mood, and I had to find a way to end it . . . for a little while at least.

After dinner, James and I went to a movie and only ended up seeing half of it before I started riding him in the back of the mostly empty theater. We were into the film, or at least I was. James kept kissing me behind my ear and fondling my breasts through my shirt. At one point he reached between my legs and stroked my clit until he had to kiss me to keep me from moaning too loud. There were only about twelve of us in the theater, but we were the only ones sitting in the back.

To make up for my stank attitude, I removed his fingers from between my legs and placed them in my mouth to remove any juices from them. Then I tongue kissed him so that he could taste it because that was a major turn-on for him. While doing so, I removed his erection from his pants and began to stroke him softly. I ended the kiss to wrap my lips around him, and his head met the wall as soon as my tongue met him.

I traced the head of his penis before taking him into my mouth completely. He touched the back of my throat with no effort, and I made sure to keep his testicles warm in my small hands. He held me by the back of my neck pushing me down on him, and I silently thanked God for giving me skills because an amateur baby drinker would have choked.

I released his hold on my head and straddled him with my back facing him. I sat all the way down on his length, only lifting up a little before he was back in me. He held me by my waist as he met me stroke for stroke until he exploded inside me. The best five minutes I ever had. Afterward he wiped me as best he could with the few napkins we had from the popcorn, and instead of letting the movie finish, we got into the car to go home. On the way home, we stopped the car and parked behind a Dunkin' Donuts, where he bent me over the hood and handled his business. We continued our session in the shower and finished up in the bedroom, where we got it on for two more hours. By morning, I felt like I had run a triathlon, but it was worth it.

I got up early and made breakfast while James was taking a shower. The kids and I were at the table eating by the time he came downstairs. He looked tired but thoroughly satisfied as he kissed me on the lips before taking the seat across from me.

"Oooooh, Mommy and Daddy kissin'," my 4-year-old daughter, Jaden, said, covering her mouth in a cute giggle. Jalil, her fraternal twin brother, just giggled and continued to eat his French toast sticks.

"That's because Mommy and Daddy love each other, ain't that right, honey?" James replied after giving Jaden a kiss on the cheek and Jalil a pound. We were like the Huxtables in here that morning.

"Yep," I replied nonchalantly. I was itching to call Monica and was trying to hurry up out of the house.

"Daddy, can you take us to school?" our son replied as he crammed eggs into his mouth. I was just about to ask James that very question, but it sounded a lot better coming from Jalil.

"Sure, buddy. I'll drop you off," James said as he stood up to gather his belongings. "Last one to the car is a rotten egg."

Both of our kids jumped up, neglecting the rest of their breakfasts, and ran to their rooms to get their jackets and backpacks. While they were upstairs, James stooped down on the side of me. He just kind of looked into my eyes like he was trying to read my thoughts. I looked back, not wanting to seem like I was nervous about anything. He looked like he wanted to say something, but instead he kissed me softly on my lips. I was just about to slip him some tongue when the kids came back into the kitchen.

"They kissin' again," Jaden tried to whisper to Jalil as they walked around the table to the door. James smiled at me and pecked me on my lips one final time before standing.

"Give Mommy a hug so we can go," James instructed our children as he took one last piece of bacon off the table. They both hugged me around the neck and kissed my cheeks. I kissed and hugged them back, and I could hear Jalil tell Jaden that you got cooties from kissing as they walked out of the door. James was going to have a time with them this morning.

Before leaving out for work, I decided to go ahead and call Monica up so she could say what she had to say and get it over with. I tried to prepare myself for the tears that I knew would come, but her tears made me weak. I couldn't think straight and hold a level head when she was hurting. Although I came at her strong, it tore me up on the inside seeing her like that. I was determined not to fall for her, and it took everything in me to hold it down. I had two kids to think about, and my career was not to be messed with. James was also the love of my life, and I married him for better or worse. Something like this could snatch everything away from me, and that wasn't happening.

I knew I would need at least a half hour to deal with her. I got comfortable on the love seat before I made my call and decided that I would just get right to the point and let her know we couldn't see each other anymore. I reasoned that she had to be tired of me canceling on her all the time, and I was tired of the entire scenario anyway. I couldn't swing two lovers, and I knew my best bet was to stay with my husband.

When I called her, she picked up on the first ring. I didn't have time to practice what I was going to say, and she caught me off guard a little. She didn't sound too upset, and that had me shook. If anything, she sounded too damn cheerful.

"Hey, Monica, it's me," I breathed into the phone. I was hoping to make a clean break and didn't want her to start getting all hysterical on me.

"Hey, Jazz, what's good? What can I do for you?"

I had to look at the phone for a minute to make sure I was talking to the right person. This didn't sound like the Monica I knew.

"Well, about yesterday—"

"Don't sweat it. It's cool." She just cut me off on some real nonchalant shit. I didn't know whether to be happy she was chillin' or ask her what the hell was going on.

"Okay, well, if you want, I can make it up to you tonight."

"It's cool, no worries," she just kind of mumbled into the phone. Something was definitely up. I figured I might as well break the news to her so that we could be done with it. She didn't seem interested anymore anyway.

"I get off work at five tonight. Can we talk then?"

"Actually, I was just about to call you to give you your dismissal papers."

"Excuse me?" I knew this chick wasn't dissin' me. I was starting to get an attitude.

"I've decided that I'm done with this situation. After yesterday I realized that it just wasn't worth it. So, you're free. Go spread your wings," she said dismissively, and she was serious.

"Are you kidding me?" I asked in disbelief more to myself than her. This was what I wanted, but I didn't think it would go down like that.

"No, and actually I have to tend to my company, so I'll see you around. Don't worry about calling me back. After today this number won't work," she said, and she just hung up.

I must have sat on the couch looking stupid for like ten minutes. I knew I wasn't just handed my walking papers by needy-ass Monica! Then she had the nerve to get igno-rant with the shit. I called back to give her a few choice words, but when her phone rang, the operator informed me that she had blocked my number. I tried calling from my cell phone, and that was blocked too. I had a numb feeling all over my body that I couldn't quite shake as I readied myself to leave for work. In a sense I was glad it was all over, but I was a tad bit salty because I didn't think it would end like that. Like, damn. We couldn't at least be friends? This was the bipolar shit I was talking about with her. One minute she couldn't breathe without me, and the very next second she was avoiding me like the plague. Ugh, this girl got on every nerve that I owned, and if I was being honest with myself, I was pissed about it. *It's cool, though. God must've known that I wouldn't be able to do it, so He had her do it for me. Good looking out on His behalf.* Now I could tend to my husband and kids in peace, and that was exactly what I wanted anyway. Wasn't it?

Chapter Five

Jasmine

It'd been one hell of a day. My morning started off all wrong, and it'd been going downhill ever since. James woke up with a pissy attitude and had been waking up that way for the last four months. It was almost like he and Monica had the same shit for breakfast, because about three weeks after she and I parted, his attitude went from sugar to shit. Every time I asked him what was up, he gave me short one-word answers and some bull about being stressed out at the news station. I tried to be peaceful, but I didn't feel like the aggravation, so I just stayed away from him. He'd been stressed out at that news station many times over the years, and never had he flipped the script on me like this. There was something else going on for sure, but guess who wasn't putting any energy in it to find out what? My ass. *I'm not begging a grown-ass man to express himself.*

What pissed me off the most was I would still try to be courteous and make him breakfast when I fixed the kids and me some, but he would walk in the kitchen, kiss the kids goodbye, and leave like I didn't even exist. I asked him on a couple of occasions what the hell his problem was, and he would just act like he didn't hear me say a word to him. So I just said fuck it, and let it be.

I entertained sleeping in the guest room, but since my sleeping next to him made him miserable, I made sure to lay my head there every night and stayed with my ass on his side of the bed for good measure. I was the queen of making shit uncomfortable. *Play with somebody safer. I've never been the safe choice.* I would throw my legs over his and elbow him in his ribs just to be smart, knowing damn well I was nowhere near sleep, and it just pissed him off. When he would finally get out of the bed to go to the bathroom or something, I would stretch out in the middle so that he would only have the edge to sleep on when he got back.

Instead of his stubborn ass asking me to move over, he would ball up on the very edge so that he wouldn't have to touch me, and I would move closer to him so that he had no choice. After a while he would get so frustrated that he would either lie on the floor beside the bed or go into the den and rest because he claimed it was too cold in the guest room. Who cared? If I had it my way, I would pack the hell up and be over there with Monica in a heartbeat, but this wasn't television, so it wouldn't go down as smoothly as that. Not that I wanted to, but every so often I would find myself thinking about Monica.

One day I wasn't even paying attention and was just driving home. Well, I thought I was driving home, but when I looked up I was sitting in front of Monica's house. Since she played me, I decided I wasn't going to deal with her anymore, but deep down I really did care about her. I still didn't feel like I loved her, but there were some deep feelings involved at this point. I just couldn't leave my family out of nowhere, and I didn't think she understood that. There were rules to this shit, even when you didn't want to play by them.

I started to just pull off when I noticed her porch light come on. I didn't want her to think I was a peeping Tom or anything like that, so I started to put my Jeep in drive.

For some reason my foot wouldn't step on the gas. I tried to be out, but my body wouldn't let me go. Before I knew it, she was down her steps and looking through the passenger side window of my Jeep.

I rolled down the window and looked at her. She was even prettier than I remembered, and all of the good times we had flooded my mind. We looked at each other for what felt like an eternity before I got out of the Jeep and walked around to where she was. Without any hesitation we stepped into each other's arms, and my tears flowed instantly. I cried because things were a mess at home, and I felt powerless in trying to fix it. My heart hurt because I hurt her, and to my surprise I wasn't ashamed to admit that I was in love with her. I had been for some time, but I still couldn't say it. Partly because I didn't want to believe it, but there was no denying it anymore. Maybe, just maybe, I did love her.

"Let's go in the house and talk for a while," she offered as we stepped back from each other.

"Sure, let's do that," I responded through watery eyes and a weak smile. I didn't even realize I cared this much about her until we came face-to-face, and I hoped we could come to some kind of understanding before the night was over.

Her home was still beautiful, and I felt at peace when I sat down in her living room. Just like old times, she sat at the other end of the couch and gave me a foot massage while we talked. I didn't want to end up with her head between my legs, so I kept my thighs tight so that she wouldn't get any ideas. I was trying to clear my heart of some pain, and I really needed her to listen.

"So, do you think he's cheating on you?" Monica inquired while she worked her magic on my calves. Who knew someone with such soft hands could get a firm grip the way she did? I felt like putty in her hands, literally.

"I never even thought about it. Out of nowhere he started acting all crazy like the mere sight of me was killing him. A few times he was back to his usual five minutes, but it was only in the morning. Then when it got to be every time we had sex, I asked him what the deal was. At this point we're avoiding each other completely."

"And what did he say?" she asked, sounding concerned. Meanwhile, her massage had found its way halfway up my thighs, and her fingers were damn near dipping inside me.

"He didn't say anything. He just gave me a dirty look and walked out of the room."

"Hmm, I don't know what to say about that. You know I would never do you that way."

"Is that so?" I asked just to be smart. I was trying not to go there, but she pushed me into it.

"Basically. My love for you is unconditional. I just wish I could get the same in return."

"If it's like that, why did you brush me off the way you did after you came to the courthouse that day?" I asked the million-dollar question I'd been wanting to know the answer to for months.

"At that point I was just tired," she responded with a sad look on her face. I waited for her to continue, but she just went on with her massage.

"Okay, do you care to elaborate?"

"Well, even though I knew you had a family already, I still hoped that it could just be you and me exclusively. I know James is wonderful in the bedroom, but I pay more attention to your needs than he does. You never have to worry when it comes to me and satisfaction." She had a point there, but sex wasn't the most important thing in a relationship. There was so much more to it than that.

"Monica, I know all that, and that's why I love you. I just need you to understand that . . . What's wrong?"

Tears were threatening to fall from Monica's pretty eyes, and I had no idea as to why.

"You said you love me. Do you know how long I've been waiting for you to say that? I didn't think it would ever happen."

"Monica, I love you. I just need you to understand that I have a husband and kids at home. I just can't up and roll out like that. It's not just my life at stake here. We got kids," I emphasized, trying to drive the point home. Hell, we also had a mortgage and bills and a whole bunch of other shit that married couples had. This wouldn't be a clean break.

"Jazz, I know that. All I'm asking is that we get to see each other more often. James wouldn't know. He would think we're just hanging out. I just need you to be around."

"Monica, I wish it were that easy."

I didn't want to love her, but I did. Now I was all confused, and I didn't know what move to make next. Who thought that I, Jasmine Cinque, would ever love someone of the same sex? Good thing I'm not a betting person, because I definitely would've lost. This wasn't me. Or maybe it was and I picked wrong with James. I was starting to get confused, and it was stressing me out.

"It can be if you would just try it. The least you can do is think about it. That's all I'm asking you to do."

"Look, I'll think about it, but you have to promise to give me time to do just that. Stop asking me for updates and shit. Give me room to make decisions, and don't crowd me like you usually do. All that does is push me away."

"I can do that. Just keep loving me."

"I will."

She kissed me softly on the lips while her hands explored the rest of my body. I was dripping wet by the time her fingers made contact with my clit, and I wanted more. Usually she did me first, but tonight I felt like getting into trouble. I pulled her thong to the side, and I motioned for her to lie back on the couch. She put one leg over the back of the couch and the other on the floor as I made myself comfortable between her legs.

I inserted two fingers into her, and I sucked on her clit softly the way she liked it. She ground her opening into my face, and her body shook as she released herself on my tongue. That was amazing because I hadn't been down there that long. She was moaning like crazy, and just to make it up to her for being nasty toward her, I pushed her legs up so that they were touching her chest and dipped my tongue into her asshole until she exploded again. She had to practically beg me to stop, and I did after she had her fifth orgasm.

Monica got up off the couch on wobbly legs and asked me to follow her upstairs. I thought we were going into the bedroom, but she walked past that door and went into the one at the end of the hallway. When she opened the door and flicked the switch, the room seemed to glow from my viewpoint. Upon entrance I saw that she had several cameras set up, ready to take pictures. The room was all white, with a few photos here and there. One wall had a few amazing backdrops and a stool set off to the side. It looked like a professional studio built right into her home.

"Take off your clothes and lie right there," she said, pointing to a large, fluffy white area rug in the center of the room.

"Monica, I am not in the mood for taking pictures," I said, a little irritated. Shit, I was ready for back-to-back orgasms. We could play photographer another day.

"Just a couple, I promise. These are for my private collection so that I can look at you when you're not here."

"Let me end up on the internet and see what happens," I said to her as I disrobed and made myself comfortable on the floor.

"Panties, too," she said, pointing at my thong.

"I thought I could get away with that." I smiled sheepishly as I took them off and tossed them where my clothes were lying. I made a mental note to keep track of them because my panties always did a disappearing act when she was around.

"Now, I want you to relax. Look seductive, as if I'm tasting you right now. Play with yourself and cum for the camera. The flash is off, so it won't distract you. Just act like I'm not even here."

I started out leaning up on my elbow and stroking my clit. I held my lips open with my thumb and middle finger while my forefinger dipped into my cave and teased my clit. My eyes were closed. My head rolled back. Thoughts of James kept trying to surface, but I blocked them out and pretended that my finger was Monica's tongue.

In the background, I could hear Monica make comments on how I was doing, and she got so close a few times I thought she took a picture of my uterus or something. I could feel the camera lens press against me. I spotted a bowl of wax fruit and vegetables on a table in the corner, and I walked over to see what I could use. Selecting an oversized cucumber, I stretched back out and continued my journey. Using the cucumber made for some very interesting pictures.

"Let's take this to the shower."

I got up without saying a word and followed her to her bedroom. She was still snapping pictures as I bent over to turn the shower on and then fixed my hair in a bun so it wouldn't get wet. After adjusting the water temperature, I stepped under the steady stream and began to seductively lather my body with the loofah that was resting on the side. I sucked on my own nipples, moaning in the process. She was moaning too, but she never put the camera down.

After a few more shots she joined me, and we devoured each other until the water got cold. Monica dried me off and laid me on the bed. I fell asleep instantly when my head touched the pillow. I knew taking the photos was a bad idea, but I wanted to make her happy.

I woke up to her kissing me on my stomach an hour later. Stretching to get the kinks out, I smiled down at her as she made her way down toward my feet.

"Sleep well?" she asked, helping me sit up on the side of her bed.

"Yes, I did. Thanks for asking."

I got up and noticed that my clothes were folded neatly in the lounge chair by the door. I walked over and started to get dressed. Once again I couldn't find my panties, and I had to wonder what was up. *Is this an invasion of the panty snatchers or what?* It was like I was losing a sock in the dryer or something.

"Monica, have you seen my panties? They're not over here."

"Yes, I put them away for safe keeping," she answered nonchalantly like that was the right thing to do. This girl wore me out in more ways than she knew.

"I need to put them on. I can't go home without panties on. James will know I was out doing something I had no business doing."

"I need them. That's all I have of you when you're away," she pouted, looking irresistible.

"That's fine, but every time I come here you keep them. You must have at least ten pairs of my underwear. How many memories do you need?" I was still getting dressed while we were talking, minus the undergarments. I just knew I needed to get home, and I didn't have time to argue.

"Are you mad at me?" she asked like she was about to cry.

"No, sweetie. I'm not mad. I just want you to keep what we talked about in mind."

"I am and just wish you could stay."

I gathered my suit jacket and hair barrette and made my way downstairs. She followed me slowly, and I waited impatiently by the door, although my face didn't show it. I wanted to scream for her to move a little faster, but I didn't want to hurt her feelings. When she got to the door she had tears on her cheeks, and I wanted to drop my bag and never leave, but I had to go.

"Monica, don't do this to me. I need you to be understanding."

"I'm fine. I just miss you already."

"I'll be back, and I'll call you when I get home. Just don't cry, okay?"

"You do love me, right?"

"Yes, Monica, I love you."

"Okay, drive safely."

"I will, and I'll call you."

She watched me until I got to my car. I waved at her as I pulled off, and I jetted home to be with my family.

I said I didn't want this, but for some reason I couldn't walk away. She wouldn't let me. An old saying that my grandmother used to say to me came to mind as I went well past the speed limit on the expressway: "The first time you hurt me, it's shame on you. The second time, it's shame on me. All the times after that is plain foolishness." I felt like a fool, too. I knew that all of this would blow up in my face sooner or later. What you do in the dark will come out in the light whether you want it to or not.

When I got home, James and the kids were in the den watching *Finding Nemo*. I kissed the kids on the cheek and said hello to James. He gave me a weak response, never taking his eyes off the television. I wasn't in the mood for his bullshit, so I went on upstairs and hopped in the shower. When I came out, he was already in the bed reading a magazine. I tried my best to ignore him as I moisturized my body so that I could put some nightclothes on and chill. I saw him peeking at my naked body, and I also saw him rise to the occasion. *He better go to the bathroom and get to whacking because ain't shit poppin'.*

I stepped into my knee-length chemise and climbed under the covers. Turning my back to him, I chilled on my side and closed my eyes, thinking about how I was going to deal with Monica. I almost didn't hear him talking to me until he repeated his question for the third time.

"What did you say?" I asked with my back still facing him. I wanted this to be quick and done with.

"I asked, how was work?"

"Fine," I said, and left it at that. He still wanted to talk, and I felt like we were playing *Jeopardy!* with all the questions he was throwing at me.

"Is the case coming along okay?"

"Yeah."

"What's with the short answers?" he said, a tad agitated. I didn't even give a damn, and I told him just that.

"I've been wondering that same thing for the past four months. Just giving you what you've been giving me," I responded with a smirk on my face.

"I told you I was stressed at work."

"That's the same excuse I have then."

"You weren't at work. I called there six times."

"And what, you're checking up on me now?"

"No, it's not like that."

"Then what is it like? You've been giving me your ass to kiss for months. Now all of a sudden you care about my well-being? James, please, tell that shit to someone who gives a damn."

"I do care. I've just been going through stuff."

"I tried to help you."

"I know that, and I apologize. I just don't want to lose you to someone else."

"Like who, James?" I started to sweat a little because I thought maybe he found out about me and Monica, but I wasn't going to be the one to say it first.

"I don't know who, but I need to know that it's just me and you."

I turned to face him and asked with a straight face, "Have I ever cheated on you before?"

"No, but—"

"Then I have no reason to now."

"Are you sure?"

"Are you? Usually when you start pointing the finger it's you who's doing it," I replied with way more attitude than what was required for this level of conversation. If deflection were a person, I was she.

"I would never do that."

"Neither would I."

"Then how come we haven't been having sex lately?"

"Because you've been acting like a dickhead, and I'm just not in the mood for it. That five minutes you dishing out I can do myself." I regretted it as soon as it left my lips.

"So, is that how it is? Is that what you think of me?"

"James, it's not like that."

"If it wasn't like that, you wouldn't have said it," he responded while he put on the sweat suit he had on earlier.

"James, why are you leaving?"

"I just need to clear my head. I'll be back. The kids are still watching the movie, so check on them in another half hour."

I was left speechless with a dumb-ass look on my face as he walked out of the bedroom. I heard him get in the car and pull away, and I resisted the urge to jump in my Jeep and go after him. I wanted to, but I couldn't leave the kids here by themselves, and by the time I would have gotten dressed and got them to the neighbors, he would be long gone. Besides all that, I didn't want them in my business, and I didn't know where he was going. I just sat on the bed and thought about the last couple of months and what our future held. At this rate it didn't look too bright, and I was hoping our vows "for better or worse" held up.

How It All Went Down . . .

Chapter Six

James

I pulled up in front of Monica's house after riding around in circles for two hours. I had no intention of ever seeing Monica again, but her body was calling me. The creeping we had been doing for the past four months had started to wear me down, and my relationship with Jasmine was suffering because of it. Taking all of that into consideration, I still walked my stupid ass slowly up the path to Monica's house. Standing outside the door, hesitant to ring the bell, I finally leaned on it until she answered. I had no business being there, this I knew. I felt terrible about it, but the things my wife said made me feel even worse. I knew that if no one else in the world could make me feel wanted, Monica would.

When she opened the door, a pleasant smile spread across her face. She hadn't expected to see me this evening, especially since I just told her earlier that I had to rethink some things at home. Standing in front of me in crotchless French-cut boy shorts and three-inch stiletto heels, she waited for me to stop staring at her exposed breasts and to make contact with her eyes before she said anything.

"To what do I owe the pleasure of seeing your handsome face this evening?" she purred in my ear as she ran her hands up under my shirt and across my nipples.

I tried to act like I wasn't fazed by her actions, but my evident erection spoke volumes.

"I needed to get out of the house. Jazz is trippin' again," I said, remembering my reason for being out that time of night in the first place. My erection faded to nothing as I stood with my head bowed down, feeling vulnerable, waiting for Monica to invite me in.

"Really?" she responded, looking like she was trying to decide if she wanted to deal with me. "Want to come in and talk about it?" she finally asked.

"Yeah," I said, stepping into her living room, brushing against her to get by.

I could tell by her actions that Monica already had her mind set on getting some before I left, and she made sure that I knew it, too. Before I knocked on the door I could hear Monica was upstairs entertaining, but I didn't know who. I knew she was messing around with other women, because we'd had many threesomes, and not just with Jasmine. She also had a thing for Sheila, Jasmine's secretary. Neither Jasmine nor Sheila knew about each other, and that made for a perfect playing field for Monica. With Jasmine she got her cake, I gave her the ice cream, and Sheila was the cherry on top. It would make for the perfect sundae if she could get us all together at one time.

We sat down in the living room, and she removed my sneakers before placing my feet in her lap and giving me a foot massage. She always gave the best massages that always led to something else. I was trying to stay focused, but she was making it difficult. I got into detail about what happened with Jasmine and how our sex life was next to nothing since I had been dealing with her. I went into how I didn't think we could continue the affair because I needed to make my home life work.

"Honestly, I don't know what to do," I said to Monica in a defeated voice.

"You know what your problem is?" she asked me softly. By her tone I could tell that she didn't want to ruffle any feathers because she wanted to at least fuck me one more time before I decided to stay away for good. Monica was greedy like that. She probably didn't think we would hook up again after the threesome she talked me into having with Jasmine, but it kind of just worked out that way. I dropped $3,000 on that night, and the money just kept coming. When I gave her the money for the threesome, that was supposed to be it, but months later I still found myself paying for her services.

"My problem?" I responded, sounding annoyed. "Why do I have to have a problem?"

"James, relax. I'm not saying a problem like that. I'm just going to point out what you're doing wrong. Shall I continue?"

"Please do!" I responded, ready to leave. After all, I didn't come here to hear what I was doing wrong. I knew what I was doing was unacceptable.

"The issue is your sex life has changed at home, right?"

"Yeah, she doesn't do what you do. Not to say that she's not good, but with you it's always something new."

"Does she have sex with you every time you want it?"

"Yeah, even when she doesn't want to," I said, wondering where this conversation was going.

"Are you still doing the same things for her that you used to? And don't lie," Monica warned me. Her massage was now up to my calves, and I was having a hard time concentrating.

"I'd like to think so."

"The thing is, James, when a man cheats on wifey, he tends to neglect her because he's concentrating on his new toy. What you don't realize is your wife can do the same things I do, probably better if you took your time with her. Don't change up your sexual habits with her because all you can think about is how good I'll fuck you. That's exactly how wives always find out that men are cheating. You change, and that's not good."

"So what am I supposed to do?" I asked, wanting desperately to make things right.

Monica was good to me. I couldn't deny that, but Jasmine was my wife, the mother of my kids, my soulmate. I couldn't see messing up everything we'd built together over a booty call.

"After you're done here, go home and make up with your wife. Don't rush it, but let her see that you're changing. You can have your cake and eat it, too. You just have to know when to do it. Everything is better in moderation," she explained like there was nothing to it.

"I understand that, but are you going to be okay with us not seeing each other for a while? I don't want to hurt you in the process," I asked, trying to make sure I still had her in the tuck just in case this Jasmine shit blew up in my face.

"I'm cool with it. I have someone else occupying my time right now. Want to go upstairs and unwind before you go home?"

"Do you think I should?"

"I don't see why not. You won't be here for a while, so you might as well get one for the road."

Monica stood up and walked toward the stairs. I followed like a little puppy dog, feeling kind of guilty on the inside. I had started seeing Monica months before I brought Jasmine in on the threesome. I told myself that after they got together in the hotel that night I would be leaving Monica alone, and I did try. I promise I did everything in my power to let this go. Monica just had a way of making you feel like you were missing out on something when she wasn't around.

I looked at the drawings on the wall as we walked by, and I stopped when I noticed one of the men in the drawings looked like me. In the drawing, I was lying on my back on pink roses, and Monica was riding me with her back facing me. Her head was thrown back, and her arm rested on my chest for support. Monica's hair was long in the drawing and a rose rested at her temple. I didn't know what to say. I just kind of stood there gazing at it.

Monica made her way to the top of the steps and yelled for me to hurry up. I tore my gaze from the drawing and made my way up the stairs a little puzzled at how I became a part of her collection. I knew that Monica was an artist and that she drew black art and sold it for big money. I also knew that she was a professional photographer and took pictures for a number of different agencies. I never thought that I would be in one of them and was going to question her once I got in the bedroom.

When I walked into the bedroom, all thoughts of questioning Monica left my mind as I laid eyes on Sheila, to my dismay. I remembered her face, but I never thought I'd get the opportunity to see it in this capacity. I wished that I would come home one day and find Jasmine in our bedroom with a beautiful woman. I also knew Jasmine didn't get down like that, and that she only dealt with Monica that night to make me happy. I didn't have the nerve to ask her to do it again.

"Hello, so glad you could join us," Sheila said before she kneeled down on the side of the bed between Monica's legs. Monica closed her eyes and leaned her head back, enjoying the tongue-lashing Sheila was giving her. I undressed immediately, then walked over and joined them on the bed.

I kissed Monica's lips briefly before finding my way to her chocolate nipples. Sheila's mouth had already wrapped around my erection, and I almost exploded instantly when her tongue ring made contact with the head of my dick. I remembered thinking she was better than Monica before I lay back on the bed, allowing Monica to sit on my face.

Monica held her lips apart as I flicked and sucked her clit until she came in my mouth. Standing up on the bed, she motioned for me to move back so that my entire body was on the bed comfortably. Switching places, Monica straddled my length, and Sheila sat on my face. The two women kissed and fondled each other until we all exploded together. My seed dripped out of Monica when she stood up off me, and I regretted it immediately.

Now in the shower I was beating myself up on the inside because I never ever had sex without protection with anyone but my wife until Monica came along and debunked that theory. I never bothered to ask Monica if she was on any type of birth control, and I feared it was too late to inquire now because I knew she would be offended. Sheila and Monica scrubbed me clean while I was in a daze and helped me dress so that I could get home.

"Where are my boxers?" I asked Monica while Sheila was putting my socks on my feet.

"I put them away for safe keeping," she responded nonchalantly as she pulled my undershirt over my head. Sheila already had my pants halfway up and was waiting for me to stand so that she could finish the job.

"Every time I come here you keep my boxers. What do you have now? About ten or twelve pair?" I asked, a little annoyed. I could not go home without any underclothes on, and I hoped my credit card was in the car so that I could stop and get some on the way back from a gas station or Walmart.

"That's all I have to keep me close to you," Monica responded as she pushed me toward the front door.

When we got downstairs, I turned to get one last look at her. I gazed into her eyes and then down at the rest of her body, stopping at the red lace boy shorts she had on. Kissing her one last time, I looked down at her underwear again, trying to remember if I'd seen them before.

"You know, my wife has a pair of panties just like these," I said while pulling lightly at the band around her waist.

"She has good taste," Monica said, smiling up at me.

"Yeah."

I looked at the door and then turned to face Monica again. "About that drawing on the wall . . . I don't remember posing for it."

"You didn't. I remembered one of the nights you were here and decided to put it on canvas. Is that okay?" she asked, daring me to say otherwise. If I had said it wasn't cool, she would probably send it to Jasmine in the mail to let her know I had been there. Luckily for me I didn't have a problem with it.

"No, it's cool. Just don't let it get out, okay? You know, with my career and all," I said, my voice slightly quivering.

"It won't. Now go home," Monica said while opening the door. She clearly wanted me out, and I was obviously starting to get on her nerves. I had already served my purpose for these two, I supposed. She didn't need me anymore, so there was no use in wasting her time talking about shit she didn't care about.

"One more question, and then I'm gone."

"What, James?" she spat at me, her annoyance showing.

"Is that woman Jasmine's secretary?" I asked just to confirm that who I saw was indeed who I saw.

"Yes, why do you ask?" she replied with a slight smile on her face.

"She won't tell, will she? I don't want any trouble with them on the job."

"No, your secret is safe. Now go home!"

"Okay, okay, I'm going. I miss you already."

"Yeah, yeah. I miss you too. Now go."

I made my way to the car slowly, trying to make sense of what just happened. With me busting a nut inside of Monica and orally pleasing my wife's secretary, I was sure this wasn't the end of it. I just prayed that I could fix things at home before shit got too far out of hand. I played myself tonight for sure, and now it was time to go do some damage control while I could.

Chapter Seven

Sheila

I listened to everything from the top of the stairs and crept back to the room when I heard Monica closing the front door. I liked Jasmine as a person and didn't want anything to do with this bullshit Monica had cooking up. No, I didn't know him personally, but he was my boss's husband, and that was more than enough to stay away from him. I was sitting on the edge of the bed contemplating all of this when Monica walked in the room.

"So, Sheila, did you enjoy yourself tonight, sweetie?" Monica asked before she reached behind the mirror and pulled out the camcorder. I didn't know we were being taped, and I didn't know what to do. I had just gotten myself into some serious shit and was clueless as to how to get out of it. Like, what the fuck did I just do? This was really bad, and I couldn't afford for Jasmine to find out about this.

"Yes, it was nice, but I need to be heading out. I need to pick up my son from my mom's house before she starts calling around looking for me."

My son was at home with my sister, but I was trying to find any reason to leave. I knew I would never step foot into Monica's house again, but I had to get out first. This shit felt creepy all of a sudden, and my body quaked in anticipation to be free of this place.

"No problem, sweetie. Call a cab and get yourself dressed. I want to download some of these pictures onto my laptop before I forget. Let me know when you're leaving," Monica replied before leaving the room. She never even made eye contact with me as she talked.

Instantly I felt stupid as hell. This bitch used me, and I definitely let her. I mean, James wasn't a part of the original plan, but Monica's slick ass was quick on her feet with this one. I got played, and now I had to figure my way out of it.

I got dressed as quickly as possible after calling a cab from Monica's phone. I sat in the living room as I was instructed and didn't budge until the cab driver honked his horn out front. Monica came into the living room and gave me money to get home in one envelope and money for the evening in another. I was confused as to why I was getting paid for being there, and it showed all over my face. I had never gotten paid before. What was up with that?

"Now, this night is our little secret, right?" she warned more than asked me as she waited for me to reply.

"Yes, I won't say anything."

"Okay, I'll call you later. Be sure to answer the phone."

I walked out of the house, and Monica watched me from the doorway, not seeming to care that she was still topless. Just as I was opening the cab door, Monica called out to me. I looked at Monica, puzzled at what she was calling me for.

"Just a heads-up," Monica began with an evil look on her face. "Don't fuck with me!"

I got into the cab quickly and instructed the driver to take me home. My heart didn't slow down for a couple of blocks, and for once in my life someone other than my mother put real, genuine fear in me. I never suspected Monica was crazy, just a little obsessive with all the pink and white going on. Now that I knew for sure Monica was in fact crazy, I had to find a way to tell Jasmine without her finding out that I slept with her husband, too. I didn't know what to do and was in tears by the time I got home.

Grabbing my son, I lay in the bed holding onto him for dear life as tears ran from my eyes. How in the hell did I end up in this shit? Monica was supposed to be just something to do. I ran into her one day while I was at the courthouse getting documents filed for Jasmine and gathering info from the law library for upcoming cases. It was so innocent how she approached me, and I fell for the okey-doke.

"Sheila, right?" she said to me as she joined me at the table in the law library. I looked up with confusion covering my face, wondering who this woman was and how she knew me. Monica was . . . yummy. I mean, if I had to pick a word to describe her. Milk chocolate and flawless, and she smelled delicious. As much as I loved the dick, every so often I could be found playing in a split as well. I had to make myself look away as I got lost in eyes nearly the same warm color as her flesh.

"Yes?" I responded more like a question than an answer. I was sure I sounded dumb as hell, but she caught me off guard. "Do we know each other?"

"Not yet," she responded with a sly smile on her face. She introduced herself as a photographer who was looking up old photos of criminals because she had an idea for a photoshoot theme she wanted to produce.

Did it sound dumb as all hell? Why, yes. Yes, it did. However, I was so caught up in her beauty I couldn't get my thoughts straight. She told me that she recognized—wait for it—my voice from when I answered the phone when she called the law office. I was one of a few secretaries who answered the phone at any given time, but my voice stood out. No way I should be this damn gullible, but I was. At any rate, we conversed more, and she somehow managed to talk me over to her crib after work that day.

"It's the only pink house on the block," she instructed as she left my side that afternoon. When I got to the block, I saw it was technically a white house with pink accents, but I got the point. The pink rosebushes, mailbox, and other accessories made hers stand out from the rest.

By the time I left there that night she had my body twisted in ways from orgasms that I couldn't even explain. She licked, sucked, and fucked on every part of my body, and my limbs felt like wet noodles by the time it was said and done. I was hooked and couldn't wait to do it again. Monica was nasty as fuck, and I was there for it.

Just my damn luck, the second time I went there, my boss's husband popped the fuck up. What else was I supposed to do besides what I did? Before Monica answered the door she told me what was going to happen when she saw him pull up. I was shocked to see him, but she was ready to put in work. I felt horrible about this entire night, but it was okay. *I'm going to sleep this off and come up with a plan in the morning.*

Pulling my son closer to me, I kissed his forehead before I finally dozed off to sleep. I was not going to let her put fear in me. All was fair in love and war.

Chapter Eight

James

I had left my credit card in another pants pocket and didn't have any cash on me to replace the underclothes that Monica took from me. I decided once I got in the house that I would hop in the shower and sleep in the guest room. I wanted to make up with Jasmine for the way I had been acting, but tonight wouldn't work. I smelled like I just came from Monica's house, and I didn't want Jasmine to think I was stepping out on her.

When I walked in, Jasmine was lying on the couch, asleep. She must have been waiting for me to get back and dozed off. Looking at my watch, I saw that I'd been gone for at least three hours, and I knew that Jasmine was going to have a fit when she woke up. I also knew that if I tried to sneak past her and hop in the shower, she would definitely know what I had done.

Stuck between a rock and a hard place, I decided to wake Jasmine up and try to apologize to her. I stood over her, watching her sleep, and silently wondered what I had gotten myself into dealing with Monica. I knew I had to stay away or Jasmine would find out I was creeping. I honestly couldn't think of a reason to cheat on my wife, and I did feel bad. I decided at that moment that I wouldn't contact Monica anymore. From what I could see she was nothing but trouble, trouble that was easy to get into. Trouble that I low-key liked getting into, but I'd deny it if anyone ever asked me.

"Jasmine, wake up," I whispered in her ear, shaking her a little to get her attention. When she opened her eyes, she looked at me like she wanted to punch me clean out.

"What time is it?" she asked while she sat up on the couch and got herself together.

"It's one thirty in the morning," I responded while bracing myself to be cursed out. Jasmine had a sharp tongue and could slice you up with just words alone.

"So you've been gone for at least three hours. Why did you leave like that without letting me explain myself?"

"Jazz, I really don't know. You hurt me."

"I hurt you? You've been acting like you hate me for the last few months. How did I hurt you?"

"I know I've been treating you wrong. I've been stressed at work and tired when I get home," I said, avoiding her question. I didn't have a real reason why I was treating her bad other than me just being stupid.

"I'm tired when I get home too, but I make sure you and the kids eat, and if you want to have sex, you get it no matter how late I'm at the office. I bend over backward to keep this house running smoothly no matter how stressed I am."

"Baby, I know, and I'm sorry about the way I've been treating you. I'm sorry I stormed out of here the way I did. I just needed to breathe for a second."

"James, I need to breathe too. You say shit to me that I don't like, but I stay here and deal with it! I just can't up and leave because I have kids to think about. Mommy can't afford to have a breakdown when things don't go right," Jasmine said between her tears. I briefly wondered what real reason she was crying for, but that was just me projecting my insecurities on her. I checked myself before I played myself.

"I know that, Jazz. I know I need to change, but I need you to stick it out and help me. I need you to love me like you used to."

"James, that will never change, but you need to get it together. I can't do this by myself."

"Baby, I know. I love you so much, and I need you. Whatever you do, just don't leave." I was begging her, damn near in tears. I had to leave Monica alone, and I vowed to myself right then that I would never be alone with her after this day. I had to if I wanted my marriage to work.

Chapter Nine

Monica

I placed the photos that I downloaded from my camcorder into a hidden safe behind the picture I drew of myself and the mayor of DC. I had my hooks in his wife also, and I decided that it was about time to call for my money. He had paid me to keep quiet about him sleeping with me on occasion, and he didn't know that I was having sex with his wife and his oldest daughter also. I also knew I had to keep Sheila in check before her paranoid ass messed up everything. I had work to do, and I went to relax in the tub before putting my plan into action.

There were starting to be way too many variables, but if nothing else, I knew how to work shit out. The plan was to get rid of James for good. Jasmine wanted me. I was sure of it. I just had to get her to see things my way. I could understand that she felt like what she was doing was horrible to her family, but in reality, it wasn't that bad. I mean, she could still coparent with his raggedy ass, right? I wasn't trying to completely dismantle the entire household, but she needed to understand that her safest place was with me. Not James's nut ass.

Sigh. A girl's work was never done.

Sinking down into the hot water, I allowed the warmth to relax me as my mind raced with what moves I would make next. I had to be smart about it, and after a while

I knew exactly what I needed to do. A smile crossed my face as I sank deeper into the water until I was completely submerged. If this played out the way I was expecting it to, I would have everything I wanted and more.

It appeared that, for James, staying away from me was nothing. I knew he thought I was trouble, and to avoid losing his wife, he just simply avoided me. I called his cell phone on occasion to hook up, but he always had a reason why it wasn't a good idea. This of course frustrated me to no end, and I wasn't one to let things go easily. Deciding to pay James a little visit at home, I got into my hot pink convertible Benz dressed in a trench coat and stiletto heels. Hair freshly done, makeup perfect, and nothing underneath was sure to get James's attention, and I almost burst with anticipation as I zigzagged in and out of traffic on a twenty-minute ride to the Cinque household.

Deciding to park a block down from the house so that he wouldn't hear me pull up in the driveway, I made my way to the front door, my heels echoing loudly on the sidewalk. First glancing through the window, I spied James sitting on the couch in boxers and a T-shirt, watching television. I knew Jasmine and the kids were away because Sheila had informed me that Jasmine went to visit her mother in Virginia on a three-day weekend vacation. James couldn't go because it was sweeps week at the station, and he had to be there to make sure everything ran smoothly.

Ringing the doorbell, I loosened the belt on my coat so that when he opened the door I could surprise him. I felt in my pocket for the pair of panties I had in there, then posed for him once the door opened.

"Monica, what are you doing here?" James asked as he leaned out the door and looked from side to side to make sure none of his neighbors were out. It appeared that things with him and Jasmine were starting to get better, and the last thing he needed was one of his nosy-ass neighbors seeing another woman entering his house. They would probably tell Jasmine no sooner than when she set foot on the block, and that would be something else he would have to explain. They were finally talking out their differences from what I could tell, and although it wasn't back to normal, it was damn close. At least that was the reason in my head why I hadn't heard from him for some time now.

"I came to see you. I miss you," I responded, revealing myself to James. The look on his face said it all, yet he hadn't invited me in. Rubbing my hands down my body, I looked James in the eye, waiting for him to say something.

"I told you we had to chill for a while. I thought you understood that," James responded with his eyes still roaming all over my naked body. My trench coat was falling off of my shoulders while I fingered myself. If he didn't invite me in soon, I would be standing in front of him, naked for the entire neighborhood to see.

"Yeah, but Jazz and the kids are out of town, and you know what they say," I responded as I walked up to him in the doorway and took hold of his erection. "When the cat's away . . ."

"Monica, we can't do this. Jasmine would have a fit!" James tried to keep his cool as I was backing him into the house, but it wasn't working. By now I had the door closed and him sprawled out on the couch with his boxers down around his knees.

"What she doesn't know won't hurt you. You know you want this."

I kissed him behind his ear and stroked his length against my clit at the same time. My wetness covered the head of his penis, and James struggled to gain control of the situation.

"Monica, you shouldn't be here," James responded weakly as he pushed me off him. He stood up, pulling his boxers up with him, and tried to clear his head. I was set on getting it whether he wanted to give it or not, and instead of arguing with him, I turned and went upstairs.

James was left standing in his living room with a hard dick, not knowing what to do. I heard his footsteps as he went over and locked the door. I wasn't leaving until I got what I came for. He had no choice but to knock me off real quick, and his best bet was to get it done quickly so that I could leave.

By the time James came up to the room, I was spread out on the lounge chair by the window with both sets of my lips spread open. My eyes were closed, and I didn't open them until he was right up on me.

"Monica, we have to make this quick. I don't know what time Jazz will be back, and she can't see you here!" He got down on his knees on the side of the chair so that we could talk face-to-face. A man will choose pussy every time, ladies. He could have put me out and rejected me, but he didn't want to. The pussy was too powerful to pass up.

Instead of responding, I took my finger out of my walls and placed it in his mouth. His eyes closed as he tasted my wetness with a hint of chocolate body butter mixed in. He stood at attention immediately, and I moved up so that the head of his penis was just inside of my throbbing walls.

James moaned as my muscles contracted around his head as I ground on him slowly, not letting more than that go in. I wrapped my legs around his waist, still not letting him fully penetrate me as I tongue kissed his nipples and rubbed his back.

Slowly at first, we pushed and pulled on each other. I fed James my nipples one at a time as his strokes quickened inside of me, making me lean against the windowsill for support. We moaned like crazy, and James was just about ready to explode until we looked out the window and saw Jasmine's Jeep pull into the driveway.

"Monica, you have to go! Jazz just pulled up."

Scared to death, James pulled out and ejaculated on me. Grabbing the Glade air freshener, he started spraying the room to get the smell of sex out after pulling on his boxers. I grabbed one of Jasmine's blouses out of the closet and wiped the semen off my stomach, leaving what was on my pubic area there. I knew if I got pregnant, Jasmine would leave him, and I was ready to do anything to make it happen.

I made my way to the kitchen and could hear Jasmine getting the kids out of the car. James had hopped in the shower and probably planned to stay there until Jasmine came upstairs looking for him, like he was in there the entire time. I slipped out the back door just as Jasmine was opening the front, and I crept around the side of the house and down the street into my car unnoticed.

Pulling up in front of the house, I parked my car, grabbed the binoculars that rested on the passenger seat, and stared up at the window that led into Jasmine and James's bedroom. I watched James walk into the bedroom with a towel wrapped around his waist. I was so angry as I watched James embrace Jasmine and kiss her slowly. I wanted Jasmine to come home to me and to kiss me that way. Briefly, I pictured myself in Jasmine's arms, and before a tear could drop, I peeled off down the street and onto the expressway, thinking of how to put plan B into motion. I had to make her mine sooner rather than later. Otherwise, I didn't know what the future held for James and those kids, but it wasn't looking good for him.

Chapter Ten

James

I held my wife like I hadn't seen her in ages. Jasmine thought it was because we were apart for the weekend, but I was just relieved that Monica made it out in time. I sat down on the side of the bed after I was sure that Monica was gone. I saw her sitting outside the house from the window. I knew kissing Jasmine would piss Monica off, but I didn't care as long as she was gone.

"I missed you too," Jasmine said once I pulled back from the kiss. She smiled. She wasn't expecting this, and she was pleasantly surprised.

"What are you doing back so soon? I thought you guys weren't coming back until the evening," I said as I sat down on the bed to moisturize my body. I didn't want any traces of Monica on me or in the room, and I sprayed cologne on my body just to make sure.

"It started raining pretty heavy down there, so I wanted to make it back before it started to flood. You know how it is down my mom's way with the dirt roads and everything," Jasmine responded, taking a seat on the lounge chair and leaning back. Her arm fell over the side lazily, making contact with the blouse Monica used to wipe her stomach off. I spotted it, but Jasmine was already leaning over to pick it up.

Holding the shirt up and feeling the stickiness on her hand, she looked at me, puzzled. I continued looking down at my legs and moisturizing my body like I didn't see her pick the shirt up off the floor. I wasn't going to say anything until she asked, and I hoped I could come up with a good excuse as to why there was a sticky substance on her favorite Donna Karan blouse.

"James," she said with a little attitude in her voice, holding the shirt close to my bowed head, "can you explain this to me?"

Looking up guiltily, I examined the shirt that she was holding with her fingertips up to my face. I didn't really know what to say, and I didn't want to lie. I also knew I couldn't tell her that I'd just finished having sex with Monica on the lounge chair she was lying on and had exploded all over her stomach when she pulled up, and just to be a smart-ass Monica used her shirt to wipe off. That would get me jacked up for sure.

"Before you came, I was thinking about what you did to me before you left. You know your riding skills are the bomb, and I wanted something of yours near me. I was handling business and let off on your blouse because I didn't want to get it on the bed. I was gonna have it cleaned before you noticed it."

"Then why was it under the lounge chair?" Jasmine asked suspiciously. Maybe she saw Monica's car as she was riding up the street, but I wasn't sure. We didn't know too many people with a hot pink convertible, but I opted to pay it no mind.

"Because that's where I was. You know how I do, and I would have exploded all over the place if I didn't have something to cover up with. I didn't think much about it and was going to put it in the bag for dry cleaning when I got out of the shower. You pulled up as I was getting out, and it totally slipped my mind. I can buy you another one, though. Two if it'll keep you from being upset with me. I just missed you, that's all."

With all that said, I bowed my head down like I was in some serious trouble and waited for Jasmine to snap. Instead, she just threw the shirt in the hamper by the door and moved closer to me. Lifting my head up by the chin, she kissed me softly, straddling my lap in the process.

"Okay, James, it's cool. The next time, use something that didn't cost so much, please. Semen isn't all that easy to get out of silk," Jasmine replied with a smile before standing up. "I'm going to put the kids down for a nap. Be ready to make it up to me when I get back."

"I will," I responded as she left the room.

I didn't know how I made it out of that one, but I knew I would be staying as far away from Monica as possible. That girl was trouble with a capital T, and if I didn't play my hand right, Jasmine would leave me without thinking twice about it.

Jasmine came back in the room dressed in a pink thong and sandals that strapped to her knee of the same color. She hit the power button on the stereo, and the slow version of "Sumthin' Sumthin'" from the *Love Jones* soundtrack played right on cue. Jasmine danced her way over to the bed, sensuously keeping constant eye contact with me. Topless, she crawled up to me on her knees, kissing my body on the way up. I couldn't help but think that the show I was watching was something that Monica would do, but I was glad to see my wife broadening her views on creative lovemaking.

Squatting down onto my erection, Jasmine rode me slowly with her hands on the headboard for support. While we tossed and turned into different positions, I recalled thinking about Monica only once and saying to myself that this was going to be one hell of a night.

Throwing her legs up on my shoulders, I made sure to pay special attention to her clit, pushing deep just the way she liked it. She felt good as shit, and the warmth that surrounded us both like a cocoon had me feeling lightheaded. Grabbing hold of her ass, I leaned back, dragging her forward. Her legs were straddling me, but her body was spread out, shaking like a leaf in the wind. The top of her back and shoulders were on the bed, and the rest of her was basically in my lap. Damn, I wanted to taste her, but she felt so good I didn't want to pull out.

"Tell daddy what you want," I moaned out as I pulsed inside of her. I was losing it slowly and trying to maintain composure. She was extra juicy tonight, dripping all over my balls and pelvis. Much wetter than Monica had ever been. She was so slippery, and my thumb slid across her clit with ease. I sat still, no movement, and the clenching she was doing matched my pulse as she tried to catch her breath.

I pulled all the way out until just the head was in. The veins in my dick glistened with her juices, and I didn't think I could get harder, but I did. Her moans were driving me crazy as she tried to grip me and pull me back inside. I would give her an inch and pull back out to the tip. I would then give her a little more, then pull all the way back out. She was going crazy, grabbing her hair and gripping at the air, trying to gain some form of control.

"You must don't want this dick," I threatened as I lifted her from me and slammed back down balls deep. That move almost caused me to nut, and I had to gain control quickly.

"I want it! I do!" she yelled out, wrapping her body around me and grinding into me. I pushed myself up from the bed, carrying her to the wall, using it to support her body. Stepping into my Timberlands, I gave myself some leverage so that I wouldn't slip while holding her.

I drilled into her at a steady pace, the sounds her pussy was making taking me over the edge.

"Go deeper. Push all the way to the back. Make me cum on it." She whispered some real dirty, nasty shit in my ear, making me blush low-key. I was able to bring us both to a climax without dropping my girl on the floor. When she climbed down from the wall and dropped to her knees to suck out the little bit of cum I had left in my balls, I knew for sure that this Monica shit had to stop. Jasmine was coming with her A game, and I could only pray that she kept up the good work.

We went one more time in the shower before we took it down for the night. As she lay under me, sleeping and snoring lightly, I stared at her. *I love this woman, I really do. For the life of me, I just can't figure out why Monica is so appealing.* Finally succumbing to sleep myself, I made up my mind to do right by her.

For real this time.

Chapter Eleven

Monica

I ate ice cream and waited for the results of the pregnancy test I just took. Who knew three minutes could be so long? As I paced outside of the bathroom door, trying patiently to wait for the timer to sound, indicating my time was up, my thoughts were all over the place. When I got home, I did a headstand for about three minutes, hoping whatever semen was on me would find its way to my insides. Never mind most of it was rubbed off on the way home. Thinking rationally was not a priority here. Having James's baby would be a scandalous thing, but I couldn't care less. I lived for drama, and scandal was my favorite pastime.

Finally the buzzer sounded, causing me to almost drop my dessert on the floor. Walking quickly into the bathroom, I set my pint of Ben and Jerry's on the vanity and stared down at the test on the back of the toilet. Not sure what the line meant, I picked up the box to read the instructions.

"'One stripe means not pregnant, two stripes mean baby on board,'" I said aloud. Looking down at the test, I only saw one line.

"This is bullshit! Is the nigga shootin' blanks or what?" I said to my frustrated reflection in the mirror. I knew

James could make babies because he had twins now. I made sure he was inside of me the first time, and the second time he pulled out, but I still got some on me. I felt pregnant, or so went my imagination.

"Maybe the test is old," I said, continuing my one-sided conversation. "Who knows how long they sit in the back before they are put out for sale?"

Grabbing my jacket, I decided to go to the drug store near my house. Pulling up with a screeching halt, I jumped out of the car before it stopped moving completely. Going directly to the feminine products aisle, I picked up four different brands of pregnancy tests just to make sure there wouldn't be any issues. The cashier looked at me kind of crazy as she rang the items up, and I gave her a "don't go there" look as I paid for my stuff and I ran out of the store.

On the way home, I hit ninety miles an hour, and as soon as I turned the corner to my block, a police car was right on my tail with flashing lights going off. I pulled over, mad as hell, not wanting to stop, and at one point I thought about jetting off. When the officer got to my car, I made sure to keep my hands on the steering wheel just in case this one was trigger-happy. I didn't want to become a statistic because of speeding and a few pregnancy tests.

"Can I help you, Officer?" I said to the cop standing outside my car door. I hoped he would make it quick. I had things to do.

"Ma'am, are you aware of how fast you were going?"

"No, sir, I'm not. I have to pee and was in a rush to get home. I only live a few houses down on this side of the street." I gave him my most pitiful look, but he didn't seem to be buying it.

"License, insurance, and registration, please," the cop said, looking into the car window.

"Sir, please. You can't give me a ticket. I just got this car. Let me make it up to you."

"Ma'am, are you soliciting me? I'm an officer of the law, and I can lock you up for prostitution."

"I'm not a prostitute, sir! I'm just trying to get out of this ticket. I only live a few houses down. No one has to know but me and you."

The officer looked at me for a second to see if I was serious. I started unbuttoning my shirt, exposing my chocolate breasts to the rookie cop. I had already slept with most of the guys on the force, and this one I didn't remember seeing before. His evident erection let me know I had him hooked. That was exactly how I got the mayor to sleep with me, and my little flash trick worked here too.

"Pull up at your door and go in," the officer said. "Leave the door unlocked. I'll be coming in right behind you."

Pulling off, I made my way down the block, parking my car in the driveway. Doing exactly as I was told, I went inside, stripping down to nothing as I waited for the cop to come in. Forgetting about the pregnancy and my earlier dilemma, I sat on the floor in front of the fireplace with my legs open, tugging on my clit. When the cop walked in, he spotted me and almost came on himself right then. Undressing quickly, he joined me on the rug, his head falling directly between my legs.

"Eat up, Officer," I spoke to him while holding the back of his head.

The cop kissed his way up my stomach, inserting himself unprotected as he kissed my breasts. Not even a minute later, he spit his seed inside of me, collapsing heavily on top of me. I held my breath and waited for him to move.

Rolling off of me, he snatched my shirt from the floor beside us and wiped himself off before stepping back into his uniform. I looked up at him from the floor with a smirk on my face.

"Now, be careful how you drive from now on. I wouldn't want you to tear that pretty car up," he said as he placed his state-issued hat on top of his bald head. Looking back at me one more time, he opened the door and stepped out just as his radio sounded.

"Officer Hill, what's your location?" the captain called from the precinct.

"I'm on Bellevue and Thompson on my way to City Avenue," the police officer answered, still staring at my naked body.

"There's a three-car pileup on Route 23. Get there ASAP. It looks a bit messy."

"Roger that, I'm on my way."

"Okay, ten-four."

"Ten-four."

I just looked at him, wishing he would hurry up and close the door. This was such a waste of time. After all, I was ass naked and there was a breeze outside, even for the middle of May. Officer Hill looked back at me once more before closing the door. Getting up to lock it, I almost laughed out loud at his silly ass.

"He had the nerve to look like he just did something," I said on the way upstairs. Totally forgetting about the pregnancy test at this point, I filled the tub with hot water and soaked my tired body. Thinking about Jasmine and how I was going to steal her from James was still on my mind as I rinsed off and went to lie across my bed. Before I knew it, I was drifting off to sleep, already making up my mind to visit Jasmine in the morning.

The next morning, I was parked down the street from Jasmine's house, waiting patiently for James and the kids to leave. I knew they rotated mornings on who took the kids out, and I hoped it would play in my favor today. Dozing off for a minute, I woke up in time to see James and his twins get in the car and pull off. Ducking down some in my seat so that he wouldn't see me when they passed by, I waited about five minutes before I got out of the car and went up to the door.

I was dressed similarly to what I had on for James, but this time I had on the red French-cut boy shorts that Jasmine liked me in. Tying the belt tighter around my waist, I rang the bell and waited patiently for Jasmine to answer. When Jasmine came to the door, all she had on was a bathrobe, and half her hair was pinned up because she was curling it. Half dressed, she still looked like a goddess to me, and I wanted so badly to just have her to myself for once.

"What are you doing here?" Jasmine asked, looking both ways to see if anyone was outside, just as James had. I was sure she didn't want to have to explain to James later why I was there.

"I came to see you, silly," I replied playfully. "It's been a while since we . . . you know, and I decided to catch you before you left. Maybe give you something to smile about while you're at work."

"Okay, Monica, that's cool and all, but what if James were here? How would I explain that?" Jasmine said, a little frustrated, although I could tell by the way her nipples hardened under her robe that she was getting wet just thinking about what I would do to her.

"I figured he would be gone around this time. That's why I waited. I'm sorry if I caused a problem." I began looking like I was about to cry. I had that shit down to a science at this point, and it worked on the Cinques every time. "I just miss you, and I needed to see you, so I came over."

"Look, don't cry," Jasmine said after the first tear fell. "Come on in, but we have to be quick because I have to get to work soon."

"No problem. Just lie back and let me make you feel good."

Jasmine, still a little irritated, went upstairs with me following close behind. Going to the bathroom to unplug her curling iron, she brushed her hair back into a bun and tied a scarf around it because she knew by the time me and her got done she wouldn't have time to curl her hair over.

While Jasmine was in the bathroom, I checked behind the bed to make sure the panties were still there. I also felt in my jacket pocket for the clay I brought with me. I knew a guy who made keys, and he told me all I needed was a good print of the key I wanted duplicated and he could make me one. As I looked around from my spot on the bed, I hoped Jasmine's house keys would be lying around somewhere so that I could get a print.

Jasmine entered the room naked and took a spot on the bed next to me. Scooting over in the middle of the bed and spreading her legs, she waited for me to do whatever I was going to do. I hoped James wouldn't turn around and come back to the house for anything as I began at her toes and worked my way up.

I had already taken off my panties and had them on the side of the bed. Pleasing myself in the process, I spread open Jasmine's lips with my free hand and immediately took hold of her clit, making Jasmine explode instantly. Holding her legs up, Jasmine held on to the back of my head while I devoured her. Moaning like crazy, and exploding all over the place, Jasmine took her nipples into her mouth one at a time, adding to the excitement that was already playing all over her body.

I made sure to put my tongue inside of Jasmine, lapping up all of her honey until there was nothing left. Jasmine started squirming under me, indicating an orgasm was fast approaching. Taking my hand from my own clit, I licked off my juices before inserting my fingers inside of Jasmine's tightness, her body barely on the bed as she rained all over my hand and tongue.

Reaching over into my coat pocket, I pulled out the strap on that I brought with me and stepped into it. Getting as close to Jasmine as possible on my knees, I threw her legs over my shoulders, plunging into her deeply, hoping that I was doing a better job than James. Jasmine held her lips open, begging me not to stop. I threw her legs over to the side, taking her that way, with Jasmine holding on to the headboard.

"Whose pussy is this?" I asked in a low tone but loud enough for Jasmine to hear me.

"It's yours," Jasmine replied between breaths. I was doing the damn thing to her, and I was sure it was almost better than what James could do to her . . . almost. A dildo can't really compete with a dick with a pulse, but it still did what it came to do.

"Tell me it's my pussy. Say it!" I came back, enjoying the control I had over Jasmine at this point. If Jasmine had any doubts that a woman could please her the same as or better than a man, I wanted to make sure that she knew she could have the best of both worlds.

"Monica, it's your pussy. It's yours, baby," Jasmine responded as I turned her body so that she was on her knees in the doggie-style position.

"It better be."

I started kissing Jasmine down her back, running my tongue up and down her spine, making Jasmine go crazy. Using some of the KY jelly from the nightstand, I applied some on Jasmine's asshole, never losing my rhythm with Jasmine throwing her ass back like crazy. I slowly pushed my finger into Jasmine's ass and slowed down my stroke. Jasmine's back stiffened.

"Jasmine, just relax. I won't hurt you. Just enjoy it."

Every time I pushed in, I pulled my finger out, and vice versa, building up an orgasm so big Jasmine just about passed out from the explosion. Feeling satisfied that I handled my business, I pulled out of Jasmine and stepped out of my strap-on. Jasmine was lying face down on the bed, trying to catch her breath as I dressed. Smiling to myself, I walked around the side of the bed and kissed Jasmine on the forehead.

"I'll call you later," I said before leaving the room, "and I'll lock the door behind me. Don't oversleep. It's nine o'clock."

Jasmine just kind of grunted her goodbye and remained sprawled out in the bed, trying to get herself together.

When I got downstairs, I spotted the peg block hanging by the door. Coming closer to it, I saw several keys hanging from it. There were numerous tags listing what the keys were over each peg, and the last one that read SPARE HOUSE KEYS had two of the same keys hanging from it. I started to just take a key, but that would be too easy. Testing the key in the door to make sure it was the right one, I did as I was told and pressed the key firmly into the clay. The shape and name on the key came out perfectly. Smiling to myself, I slid the clay into one of the sandwich bags on the table and left the house, whistling.

On my way back home, I went by the locksmith's office and dropped off the print. After I knocked him off quickly, he told me I could come back and get the key that afternoon. I went home and all of a sudden felt very sleepy. Deciding to take my shower after a nap, I would stop by and get the key before I made my way to the studio. I was shooting Usher for the June cover of *Essence* magazine, and I could not be late.

Chapter Twelve

Jasmine

I finally got out of the bed a half hour after Monica left. I pulled the sheets with me, and the pair of underwear popped out. I couldn't really remember what Monica had covering her ass when she got here, but I couldn't leave evidence for James to find, so I put them in the bottom of the hamper, mentally writing myself a note to get them out later before James saw them. Already late for work, I quickly refreshed and dressed and headed for the office, smiling just as Monica said I would all the way there.

She definitely knew how to get the party started, but after that performance that James put in last night, she wasn't really holding a candle to my man. I mean, it was good, but that shit last night was great. Monica was just bad news, and I shouldn't have let her in. I needed to find a way to get rid of her for real this time. Fuck those fake-ass tears that she thought were controlling me. They used to, but not anymore. We needed to make a clean break if my marriage was going to work. As much as I liked tasting her pussy, I loved sucking my man off even more. I needed a pulse. She would never have that.

An hour later, I walked into the office with a smile so bright I could be the star of a Colgate commercial. Unusually friendly to everyone, I practically skipped into my office, flopping down in my chair when I got there.

Not that I was a mean person, but I was very professional at all times, not wanting to blur the lines between what I contributed to this company and what anyone else did. It was rare that I was as giddy and carefree as I was now. I didn't know Monica had it in her to turn me out like this, but I was low-key hooked. Never in my wildest imagination did I think a girl could leave me feeling sore and completely drained at the same time, but then again Monica wasn't just "any woman," and you could never be too sure of her capabilities. Either way, it was cute while it lasted, but it was time for me to wrap that part of my life up. I was playing a dangerous game with Monica, and surely nothing good would come from it.

"Sheila, can I see you in my office please?" I called from the intercom. I had several meetings I needed to attend over the course of the day, and if Sheila could download a couple of subpoenas for me by the time I got back, that would take a few things off my plate.

When Sheila walked in, her face was red and her eyes were puffy like she had been crying all morning. Trying to hide behind her hair, she sat down with her pen and notepad ready, looking into her lap and not at me like she normally did.

"Sheila, are you okay?" I asked, concern etching my face, stealing my jolly mood away completely.

"I'm fine," Sheila responded, starting to cry again. "Let's just get on with the meeting."

"If you were fine, you wouldn't be sitting here in tears," I said, deciding to ignore her attitude and go around to sit in the chair opposite Sheila with my tissue box in hand. "I'm a lawyer. I can help you," I offered, assuming her issue was domestic. We allowed these men to drag us down every chance they got, and I felt for Sheila.

"It's nothing really, just some issues I have to work through, that's all," Sheila said, trying to steer the conversation away from her.

"Sheila, whatever it is, you can tell me. I'll try my best to help you, and I know others who can also. Is it your son's father? Is he abusing you?" I went on trying to draw a conclusion from her feelings, at the same time going through my mental Rolodex thinking of who could help Sheila out with the situation she might be in.

Sheila probably just wanted to go home. I could not help her out of this one because I had my own shit I was trying to figure out. I had to do what was necessary to get Monica off my back, and although I didn't know what Sheila's situation was just yet, I knew she had to think fast before things got out of hand. Anytime somebody got you at work crying, it's not looking good.

"No, I'm fine, really. I think I may end up taking a half day if you don't really have anything for me to do. Honestly, my head is pounding, and I probably won't be any good around here anyway."

"That is not a problem. All I need you to do is pull up and send out a few subpoenas for the files in the corner over there, and then you can head out. Leave me a note on top of them when you're done and your number so I can check on you later."

"Are you sure? I can stay if you need me."

"No, Sheila, go on. Every so often a woman needs to just lie down and rest for a second. You have my cell. Call if you need me."

"I will. Are we done now?" Sheila asked, looking like she wanted to get out of my face as soon as possible. She got up to leave before any more tears fell.

"Yeah, we're done. I'll give you a call tonight, okay?"

"Cool."

I gathered a couple of folders for some cases I had to view and put the one that I was about to start on top. On my way out the door, I walked slowly by Sheila, looking to see if she was okay. Sheila was having a heated debate

over the phone, and it was getting loud. Knowing how
the senior partners were and not wanting Sheila to lose
her job because of her personal problems, I waited by
Sheila's desk for her to end the call.

"I told you to stop calling here!" Sheila said sharply
through the phone. She was holding the phone tightly to
her ear, tears just streaming down her face. Whomever
she was speaking to was disrupting the atmosphere in
the workplace, and I simply couldn't allow that.

I touched her shoulder to let her know I was standing
there and that she was starting to get weird looks from
the other workers in the office. Sheila held up one finger
to indicate she was almost done with her conversation
and that she wanted to talk to me.

"I'll meet you there, but this is the last time," she said
into the phone. Sheila placed the phone back on the hook
slowly and followed me back into my office.

"Sheila, you got everybody looking at you crazy, love.
Do you want to share what's going on?" I asked, concerned about her safety. I knew harassment when I heard
it, and that conversation led me to believe that Sheila
might be in some kind of trouble. I probably should
have been minding my business, but the lawyer in me
wouldn't let it slide.

"I wish I could," she responded, looking exhausted.

"How can I help you or get you help if I can't do it
personally? That interaction was concerning." I pressed
the issue, trying to get her to say something. All she did
was cry. After twenty minutes of her convincing me that
she would be okay, I recommended that she take some
time off to get herself together. I informed Sheila of the
procedures for a sick and a personal leave and told her to
let me know what she would do by the next day.

"I'm just looking out for you," I said while offering
Sheila more tissue for her never-ending tears.

"I know, and I really appreciate it. If you could get the paperwork for me, I'll come in tomorrow and fill it out so you can put it through."

Not that I wanted Sheila to leave work, but her snapping out in this atmosphere was too much to handle emotionally and physically, and if any shit went down, I didn't want to be there for it.

"No problem, just go on home. I'll get one of the temps to do the subpoenas for me, and we'll talk tonight, okay?"

"Okay," Sheila responded after giving me a hug.

She gathered her stuff and followed me out to the elevator. On the way down to the street level, I offered her a ride to wherever she needed to go. I still had some time before I had to be at the courthouse, and I didn't know how far out she needed to travel.

"That's okay," Sheila said. "You've already been a big help."

"Just let me know if you need anything."

"I will."

As the elevator doors opened, Sheila tried to quickly step through them and managed to bump her right arm against the door. She winced and dropped the folder she was carrying. Photos spilled out of the folder. We both bent down at the same time to pick them up, but before I had a chance to put my hand on one, Sheila scooped them all up in a big pile. I peeped a few but not close enough to notice anyone I might know right offhand. I handed Sheila the hat she dropped.

"You sure you don't need a ride?" I asked one last time.

Sheila pulled the folder close to her chest. "Yeah," she muttered. "I'll just take the bus."

She waved, turned, and walked off. I didn't know what to think of the interaction, but I'd be lying if I said this didn't irk me a little. I hated domestic situations, but I knew enough about them to know to mind my damn business. I did in fact offer help, and she didn't take it. I did my part. Right?

Chapter Thirteen

Sheila

By the time I got to Monica's house, I was a nervous wreck. I opted to take the bus over there for two reasons. One because I needed time to clear my head. I had to put Monica in her place, or at least try to. I was determined to make Monica understand that I wanted no part of the bullshit she was brewing up and that I wanted to be left out of the entire situation. The second reason I caught the bus was because I knew Jasmine and Monica were cool, not exactly how cool they were, but I knew they were friends, and I didn't want Jasmine to know I was chillin' with Monica like that. I wasn't sure why though. It's not like I had to explain my friendships to people, but I just preferred to keep my private life just that. Jasmine didn't need to know that much about me.

Walking up her block slowly, I made my way to the only pink and white house on the block. Monica's house stood out, seemingly making the neighborhood look a little brighter. Approaching the door, I raised my hand to knock. Monica swung the door open before my fist could make contact with the wood, and I accidentally punched her in the mouth. She immediately covered her mouth with both hands, being caught off guard by the blow. She had to know it was an accident by the look on my face, but she snapped anyway in true Monica fashion.

"Monica, I'm so sorry!" I reached out to hold her face, but she stepped back. The hit wasn't as hard as she was making it out to be, but being the drama queen that she was, she milked it for all it was worth.

Instead of answering, she just turned around and went toward the kitchen to get some ice for the nonexistent swelling she thought would take place. I was so close on her heels that when Monica stopped suddenly, I bumped into her, causing the back of her tennis shoe to flop off. Trying to keep her cool, Monica kicked the shoe off and continued to the freezer to get the ice that she came there for. I waited silently at the kitchen table for Monica to wrap her ice in a towel, put on the house shoes that were by the back door, and examine the back of her foot.

"Monica, I'm so sor—"

"Bitch, just be quiet! You have just about worked my last nerve, and you haven't even been here that long. Relax!"

That shut my ass right up. Monica was a tad on the demanding side, but she never talked to me in that tone before. I wanted to say something, but for reasons even I didn't understand Monica scared the hell out of me. She had this underlying crazy that crept to the surface every so often, and I just didn't know what to do with that kind of energy. Even if I wasn't scared, I couldn't think of a snappy comeback in time anyway, so I did as I was told and fell back. After about five minutes of silence and Monica giving me dirty looks, she finally joined me at the table and got down to why I was there in the first place.

"I need you to help me out with something," Monica began in a matter-of-fact tone like she dared me to say I wouldn't do it.

"What is it?" I did not feel like the Monica drama, but I figured if I just agreed to do whatever she wanted, I could leave and not hear from her again.

"James keeps asking about you, and he wants to know if you're down with a threesome. I told him you would do it," Monica replied while closely watching my reaction. Monica explained that she had spoken to James about a threesome when she was at his house the night before, but he said he didn't want anything to do with it. Since she stopped by his house that day, she had to find some way to have sex with him again if this pregnancy thing was going to work. She had taken two pregnancy tests and both came up positive, but she wanted to be 100 percent sure before she visited her gynecologist.

"I'm not getting into that with you. Find someone else. You know his wife is my boss," I said with my arms folded across my chest. For the first time, I was seeing just how crazy and deranged Monica really was. Monica came around the table and stood close to me. She bent down so that we were face-to-face.

"You'll do it," she whispered, "because if you don't, every step you take I'll be right on your ass. Trust and believe that life for you will be nothing wonderful when I'm done with you."

"Monica, what are you going to do? So what if you sent pictures to the job? Your bedroom is in the background, and they weren't even clear shots," I responded, feeling confident all of a sudden. I tried to play the same role that Monica was playing and hoped that she would be somewhat intimidated. She wasn't.

"Dear Sheila, a lot of shit has changed," Monica said, walking circles around the table. Her facial expression seemed to turn sinister as she told me exactly how she planned to mess my life up if I didn't help her get pregnant by James.

"The photos I sent you were that way because I knew you would underestimate me. I have photos of you giving him head and everything. I can take your picture and put it anywhere I choose. Even email them to Jazz if I wanted to take it to that level. How much of a job will you have then?"

Trying to hold my ground, but so close to breaking down, I was determined not to be a part of the nonsense. Jasmine was looking out for me in a major way even though I already violated her by sleeping with her husband. I couldn't bring myself to cross her again and was damn near about to cry. I couldn't understand how Monica could act the way she did and not care about the lives of the people she was hurting.

Monica took her seat across from me and waited for me to reply. In Monica's mind she couldn't take it far enough to get Jasmine. She wanted her as much as she wanted her next breath, and she was determined to have her by any means necessary. I would be the perfect source to get Jasmine to leave James, and she figured she would have James's child so that they could both have him in common. Like, this was the plan she told me, and I couldn't help but look at her like the crazy person she was. Sick and twisted, yes, but she didn't care, and she was getting fed up because it was taking too long to get what she wanted.

"How do you plan to get James to come by? He's obviously happy at home. Jasmine came in the office today looking like he put some serious work in this morning," I said, hoping to throw Monica off.

Monica almost laughed. "You let me worry about that," she said, smirking. "Just be ready when I set up the meeting. I'll call you the day before. Now leave. Your presence is making me feel sick."

I wanted to grip Monica's ass up, but I decided it wasn't worth it. Monica could call until the cows came home. I would be changing my phone number the very next day and would be staying at my mom's house during my leave of absence. Monica was crazy, and I decided to let her be crazy all by herself. Not wanting to reveal how I would pull off my disappearing act, I readied myself to leave.

"I need a ride home," I said to Monica on my way to the door.

"There's money on the table in the living room. Call a cab and wait outside for it. I want you gone before I start getting pissed."

I just gave her a look like I couldn't believe how she was acting and walked away. In the living room I found about $200 sitting on the table next to receipts from Neiman Marcus and Strawbridge's. It only cost about $7 for me to get home from here, but I opted to take the whole $200 for my troubles. Fuck Monica and all the stupid shit she came with. Instead of calling a cab, I walked until I found one and went home. Calling my sister over to help me with my son once she got there, I gave my sister half the money to tell Monica I wasn't there no matter how many times she called. I knew getting away from Monica wouldn't be that easy, and I needed my sister there just in case I needed backup. My sister didn't play about me, and I would hate for Monica to find that out the hard way.

Before morning, Monica was ringing my phone off the hook. I didn't think she would be calling that soon, but I did take her money and instantly regretted it. Between Monica's calls, I called the phone company, but it was after hours and I would have to wait until nine the next day to do anything.

I told my sister as much as I could without incriminating myself, and my sister decided that she didn't care how many times Monica called. She would have to get over it and move on. Nobody was about to bully me in front of her, and she meant that shit.

"Hello, can I speak with Sheila?" Monica asked in her sweetest voice. She was probably calling to set up some time with me for the next night, hoping she could get me to help persuade James into having the threesome. She did say that she wanted to move on it right away, and she would have to do that shit without me.

"She's not available. Can I take a message?" my sister replied just as nicely. She knew it was Monica from her calling the house before, and whatever reason I had for not wanting to talk to her was a good enough reason for her not to like Monica either. She said there was something about Monica that she couldn't place her finger on, but she knew it wasn't good.

"What do you mean she's not there? I suggest you find out where she is and have her call me back!" Monica screamed into the phone.

"Excuse me?" My sister had to look at the phone to make sure she heard her right.

"I said Sheila needs to be contacted ASAP!" Monica came back with even more attitude.

"You need to get a better attitude before calling someone's house!" my sister said and hung up.

"Put Sheila on the phone!" Monica demanded from the other end when she called right back.

"Bitch, please! When you learn some manners, call back," she said, and she hung up again. I was real-life scared for my life at this point, but I put on a brave face in front of my sister because she would be ready to go to Monica's house, and I just wasn't built for that kind of drama. Monica would be okay. Hell, at this point she didn't have a choice. I refused to take part in these shenanigans whether she liked it or not.

Chapter Fourteen

Monica

Three weeks had gone by, and I still hadn't heard a word from Sheila. When I called the office, a temporary assistant answered the phone, informing me that Sheila was on an indefinite leave of absence. I had been trying to keep my cool, but this was the last straw. Getting dressed in a sweat suit and sneakers and pulling my hair back into a ponytail just in case I had to whip someone's ass, I got in my car and raced over to Sheila's apartment to see what the problem was. Hopefully that rude bitch who had been answering her phone would be there, too. Then I could knock both they asses out.

Double-parking my car in front of the building and not giving a damn that I was holding up traffic on a busy intersection early on a Saturday afternoon, I took the stairs two at a time all the way up to Sheila's third-floor apartment. Knocking turned to practically trying to break the door down as I screamed and hollered for Sheila to show her face. I figured Sheila was inside hiding from me.

I was making so much noise in the hallway that Sheila's neighbors started to come out in the hall to see what all the ruckus was about. After all, Sheila didn't exactly live in the ghetto, and it was normally quiet in the overpriced, working-class renters' apartment building. For a half hour I kicked and banged on the door, thinking Sheila

would come out eventually. I was so into it that I didn't
see one of Sheila's neighbors walking toward me.

"Ma'am? Ma'am, are you looking for someone?"

I turned around to stare at the elderly Caucasian guy
standing a few feet from me. Almost doubling over in
laughter, I tried to control my smile as I stared at him. He
reminded me of the cartoon character named Mr. Burns
off *The Simpsons* television show, teeth and all.

"Would I be banging on this door like a madwoman if
I weren't looking for someone?" I asked, my smile disappearing. After thirty minutes of kicking and banging,
I decided that if Sheila hadn't come to the door by now,
she wouldn't.

"Well, ma'am," the senior citizen responded like he was
getting an attitude, "it's just that you're making a lot of
noise, and some of us are trying to sleep."

"Does this look like the face of someone who gives a
fuck?" I asked him, looking him dead in his eyes. "I'm not
here for you, so take your old, wrinkled ass back to your
apartment before you write a check your half-rich ass
can't cash."

"Your attitude is not necessary, young lady. I was just
simply stating—"

"Simply stating what?" I replied, approaching the
elderly man like I was going to strike him.

"That you need to take that *hood* shit back to the *hood*.
This is a peaceful building and—"

"Old man, save it! I do what I want when I'm ready.
What are you going to do to stop me?"

"I . . . I'm going to call the police," Sheila's neighbor
responded, taken aback by what I said.

"Yeah, you do that. I'll be waiting right here for them,"
I shouted at his turned back as he shuffled down the
hallway and into his apartment.

I could hear him making the call to the police department and perched my tired body into one of the chairs to wait for the cops to get there. Periodically I would see the guy poke his head out the door to check if I was still sitting there, and I almost had to laugh. I wasn't scared of the police. Eighty percent of them had already sucked on my pussy at some point, so I doubted that any of them would arrest me. Not with the secrets I had on them in my pocket.

"I'm still here, you old bastard, and I'm not leaving until the cops come!"

He would just snatch his head back into the apartment and slam the door, disgusted by my actions.

Not even ten minutes later, who but Officer Hill and my other favorite officer of the law, Officer Collins, came strolling up the hallway to investigate the situation. Looking at me like he wasn't sure if he knew me, Officer Hill proceeded to knock on the neighbor's door to see what happened.

"Someone report a disturbance?" he asked the frail old man. He looked visibly shaken and was afraid to step foot into the hall.

"Yes, that woman right there," he said, pointing at me, "was making all kinds of noise and threatened me when I asked her to stop."

I just sat there with a smirk on my face.

"Ma'am, is this true?" Officer Hill responded, taking a closer look at me. As he got closer to me, he recognized me better and smiled in spite of the situation.

"No, Officer, it isn't. I'm just waiting for my sister to get home. This guy seems to get nervous around black people or something," I replied, smiling seductively at the cop. He remembered the night we spent together and started blushing.

"That's a lie!" the elderly man spat out between his dentures. "She was kicking the door and everything. Look at it, you can still see her footprints on it." Everyone looked at the door at the same time, and there were scuff marks on the bottom half of it. I just laughed softly to myself.

"Officer, those marks were on that door when I got here. My sister was supposed to meet me here, and I've been waiting for her for about ten minutes. That's my car double-parked out front. I haven't been here for that long." Staring at my breasts and not really paying attention, Officer Hill didn't hear much of what I said.

"Sir, do you have any witnesses?" Officer Collins asked the man, reluctantly turning his gaze away from me.

"This is ridiculous," the neighbor said. "What do you have to do to get a good cop nowadays?" Without looking back, he walked into his apartment and slammed the door. Officer Hill and I stood in the hallway, looking at each other and smiling. I was hoping he would just leave, but I was sure it wouldn't go down that way.

"And for the record," the Mr. Burns look-alike said, inching his door back open, "this is a quiet building. Take all of that ruckus back to your hood," he hollered before giving the door one final slam, clicking the locks loudly.

Both law enforcers turned to face me. Officer Collins couldn't even look at me for fear that he might snatch me up. We had dealt for only a short time, and I had managed to almost destroy his marriage. He too fell for the Jedi Pussy Trick, falling head over heels for me. The sexy vixen with amazing control of her vaginal walls.

"Hill, wrap this up. I'll meet you downstairs," Officer Collins said as he walked quickly down the hall, opting to take the stairs before his good intentions escaped him. I hid my smirk as I turned my attention to the obviously horny Officer Hill.

"So, Monica, how have you been?" Officer Hill said to me while backing me into Sheila's door. His erection, as small as it was, was pressing against my abdomen, clearly showing his intentions.

"I've been good, Officer Hill. How have you been?" I replied seductively, hoping he would get a call on his radio or something. I was not in the mood for him tonight, and I knew it wouldn't be easy to just diss him.

"Better, now that I see you."

"How's the wife and kids?" I shot at him as he leaned down to kiss my neck. That caught him off guard, causing him to stand straight up.

"My wife an . . . and kids?" he replied, stuttering, trying to remember if he ever told me about his family.

"Yes. You know, your wife, Cynthia, and your kids, Thomas and Jessica. How are they doing?" I smirked, waiting for his reply as his erection faded to nothing. I had gotten information on his background from the captain in his district. He owed me a favor and wanted me to keep his secret from his wife as well.

"They're doing great. Thanks for asking," he replied, backing away from me and adjusting his pants. "So, are you about to leave?" he asked, already walking down the hallway toward the exit.

"Yeah, my sister doesn't seem to be home."

Looking back at the door one more time, I followed Officer Hill out of the building. He waited for me to get into my car and pulled up beside me in his squad car. Lust was jumping off him like fleas on a dog as he stared at me, trying to think of a way to get over to my house.

"You go on ahead. I'll follow you to make sure you get home safely," he said, staring at my painted lips. I almost laughed at his attempt to get a booty call.

"No, it's cool," I replied through the window. "I'm not going straight home, but I'll call you when it's okay to stop by."

"Don't wait too long," Officer Hill came back, practically begging. "I don't think they have a twelve-step program for getting over beautiful women."

Instead of responding to his lame advances, I pulled off as quickly as possible, jumping on the first exit I saw, not knowing exactly where I was heading. I wanted to get away from Officer Hill as quickly as possible. It was a nice Saturday afternoon, and I did not feel like his bullshit or his thirty seconds of wack sex.

Skipping my exit, I decided to go shake things up at the Cinque household since Sheila was missing in action. I was interested in seeing how the two would act knowing they were both separately sleeping with me but neither knowing about the other. I thought maybe I could talk to James about that threesome on the sly if Jasmine left us in the room by ourselves. Smiling wickedly, I jumped off I-76 at the Lincoln Drive exit and made my way to the Mount Airy section of the city to stir up some shit.

Parking in the driveway, I got out of my car and peeped in the window on the way by. Seeing Jasmine and James cuddled on the couch gave me an instant attitude, and I almost snapped. James was stretched out on the couch, and Jasmine was lying down on top of him with her head on his chest, both watching television. They didn't see me in the window, and when Jasmine leaned up to give James a kiss, my temper went from zero to sixty in three seconds.

"I know he's not hugged up on my girl," I said to myself while I looked in the window. "Doesn't he know she belongs to me?"

Knocking on the door like I was the police, I waited for someone to open it, hoping it would be James. Putting on my game face, I waited patiently for the lovebirds to separate and finally answer the door. I wanted to scream through the window that the same lips that were kissing James were all in my treasure chest not too long ago. I hated the fact that no matter how hard I tried to separate them, they always found a way to be together anyway.

"Who is it?" Jasmine's voice sounded from the other side of the door. She sounded frustrated, but I didn't care. I hoped I messed up their little make-out session because I didn't want James sleeping with her anyway.

"It's Monica," I said into the door. I didn't know how Jasmine would react to me popping up again, but I didn't exactly care either. I banged Jasmine's back out rather nicely a couple of weeks ago, so I figured Jasmine was aware of my capabilities by now.

"Who?" Jasmine asked, not sure if she heard correctly. She swung the door open with tons of attitude.

"Hey, Jazz," I said, acting like I didn't notice Jasmine's mood.

"What did I tell you?" Jasmine said, getting right to the point. "Didn't I tell you not to be just popping up whenever you felt like it?"

"Yeah, but—"

"But what?" Jasmine said, getting heated. She liked me enough to let me eat her pussy while her husband wasn't home, but if she kept doing the stuff she was doing, she was going to mess up everything.

"I just wanted to take you shopping. I was on my way to the mall, and I didn't want to go by myself," I replied, coming up with the lie quickly. I hoped I did have at least one credit card on me because if I didn't, Jasmine would know that wasn't my reason for being there if she did take me up on the offer.

"Babe, who's at the door?" James hollered in the background. He was lying on the couch with a granite pipe, waiting to serve Jasmine properly. Pissed because he told Jazz not to answer the door in the first place, he was wondering what was taking her so long to get back.

"Look, you have to go," she said to me, ignoring James. She wanted me to leave before James got up to see who knocked, and I wasn't moving without him seeing my face. I was the queen of making situations uncomfortable, and this would be no exception.

"We won't even be gone that long, just a quick trip to the mall," I replied, stalling for time. I wanted James to see me and wished he would hurry up.

It was like he heard my thoughts. James finally got up to see what was going on. He wanted Jasmine wrapped around him in more ways than one, and he was ready to go now. When he got to the door, his facial expressions went from shocked to scared as hell when he saw me standing there. He was just with me a few days ago, and he probably still hadn't put the money back into the account that he paid to me for the sex we had that night.

I was good, but I damn sure wasn't cheap. That night cost him $700, and it was getting harder to replace it. Yeah, I gave him a couple of free shots here and there, but most of the time I wanted my money up front if he wanted me to stay quiet. I was already pissed because he was making me let him use a condom, and with that, up went the prices. I got even more pissed when he insisted on bringing his own because he thought I was putting holes in the ones I had.

"Monica, long time no see," James said, feeling the heat between the two ladies. He was just as surprised to see me, but for a different reason than his wife.

"Hey, James. I was just asking Jasmine if she wanted to go to the mall with me. You know, sort of a ladies' day out. You don't mind, do you?" I asked James with a smirk. Blowing him up would be blowing myself up, but I didn't care about consequences.

"Well, we were about to . . ." James said, looking down at Jasmine for support. He didn't want to be the one to say no and hoped Jasmine would say just that.

"Before you came, we were, um, enjoying each other's company," Jasmine began, not caring if she hurt my feelings, "so maybe next time you can call first and we can set up something, okay?"

"Are you telling me no?" I asked with a surprised look on my face before quickly checking my attitude. I didn't want to put myself out there just yet.

"I'm telling you maybe next time," Jasmine said, backing up so that she could close the door. I looked like I was going to cry, but it wasn't working this time.

"Okay then, you lovebirds get back to each other. Jazz, I'll see you around."

Instead of responding, Jasmine closed the door in my face with a hard thud and a loud click of the lock. Stunned, I stood looking at the door for about five minutes before I turned around and numbly walked to my car. I thought for sure I had Jasmine in check, especially after that last session, but now I wasn't too sure. James totally took me by surprise, and I knew for sure I would have to get him back for trying to play me.

"Hiding behind wifey," I mumbled to myself angrily as I got into my car and peeled off from the curb. "She won't be yours for too much longer, James."

Not knowing what to do with myself because I was so mad, I rode around aimlessly, trying to get my temper under control. For some reason, things weren't working out the way I planned. At this phase Jasmine should be ready to leave James, but they seemed more in love now than they did before.

I felt sick, and not sick like the morning sickness I had been experiencing lately either. I wanted to get pregnant, I wanted James's ass gone, and I wanted Jasmine now.

Slamming on the brakes at a red light, I was fixing my mouth to curse the guy in front of me when I looked to the side just in time to see Sheila, accompanied by her mom and her son, come out of the Pizza Palace.

"This must be my lucky day," I said as I maneuvered my car into the right turning lane so that I could pull into the lot before Sheila got into her mom's car.

Taking the red light, I pulled around the entrance and stopped next to Sheila on the passenger side of the car just as the door closed. Catching Sheila off guard, I had to control myself to keep from snatching Sheila through the car window. I had been trying to get in touch with her for weeks, and Sheila didn't look so happy to see me, but then again, why should she be?

"Hey, Sheila, it's been a while," I began with a false smile. The only thing that kept me from snapping was the fact that Sheila's son was in the car, and I didn't want to cause a scene in front of her peoples. I wasn't above acting up and out, but I needed her help, so it was best to just play it cool until I got what I wanted.

Chapter Fifteen

Sheila

"Hey, Monica, how have you been?" I sat in the car feeling caged in because Monica was the last person I was expecting to see. I figured since three weeks had gone by, she would have found someone else to bully by now.

"*Sheila,*" Monica responded, mocking my high-pitched voice. She wasn't in the mood for pleasantries, and her face showed just that. "I've been trying to catch you for a while. Where are you on your way to?"

"Home. My son is tired after all that playing," I responded, gesturing to my sleeping son in the car seat. I knew what Monica wanted, but I wasn't in the mood to give in.

"Why don't you let your son go ahead with . . ." Monica said, looking past me to my mother. "Is it good to assume that's your mom?"

"Yes, it is," my mom replied in the background. "And you are?"

"Please excuse me for being rude. I'm Monica. Me and Sheila are good friends from the office," Monica replied, planting a fake smile on her face. She made eye contact with me, daring me to say otherwise. My mom wasn't aware of what went down with Monica, and once Monica figured that out, she used it to her advantage.

"Yeah, we worked at the firm together before I went on leave," I responded unconvincingly.

"I was about to go into the mall. Want to hang out for a while?" Monica said as she scanned the lot for a space closer to the door.

"I really shouldn't," I began. "I need to put Devon down for a nap, and I'm a little tired myself."

"Girl, that's nonsense," my mom said, not minding her business as usual. "I can put Devon in bed. You've done nothing but cater to him since you been on leave. Go ahead with your friend. You need some adult time for a while. I have your cell number. I'll call you if I need you."

I was determined not to be alone with Monica ever again in life, and now my mom had made that virtually impossible.

"But, Mom, I need to—"

"Nonsense. Now go and have a good time. Your son will be here when you get back."

Trying to cover my attitude in front of my mom, I gathered my belongings out of the car. Before closing the door, I leaned in and kissed my son on the forehead, looking at him like that may be my last time seeing him. I know what you're thinking: why did I even go, right? Who was going to make me? I didn't want to be with Monica, but I knew if I didn't go this time, Monica's persistent ass would just keep following me until I gave in. The way I saw it, if I just got it done and over with, maybe Monica would just leave me alone, but deep down I knew it wouldn't be that simple. I had to find a way to turn the tables on Monica, and I vowed to find a way to do just that and still have my job intact. I needed my coins, and I wasn't about to let this Monica and Jasmine foolishness jack up my bag.

I got into Monica's car, and my mom wasn't even out of the parking lot good before Monica was back out on the street. I didn't have to ask because I knew we were on our way to Monica's house, and my thoughts were confirmed when I saw the only pink house on the block standing out from our spot on the corner. Neither of us said a word on the drive over, and I decided I would let Monica do all the talking while I tried to figure out how to get out of the mess I just happened to become a part of.

Walking into the house a short while later, I excused myself and went upstairs to use the restroom. Noticing the open door at the end of the hall, I let curiosity take over. I crept to the door to get a peek inside. That door was normally shut tight and locked. Taking notice of my surroundings, I began looking at the canvases placed in the corners around the room. I knew Monica was a photographer, but I didn't know she painted as well.

Sifting through the stacks of paintings, I noticed that the woman on the paintings looked just like Jasmine. I knew Jasmine and Monica were cool, but not to that extent. I figured Monica was probably just lusting after Jasmine too and painted what she thought Jazz would look like nude because there was no way my boss was bisexual. Leaving it to an assumption, I turned around to leave the room only to find Monica in the doorway, watching me.

"There's no toilet in here," Monica said, irritation displayed all over her face.

"Monica, I was just—" I began, holding my chest from the shock of seeing her standing there. I hadn't even heard her come up the steps.

"Being nosy as hell!" Monica began, taking a step into the room. "Find what you were looking for? From what I recall, the bathroom is nowhere near this room."

"I . . . I saw the door cracked, and—"

"You want to know why you see Jasmine on those paintings?"

Shocked by Monica's ability to read my thoughts, I stood in silence just looking at her. I knew she was in the middle of some crazy shit before, but it was just sinking in as to how deep the shit really was. Monica was one powerful chick, and I was suddenly feeling the seriousness of what was going on around me.

"Follow me," Monica said, turning from the room and going into the master bedroom. My legs felt like lead as I walked behind her, stealing glimpses at paintings of James and what looked like the guy from the hardware store in my neighborhood.

Walking down the hallway seemed to take forever as I really took notice of the people in the paintings hanging on the walls. All of them featured Monica, but each man was different, making me wonder how many men and women Monica had actually been with. Furthermore, I wondered if she bothered to use protection with any of them because we never did.

Upon entering the room, I took a seat on the edge of the bed as Monica hooked up the camcorder that she hid behind the mirror to the television. I didn't want to know what was on the tape for fear of whom I might see. It was obvious that Monica got around, and I was sure that we might know some of the same people.

Monica took a seat beside me and turned her face so that we were eye to eye. I thought I saw flames shooting up behind Monica's eyes, like she was the devil incarnate. Too scared to move, but curious at the same time, I waited to see what would happen next.

"Sheila, I'm going to show you this tape because I trust you. This recording is one of many, and what you see here can never leave this bedroom. Do you understand me?" Monica asked with a straight face. There were no traces of vengeance in her voice, but I did detect a hint of sadness, maybe even weakness that Monica wouldn't normally show. My mouth wouldn't move, so I just shook my head in response. Whatever it was I about to see, there was no turning back from it now. I was prepared to fight for my life though, and I tried my best to just mentally prepare for what was to come.

Chapter Sixteen

Monica

At this point, I was tired of the runaround. Going to Sheila was pretty much my only option because I had Sheila tucked safely in my back pocket. If Sheila told, she would be putting herself out there, and I doubted that she would do that. Besides, it was becoming too overwhelming trying to hold everything in. Nobody ever checks on their strong friends, and everybody in my life was pretty much here on a bribe. Not one genuine person in sight. Even Jasmine.

"I also want you to understand that if this does get out, it won't be wonderful for you. Get my drift?"

Without waiting for a response, I pushed the play button and stood by the window until the tape finished playing. I couldn't watch the tape again because in spite of what everyone thought of me, it was painful for me, too. I wanted Jasmine more than I wanted life, and I just couldn't seem to grab hold of her no matter how close I got. It was like someone was dangling a carrot in front of me, and I just couldn't reach it.

I spotted Jasmine long before I slept with James. Jasmine represented my former lover, Tanya, in the murder case for her husband. Tanya and I, much like Jasmine and I, were seeing each other on the low. I fell in love with Tanya, and her husband had to go . . . by any means necessary. Tanya didn't want to break it off because of the children they shared, even though I had more money than either of them could count. Besides, this wasn't about money. This was about being happily in love.

I was getting restless and fed up, because just as James was doing now, Tanya's husband, Marcus, was sleeping with me also. Although Marcus treated me like a queen, he was very abusive toward Tanya, often leaving her with black eyes and broken bones. Deciding enough was enough, I went to Tanya's house one night to see if I could lure Marcus away. I had a few bullets with his name on them and a roll of black plastic to roll his ass up in. This was just getting to be too much, and I needed to bust a move right quick. When I arrived, I found Marcus going through one of his many drunken fits, and he was beating Tanya mercilessly.

I used my spare key to get in, and I tried to help Tanya out. In a raging fit, Marcus then began swinging on me, leaving me no choice but to take the small revolver out of the pocket of my coat and off him right there. I wanted to do it in another setting, but I had to protect myself. One thing I couldn't do was beat a man. I was not delusional about that aspect. The one shot to the head would have done it, but I unloaded the gun into his face, reloaded, and finished him off until there was nothing but a shell left of what used to be his head.

Tanya broke down, and I fled the scene, promising Tanya that I would get her the best lawyer money could buy. Before I could act, Tanya's case was assigned to the extremely sexy Jasmine Cinque. When I saw her, it was love at first sight, and Tanya was slowly being replaced by the new, shiny beauty. I went through the motions of finding out who Jasmine was and if she was married. Getting info from my favorite judge down at the courthouse where the couple was married, I found out about James, later seducing him and talking him into the threesome with Jasmine. James was so damn easy to lure in, and I almost felt sorry for using him the way that I did. Now it was only a matter of time before I got Jazz, hopefully without having to get rid of James permanently. Tanya quickly became a distant memory as I left her rotting in jail for a crime she didn't commit and made Jasmine her replacement.

I snapped out of my trip down memory lane when I heard Sheila gasp. Sheila stared at the television with her mouth wide open in shock at the things the tape revealed. First, she saw James, Jasmine, and me at the hotel. Then, there was me and James getting wild in my kitchen, including the two of us exchanging money. Then, there was me and Jasmine with the ice sculptures. This was a lot to take in.

I found out later that Officer Hill was married to Sheila's oldest sister. Sheila almost fell off the bed when she saw Officer Hill on the tape in front of the fireplace. That info came as a surprise because their last names didn't match, and I didn't connect the two until I started going through his old photos on social media and saw a young Sheila in them. It's funny how small the world actually is.

I was sure she was feeling sick to her stomach as she watched me have my way with the obese mayor of Philadelphia. My stomach did a small flip as well just remembering the night. I almost lost my lunch when shortly after a threesome including the mayor's wife, me, and the mayor's daughter flashed across the screen.

Just as the tears began to form in my eyes, I clicked the stop button on the DVD player. Sheila didn't know what to do as a steady stream of salty tears stained her cheeks and the front of her blouse. I tried to be oblivious to Shelia's tears as I was dealing with my own pain and memories of Tanya. Breaking the silence, I turned Sheila's face around so that she could look into my eyes as I talked. I wanted Sheila to understand the significance of the situation before we moved any further.

"Now, Sheila, I know that may have been a bit much to view at one time, but I need you to understand the caliber of what's happening here. I'm in love with Jasmine, and I need your help. I don't want to blackmail James, but that may be the only way to get him out. Either that or kill him, and who wants to deal with that again?"

"What do you want me to do?" Sheila asked through her tears. I had her on tape, and if she didn't want to get exposed, she had no choice but to comply.

"Not right now, but I will need your help down the line. I just need to know that you got me on this."

"I can't do that to Jasmine. She helped me out in more ways than you can imagine. She's been good to me."

"I can get you a job better than that. I know people in high places. You can start tomorrow," I stated like her concern had no importance. I could just call one of the many judges I was sleeping with around Philly and have Sheila in a higher paying position the very next day.

"Monica, please, just give me some time."

"I don't have time!" I snapped, losing my cool for a second. I was not in the mood to negotiate with Sheila. I wasn't asking her for help. I was telling her what she was going to do. "You will do it or else."

"Or else what?" Sheila asked, not really wanting to know the answer. I took a few deep breaths and calmed down a little before answering because now was not the time to lose control of the situation.

"Fuck with me and find out," I said, and with that said, I put the DVD back in its case and put it in one of the three safes that I had built into the wall behind a painting of myself in a two-piece sheer thong set.

Before drifting off to sleep, she took one last look at me standing by the window. I was struggling with my own thoughts in my head, and for the first time, I felt vulnerable. Hopefully Sheila could understand my pain. I couldn't understand why I had to drag so many lives into it, but it was what it was.

For a second, I felt like a child, which I thought was comical because I was afraid of so many things at that time in my life. I imagined myself looking out the window dressed in a pink and white baby doll dress with my long, thick hair pulled up into two pigtails held together with pink and white flower-shaped hair barrettes. That's when my love for the color pink began. Holding a bunny rabbit tightly in my little arms, I seemed to be at a happier time in my life then, before shit changed.

Going deeper into my thoughts, the teenage Monica, braces and all, showed up. I looked so sad. I had no friends to speak of and was teased because of my absence of curves like the rest of the girls my age had. The last thing I wanted to be was alive, and my face was etched with pain and worry for reasons unknown to anyone but me. Then my present self showed up. The evil, conniving adult Monica, and I could have sworn I felt devil horns sticking up through my wrap hairstyle. Chalking it up as fatigue setting in, I saw Sheila close her eyes in an effort to stop the little man from dancing on her temple. I hoped by morning I would have figured out some way to stop this madness for good.

Chapter Seventeen

James

"When did you and Monica start hanging out?" I asked curiously, trying to get the heat off me. I didn't want Jasmine to even begin to think I was involved with Monica in any way, shape, or form. I was still scraping up the money to put back into our joint savings account that we had for the twins from the last James and Monica private party. Keeping her quiet was expensive, and I often wondered why I kept going back.

"We hang every once in a while," Jasmine responded, choosing her words carefully.

"Since when? You acted like you didn't know who she was when we saw her at the courthouse that day," I said, trying to turn my guilt into anger, not realizing that I was making a bad situation worse for myself.

"I didn't recognize her then," Jasmine replied with the beginnings of an attitude. "I ran into her again after that, and we exchanged numbers. We only had lunch a couple of times, and she picked me up from here twice. Is that a problem?"

"Are you sure all you had was lunch?" I asked Jasmine with a straight face. If I could get Jasmine to say she slept with Monica again, it would lift some of the guilt off my shoulders.

"What the fuck is that supposed to mean? Are you implying that there should be something else?" Jasmine came back almost at a boiling point. I was wondering if she wanted to continue what was started before Monica came, but I was messing it up with my accusations.

"No, I'm just saying that Monica can be very persuasive. You act like you don't know she has the hots for you."

"How would you know, James? We only shared one night. How many times were you with her since then?" Jasmine shouted, cleverly tossing the ball back into my court.

I automatically saw that I put my foot in my mouth. I should have just let it go, and my reverse psychology didn't work. I had been trying to stay away from Monica, but since day one I was drawn to her like a magnet. Deciding to bow out of the situation, I tried to come up with a lie to cover my ass before my cover was completely blown.

"I only see Monica in passing. A young lady she's dealing with works near the station, and I see her sometimes when I'm on lunch break. She asks about you all the time and once asked if you were interested in getting together for another threesome," I lied, knowing I didn't sound believable.

"And what did you tell her?" Jasmine asked with her arms folded tightly across her chest.

"I told her that I didn't think you would do it because that's not your style. You only did it that one time because I asked you to."

"And she was okay with that?" Jasmine said, not sounding convinced. If we knew anything about Monica, we knew that she didn't bend easily, and once she set her mind on something, that was it. She probably wondered if I ever went back for more because that story I told her about how we met just didn't add up.

"She didn't say anything otherwise, and it's been a while since I've seen her."

"How long has it been exactly?" Jasmine asked to see if I would continue to lie about it. The night we got into the argument, I came home without my boxers, and the only person we knew who kept underclothes after she slept with someone was Monica.

"A couple of weeks. She hasn't been coming that way for lunch lately, I guess."

"She told me you went there the night we got into the argument," Jasmine said, testing my credibility. Monica never discussed with me that she talked to Jasmine about that night, but I also didn't know they even talked like that.

"That's bullshit. I don't even know where she lives exactly, besides the information she gave me to put the packet together for our threesome. I haven't looked at that since then, and that was so long ago."

"James, this conversation is over for now," Jasmine said while retreating up the stairs.

"But what happened with us making love on the couch?" I asked as my erection began to appear through my boxer shorts.

"You fucked that up when you decided to play detective."

"But—"

I couldn't get another word in as Jasmine disappeared up the steps and into the bathroom. I heard the shower running and thought about joining her. Deciding against it, I had to figure out a way to leave the house so that I could go talk to Monica. I didn't know if Monica really told Jasmine I was over there or if Jazz was just calling my bluff, but I was getting to the bottom of this once and for all.

Racing up the stairs to grab my keys off the dresser, I walked in on Jasmine applying lotion to her skin. Trying not to stare at the beads of water still on her freshly showered skin, I slipped into my boots and searched my jacket pocket for my cell phone. Jasmine took note of all of this as she continued with her task. I was not in the mood to argue with her, but I did want to get some before she went to sleep. It wasn't often that the house was child-free.

"I'll be right back," I said without even a glance in Jasmine's direction. I was going to confront Monica before my marriage was at stake.

"Where are you going, and why are you leaving now?" Jasmine said, sounding a little disappointed. Was she going to make it up to me? It would just have to wait because I was already set to go put Monica in her place.

"I have some business to take care of."

"On a Saturday afternoon? What kind of business?"

"Business. I'll be back."

"Sure you will. Tell Monica I said hello."

Without bothering to respond, I walked out of the house and jumped in Jasmine's Jeep, hoping to throw Monica off a little because she wouldn't be expecting me in my wife's car. I had to set things straight if things were going to work out between the three of us, and I had to do it today.

As I left, Jasmine watched from the window as I pulled off in her Jeep, probably wondering why I didn't take my own car. Did she really think that I was fooling around with Monica? I wished I had been home when she changed the sheets and was taking clothes out of the hamper. I would have seen that she found the underwear that Monica had left here a few weeks ago.

Chapter Eighteen

James

There was mad traffic on the way to Monica's house, which only added to my frustration. Her audacity never failed to amaze me. She did whatever she wanted to do, and it was like we were all powerless to do anything about it but comply with her shenanigans. She consistently contributed to my headaches, more than my wife. Why did I let this mess get this far?

When I first met Monica, I was in complete awe of how sexy she was. Standing outside of The Grill, a popular fast-food restaurant that served 90 percent of the businesspeople in central Philadelphia, I spotted Monica at one of the tables outside eating alone. After placing my order, I contemplated going outside to talk to the pretty in pink vixen dining alone. Jasmine and I were going through it at home, and even though I never really entertained the idea of stepping out of my marriage, if I did, Monica would be perfect.

Hesitant at first, I stood to the side while my food was being prepared, just watching her eat. She took petite bites of her grilled chicken salad as she simultaneously sipped homemade lemonade and flipped through her copy of Complex *magazine. She had the cutest lips, the bottom slightly fuller than the top.*

Watching her movements, I thought she made eating almost look sensual even when she looked up a couple of times, catching me glancing her way. Her facial expression didn't change as she looked back down at her magazine and continued to enjoy her meal. I noticed that her salad was almost gone, and I wished the cooks would hurry up so that I would have a reason to go over to her. As if they read my thoughts, they called my number, and I quickly made my way through the crowded restaurant and outside just as Monica was preparing herself to leave.

"Is this seat taken?" I asked, flashing my most charming smile. This smile was what attracted Jasmine to me, and she was equally as sexy as Monica, if not more.

"No, and actually I was just leaving," Monica said as she pushed the remainder of her salad to the side and searched her pocketbook for her car keys.

"You can't leave. I mean, please stay. Your company is appreciated."

Monica took me in like a tall drink of water. My physique, jet-black wavy hair, and goatee connected perfectly on my smooth face. My eyes looked like pools of warm caramel that made you just want to strip down to nothing and dive into them. I'd intrigued many women in my time on looks alone, and I was hoping Monica was ready to ride the wave too.

"No, thank you, maybe next time," Monica replied as she dropped a twenty on the table and walked away.

I was speechless as I watched her walk away in silence, her sway hypnotic. I almost ran after her, but I knew if I did, it would just scare her off. When I finally set my tray down, I noticed that the gentleman at the table next to me was looking at Monica too. We both smiled at each other in recognition, and I settled down to eat my lunch.

The following day, Monica was seated in the same spot, looking at the same magazine, eating the same meal just as I hoped she would be. This time I had already ordered, and instead of asking her permission, once my food was done, I went and sat down at the table with her. Monica looked up from her magazine, no indication of a smile present. I began cutting my grilled chicken into bite-sized pieces, totally ignoring the look of disdain on her face.

"I don't remember offering you a seat," Monica snapped at me, but I took the seat anyway. Who was going to stop me?

"Oh, I do apologize. It's just that all of the other tables are taken, and I figured sitting next to someone as beautiful as you would make all of the other men here jealous," I responded with a lazy smile. I could have easily occupied one of the tables where other men were having lunch alone, but I wasn't trying to get with them. I wanted her.

What I didn't know at the time was Monica already knew who I was from her little investigation the day before. Her lover, Tanya, was locked up for murdering her husband, and Jasmine was her lawyer. Liking the sexy curves and pretty face of the female attorney, she took the liberty of doing a background check. She was surprised to find out that I belonged to her and devised a plan to get next to her through me. She had me thinking she wanted me badly for the sake of getting a chance to meet Jasmine outside of the courtroom. I was sexy to her, but Jasmine was a dime. Monica knew if she got the chance, she would turn Jasmine out in more ways than she could handle. They say hindsight is twenty-twenty, and there my goofy ass was, sitting there thinking I was winning when all that time it was a setup. That's what happens when you think with your penis and not your brain.

"*Flattery will get you everywhere,*" Monica flirted back openly. "*What's your name?*"

"*James. James Cinque, and you are?*"

"*Monica.*"

"*Monica what? I gave you both names, so now it's your turn.*"

"*Monica will do for now,*" she replied with a slight smirk, satisfied that this was the correct James Cinque from TUNN. The last name was not common, so she knew it had to be me.

"*Okay, Miss Monica-will-do-for-now,*" I joked. "*What inspires you? What do you do for entertainment?*"

"*A little of this, a little of that,*" Monica responded flirtatiously. My gullible ass was an easy target to her as she flirted while picking at her salad.

"*Cute, real cute. Well, what do you do for a living? Or does the answer remain the same?*"

Instead of responding, Monica placed a business card on the table. I picked it up, taking in the fancy script and pleasant smell, like the cards were sprayed lightly with Breathless by Victoria. My wife loved the scent, so I recognized it immediately.

"*'Specializing in You.' Are you independently contracted or what? What exactly do you do?*" I asked as I stared at the black card complete with a long-stemmed pink rose and lettering of the same color. The card looked very chic but classy, just like Monica and completely unlike my wife's boring business cards that the firm supplied her with.

"*I'm a photographer,*" Monica offered without further explanation.

"*Family portraits, children, pets?*" I inquired, getting a sexy laugh from Monica. "*Please, elaborate for me.*"

"*I photograph celebrities for several different magazines.* Essence, Complex, Sister 2 Sister, Ebony, Vibe, *things like that. I also paint and sell my work for high dollars."*

"Wow," I said, taken aback by Monica's forwardness. "So how do I go about getting a private session?"

"A private session, huh? Is that a wedding band I see on your finger?" Monica asked, already knowing it was.

"One has nothing to do with the other," I replied, trying to avoid the question. "How can a nice brother like myself take out a sexy woman like you to dinner?"

"Sorry," Monica replied. "I don't frolic with the talent. Have a good day, Mr. Cinque."

Without waiting for a response, Monica dropped another twenty on the table and left as quickly as she came. Looking down at the business card, I saw that she wrote her home number on the back of it. Tucking the card inside of my wallet, I wrapped my lunch to go and made my way back to the office.

Slamming on the brakes, I almost ran a red light as thoughts of Monica clouded my memory. I was definitely intrigued by Monica's beauty, but now I couldn't help but think bringing her into my marriage was a huge mistake. I thought back on the threesome with my wife and wondered if she and Monica ever got together after that. I thought about all the times Monica and I had sex unprotected, and I wondered what exactly I would do if she did get pregnant. How would I explain it to Jasmine? That threesome happened well over six months ago. The amount of money I spent on her was already an issue that Jasmine could not find out about, and I was set on ending what we had today.

Pulling up to Monica's door, I parked behind Monica's convertible and walked quickly to the closed door. Monica looked like she was expecting Jasmine, too, until she saw me exiting the vehicle, further confirming my suspicions. I could see her take the steps two at a time, hurrying to answer my persistent banging on her cherrywood door.

"Why are you banging on my door like you the police?" Monica said as she swung the door open.

"We need to talk," I replied coldly as I brushed past her, not waiting to be asked inside. I missed the dirty look Monica gave me as she slowly closed the door and made her way to the sofa.

"What do we need to talk about, James?" Monica inquired, already looking bored with my presence. I wanted to snatch that look from her face, but I'd never been one to put my hands on a woman on purpose.

"Monica, I can't do this anymore," I began while pacing back and forth in front of the couch. I knew if I sat down, I wouldn't get anything said. Sitting too close to Monica was dangerous at a time like this. I needed to keep a level head to get this done.

"You can't do what, James? How many times are we going to go through this?" Monica asked as she stood up and pressed her body against mine. "Are you starting to feel guilty again?"

"Did you tell Jasmine I came over here to talk about her when she made me mad that night?"

"I haven't seen Jasmine in a long time," Monica began, trying to see where I was taking this. "Why? What did she tell you?" Monica asked, taking her seat. She looked a little uncomfortable and began grabbing at her side as she leaned farther back on the sofa.

I didn't want to put it out there if it wasn't said, and I chalked it up as Jasmine trying to call my bluff. I would deal with that once I got home, but for now I had to break things off with Monica.

"She didn't tell me anything. I wanted to know if you opened your mouth to her."

"Well, I didn't," Monica said between short breaths. The pains in her abdomen were getting sharper, causing her breath to come in spurts, contorting her pretty face.

"Good, keep it that way. I just came here to tell you that we have to chill. I can't see you no more. Things at home aren't right, and being here is not going to . . . Monica, are you okay?"

I was so into my story I didn't see Monica doubled over in pain on the couch until I turned to look at her. My back was to her, and I was mainly focused on how to get things with Jasmine back on track. She was clutching her stomach with tears streaming down her face, a pool of crimson blood forming around her on the beige sofa. I ran over to her, not knowing what to do.

"Monica, it's okay, baby. I'm calling for an ambulance now," I replied while trying to hold her up and dial 911 at the same time.

"James, tell them to hurry. I don't want to lose my baby," Monica said between her tears.

"Baby? What baby?" I said as I waited for my phone to connect to the police station.

"Your baby. Now hurry up," Monica replied as the circle of blood grew larger beneath her.

I explained the situation to the cops in a moment of disbelief, and I talked to Monica once they were on their way. I was shocked because I was just thinking what I would do if Monica was pregnant, and here she was. As cruel as it may sound, I hoped deep down that the baby didn't make it. That way I wouldn't have to explain my adulterous ways to my wife. Our marriage wouldn't withstand a blow like this. Jasmine could probably get past infidelity, but a baby would be a constant reminder that she more than likely wouldn't be able to deal with. My ass would be out and alone for sure.

By the time the ambulance showed up, Monica was laid back on the couch, barely able to move. I did what I could to keep her comfortable, but I was getting more nervous by the second because of the amount of blood on the couch and on the floor in front of it. The EMTs walked in and checked Monica's vitals as they questioned me on what happened.

I tried as best I could to explain what went down as they wheeled Monica out to the ambulance. I heard Monica, as low as her voice was, telling the EMT to hurry because she didn't want to lose her baby. They jetted away from the house, moving as quickly as they could through the evening traffic, hoping they could make it in time. Monica had lost a lot of blood and was probably miscarrying as they spoke.

Not knowing what to do as the ambulance pulled away, I turned back to the house so that I could clean the mess up. I didn't even know if I should be touching the scene, but I couldn't let Monica come home and see her house like this. When I walked in, I saw Sheila standing on the top of the steps with tears in her eyes.

"I didn't know you were here," I said, surprised to see Sheila. The last time we got together we were in a very compromising position, and it made me feel a little uncomfortable with her in the room.

"We were just talking, and I dozed off," Sheila replied. She looked like she didn't want me to know that she had heard bits and pieces of what we were talking about. I was sure she heard Monica tell me she was pregnant, but by the looks of things, she might not be for long.

We stared at each other for a while. I took a seat on the arm of the chair to collect my thoughts. How could I ask Sheila what she heard without putting my business out there? Rubbing my temples with my fingertips, I breathed in deeply, the smell of blood catching in my throat, almost choking me. Deciding to just play it out and see if Sheila would talk, I moved the conversation to the next subject.

"Look, about the last time I was here," Sheila began suddenly, feeling like she had to cover herself. She didn't know what I thought of her, and she probably wanted to tell someone what she knew before it killed her.

"Don't worry about it. Let's just clean this mess up. I don't want her to come home to this mess."

Without words, we both grabbed towels and cleaners and got the mess up as best we could. We couldn't do anything about the blood on the couch, but we made sure the floor was spotless and threw the soaked pillow away so that Monica wouldn't have to deal with it when she got home. Once everything was in place, I offered Sheila a ride home, wanting to know what was on her mind because she was super quiet.

I didn't look her way once, my eyes appearing glazed over as the tragedy played repeatedly in my head. I was going through my own shit and was praying hard that the baby didn't make it. After dropping Sheila off, I went home to talk to my wife, deciding that would be the last time Monica saw me.

I heard days later that by the time Monica arrived at the hospital, they had to take the 3-month-old fetus from her and give her a blood transfusion to help her survive. She was carrying it in her tubes, and they caught it just in time. If she had waited any longer, her tubes would have burst, killing her in the process.

Pulling into my driveway a half hour later, I walked slowly up to my front door after noticing my bedroom light was still on. Debating whether I would share what just happened with my wife, I put my key in the door, not really knowing how to handle the situation. Figuring it would probably be best if I just came clean, I took the long trek to my bedroom to clear the air between me and my wife once and for all. For real this time.

When I walked in, Jasmine was sleeping quietly under the covers. I saw that she fell asleep with the television on, which was strange because the house had to be pitch-black and quiet for Jazz to get any kind of rest. She said it was so she could hear the kids, but I knew better. Smiling for a second at how beautiful my wife was, I had to wonder again how everything went wrong. We had been soulmates since day one. She gave me what I asked for without any questions and never really gave me a reason to step out. The issues we had were minimal and could have been worked out had I been a little more patient with her.

Turning off the television and light, and turning on the radio, I got into the bed and wrapped myself around my wife as strands of Luther's "So Amazing" started to play from the radio. Jasmine snuggled up closer to me as I began to sing the chorus softly into her ear.

Love has truly been good to me
Not even one sad day
Or minute have I had since you've come my way

"Jazz, I'm so sorry I hurt you, baby. I never meant to." I was trying to control my tears as I talked to my wife. I knew she was no longer asleep, and she was crying as well as I felt her tears splash against my arm.

"Baby, I know I messed up. I just need you to help me. I need you to be here for me. I can't do this by myself. You and the kids complete me."

"James, it's okay. I'll never leave you, baby. I want this to work just as much as you do, but I need the truth. I need to know what happened when you left here. I need to know everything from day one."

Got to tell you how you thrill me
I'm happy as I can be
You have come and it's changed my whole world

"Jazz, I need to come clean with you," I said, pulling her into an embrace so that she couldn't run when I started to tell the truth. At this point, the best thing to do was just get it all out and let the chips fall where they may. She didn't say a word or refuse my embrace. She simply moved closer, burying her head in my chest. As the quiet storm played on the radio, I told Jasmine everything about Monica from day one, leaving out the money, the baby, and a few other details that I didn't think Jasmine could handle.

"I've been seeing Monica on and off since our hotel date." Her body went stiff, but she didn't move. I just took that as a sign to continue, since she hadn't started swinging just yet. I thanked God quickly and continued.

"She had been blackmailing me for a while, and I just couldn't hurt you like that. At the time I felt like the easiest thing to do was to just keep the secret, but now I know better. It turned her into a monster, but I ended it tonight. She will no longer be a concern for us," I explained in a roundabout way. There was no way I could really give up the tapes on everything, but I needed to give my wife some play in the game just in case Monica tried to come to her with some foolishness. There's nothing like getting hit with something you don't know about a person you should know nearly everything about.

I knew I was still telling lies, but it felt good to get some of the stuff off my chest. I was determined to be done with Monica and get my family back on track. Afterward, we held each other until we both fell asleep, making promises to each other to work it out the best we could.

It's so amazing to be loved
I'd follow you to the moon in the sky above

Chapter Nineteen

Monica

I had been in the hospital for three weeks, trying to recover from the loss of my child and my near-death experience. James and Sheila didn't show their faces, and it was taking a toll on me mentally and emotionally. For the first time since I was a teenager, I truly felt alone in the world. In fact, ever since my mom had passed away, or rather since her life was taken, it seemed as if no one in the universe cared about me.

My depression only made my condition worse, the doctors not seeing any sign of life in me outside of the healing of my body. All I did was cry day in and day out, and I wouldn't eat, so the doctors had me tube fed so that my body could get some type of nourishment. My weight was at an unsightly low, making me look skeletal, as I pitied myself for not taking the time to make things right in my life. I was really out in these streets alone, and truth be told, it sucked. Bad. And I hated it here.

I slept most of the day, fighting off nightmares of my uncle and my sister's father molesting me as a teenager and the unforgettable incident with Keith and his friends from the tenth grade. Every man I cared even remotely about always ended up hurting me, breaking my heart. I wallowed in self-pity day after day to the point where the doctor suggested I seek counseling so that I could better deal with my anxiety and bouts of depression. I was falling apart at the seams, unlike the me everyone knew. I was the strong friend nobody checked on, and up until now, I was okay with it. I quickly found out that not only was I not okay, but I was mad as fuck that I didn't have any damn body to lean on. Fucked up as it may be, I was determined to get past this stage too. I had to if I was going to get back at everybody who ever did me wrong.

On my last day at the hospital, after I signed up for therapy sessions and the doctor saw that I was eating and actually keeping my food down, I sat in my room, thinking of ways to get my life back. I knew I had to get James and Sheila back because they definitely abandoned me. They were the only ones who knew I was here and didn't even bother to see if I was still alive. I also had to get Jasmine before it was too late. I was tired of sleeping alone, and I had to move fast if things were going to work.

While waiting for my discharge papers, I took my time putting on the new sweat suit and sneakers one of the guards purchased for me to go home in because the clothes I came in with were soiled. I had the nurse cover all the mirrors, so I had no clue how ghastly I really looked. All the guard wanted was my number and dinner, and I obliged. At least *somebody* was willing to look out for me. I was willing to do anything to get the overbearing, underpaid security guard out of my face.

Watching *Jenny Jones* on television while waiting for the nurse to come back, I almost fell off the bed when I saw Sheila walk through the door. Fixing my face to say something smart, I thought better of it, thinking I may need Sheila to help me later on down the line. Sheila came in with a small teddy bear and flowers, her facial expression showing how nervous she was in spite of her smile.

"Monica, I'm sorry I haven't been to see you. I've been so busy with—"

"Sheila, it's fine. No explanation is needed. I'm just waiting for my discharge papers so I can blow this joint," I said as I turned my attention back to the television.

I could see Sheila taking note of how frail I looked, almost seeing the teenage Monica she saw that night. Placing the teddy bear and my house keys on the bed beside her, Sheila took one last look at me before she turned to leave. Nearing the door, she turned the knob, not knowing what to do and kicking herself for coming up there in the first place.

Just as she was closing the door, she heard me call her name. When she looked back into the room, I was holding the teddy bear in my hands with tears in my eyes. Sheila waited at the door for me to speak.

"Thanks for coming up here. I really appreciate it."

"It was no trouble. Just get better soon," Sheila replied and turned away quickly so that I wouldn't see her tears as well.

Once I was sure Sheila was gone, I held up the teddy bear, taking a long look at it. Ripping the head from its shoulders, I dropped both pieces in the can next to my bed, tucking my key into my pants pocket. I continued watching my show as if nothing happened. I didn't need stuffed animals. I needed Jasmine, and that's all I was concerned about.

After signing my discharge papers, I walked out of the hospital and got into the waiting cab that was there to take me home. The driver tried to make small talk, but I just stared out of the window, taking in the city, every-thing looking new to me. To me it felt like I was in the hospital for three years instead of three weeks. I couldn't wait to get home so that I could lie down in my own bed and not the hard hospital bed that I had been in.

Once the driver pulled up to my house, I paid him and exited the vehicle quickly so that I could hurry up to my room. Upon entrance, I could smell the stale blood in the air from my recent loss. Avoiding the stained sofa, I all but ran up to my room, throwing myself on the bed in a fit of tears once I got there. I couldn't understand why things weren't going my way, and I briefly thought about praying, casting away the thought after determining God wouldn't hear me for all of the dirt I'd done.

Drifting off to sleep once my tears subsided, I thought about ways of knocking James off quickly so that I could finally have Jasmine to myself. The baby wasn't all that important to me, but if all else failed, I decided, I would try getting pregnant again as a last resort. As bad as things were going, something had to give, and I hoped it would give soon.

I slept well until the next afternoon, the ringing phone waking me from my slumber. Upset about the interference of my much-needed sleep but glad to be awakened from the nightmare I was having, I answered the phone with a groggy voice lacking any type of enthusiasm. I thought it was still morning and wondered who would be calling so early.

"This better be good," I barked into the phone as I struggled to sit up in my bed. I was still having slight pains in my abdomen, and it wasn't easy for me to maneuver around.

"You have a paid call from an inmate held in Muncy Correctional Facility. If you attempt to use three-way calling or any other features, this call will be disconnected. To accept this call, press three now," the computer voice spoke into the receiver.

I glanced at the clock, realizing it was the afternoon, wondering who got locked up and was calling for my assistance. I had just bailed my sister out only two months ago, and I hoped she wasn't sent up again. My sister was a petty thief, and I was starting to think she preferred jail to having freedom. Pressing the three, I spoke into the receiver, ready to hear some member of my dysfunctional family beg for help.

"Who needs my help now?" I spoke into the phone once the call was connected. I didn't plan on helping whoever was calling, and I was going to make this short and sweet.

"You seem to have forgotten about me." The voice came through on the other end, sounding angry and ready to explode.

"I forgot about who?" I replied, thinking my mind was playing tricks on me. I hadn't spoken to Tanya since the day she was sent up for her husband's murder almost two and a half years ago. Wondering why she decided to call now, I didn't hide my disbelief as we continued the conversation.

"After all we've been through, you don't know who this is?" Tanya came through on the other end like she wanted to snatch me by my neck.

"I know who it is," I came back with an attitude. I was over Tanya and didn't feel like the bullshit. What was Tanya going to do for me from prison? Besides, I had my eyes on a bigger prize and didn't plan on being distracted by anyone.

"Why am I still in here? You told me a couple of weeks, and that's it," Tanya said, sounding like she was starting to cry. "I been in here for damn near three years waiting for you to get me out of this hellhole. What the fuck is the problem?"

"What do you mean, what's the problem? I told you there would be some time served," I came back with just as much attitude.

As far as I was concerned, I didn't owe Tanya shit. If anything, I did her a favor by killing her abusive husband.

Who wants to live in fear every day for the rest of their life not knowing how her man was going to act when he got home? You can't be cute with a black eye and broken ribs. Ain't nothing sexy about it. I came to the conclusion that if I hadn't killed him, he would have killed her, and it's as simple as that. I saved her life. If anything, she should have been grateful I came through the way I did. No, I didn't think about the situation I put Tanya's son in, but I was never good at looking at the big picture. Everything was about me and my satisfaction. When were people going to catch on to that fact?

"So, what am I supposed to do? I didn't tell on you because I thought you had my back. I thought you loved me," Tanya screamed into the phone, her emotions getting the best of her, causing the other inmates to look in her direction. Even though she told herself she wasn't going to cry, she couldn't help it. She wanted out of the stone cage she was forced to be in and was ready to do whatever necessary to make it happen.

"What did I tell you about trusting people? Didn't I tell you no human was trustworthy? Didn't I tell you that you were the only one who had your back?" I shot the questions at her back-to-back, not giving her enough time to answer in between. "You come into this world alone, and you leave alone. How many times have we had this conversation?" I was getting frustrated with the entire scenario and was about to hang up. My main focus was Jasmine now, and I didn't want to hear shit Tanya had to say. When was the world going to understand that it was all about me and what made me happy? No one else mattered.

"So you just gonna leave me here?" Tanya asked in a quiet voice, not believing the turn of events. She thought I was her soulmate and thought about all the nights we were wrapped around each other, confessing our never-ending love. The Monica she was talking to now was a complete stranger.

"Tanya," I began, feeling kind of bad because I was the reason she was in jail in the first place, "I'll make some calls in the morning and see what I can do for you, okay?"

"Monica, listen. I need to get out of here. I can't watch my son leave another visit. It's driving me crazy knowing that he's too young to understand. All he knows is he wants his mom. He cries every time he has to leave. Can you understand the pain I'm going through?"

I began thinking about my own loss and the loss of my mother years ago. There were so many times where I needed to talk to my mom but couldn't. So many times I wished I had a gun so that I could stop my stepfather from beating my mom in his drunken state. So many times I begged my mom to leave, only for my mom to tell me it was okay as she limped to her room after being beaten nearly unconscious for reasons she didn't even know about.

So many times I wished I had the nerve, the courage to stop him that one last time as I watched my mother's breath leave her body, her attacker still kicking and punching her until she stopped moving. I thought about the recent loss of my child and how it felt to be without a mother, and for a second, I had an ounce of compassion for Tanya's situation. Never mind the fact that I put her there in the first place.

Brushing back tears, I got myself together as I listened to Tanya's soft cries and her pleas to get her home to her son. All Tanya wanted was a second chance, and she needed me to help her get it.

"Tanya, please stop crying. I'll be there soon, and I'll make some calls for you today. I'll get you home, okay?"

Before Tanya could respond, her time had expired on the call, and we were disconnected. I held the phone long after the dial tone had stopped, and the operator was instructing me to either hang up or make a call as tears stung my eyes. I didn't want Jasmine's situation to turn out the same as Tanya's or worse. Calling up Judge Stenton, the same judge who presided over Tanya's case, I set up an appointment to meet with him in private so that we could discuss a few things. He owed me a favor, and there was no time like the present to cash in on it.

Chapter Twenty

Tanya

She really left me for dead? Like, she really left me in this bitch! I don't regret a lot of things, but Monica is the one at the top of the list of people I wished I had never met. I thought she was a good thing. I low-key always liked women, but I married my son's father to save face. I was in love with him, too, but he had a mean streak that I thought I could love out of him. One thing about a pack of horses is if you see one with stripes, it's a zebra. My grandma used to say that to us all the time when I was little, and I never understood what she meant by that. It wasn't until I got older that I was able to interpret it to mean that people will always show you who they are. Show their true colors. Both my husband and Monica showed me exactly who they were, and I didn't believe them until it was too late.

I knew I was going to spend forever with my husband even before we were married. He was everything I thought I wanted in a man. Overprotective, attentive, and well endowed. He made good money, and I really didn't have to work, but I refused to just sit back and not have a thing to bring to the table. I compromised and worked part-time while I was in culinary school, and I was content with what we had. We were happy, and I was elated about where the future was taking us.

He had a drinking problem though. At first it flew under the radar, and I just chalked it up to him not being able to handle his liquor. We didn't drink like that, so I just assumed he was a lightweight like me. I definitely made an ass out of myself with that one. As time went on, my thought process moved more to thinking maybe he was stressed out at work. That had to be the reason why he was drinking more, right? He put in long hours at the office and oftentimes came home tense and angry about whatever he and his partners had to deal with throughout the day.

The first time he hit me, I was so shocked I couldn't even swing back. Did this man just put his hands on me? We were in the middle of having a conversation about him wanting me to quit school, and I refused. I had just found out I was pregnant, but it was still early on. Pregnant people cook all the time. What did I have to stop school for so early on? I was literally still in my first trimester, and I would be done training before the baby was born.

"The baby is not due until August. School is done at the end of July. I will still have an entire month to relax before the baby gets here," I argued my case as I picked at the fancy breakfast I had made us that morning. I was really enjoying learning new dishes and trying them out at home, but he was making shit difficult for both of us. He could just argue with himself, though. I wasn't quitting school for him or anybody else. I was almost at the damn finish line.

"This is not a negotiation, Tanya. You either sit your ass down, or—"

"Or what?" I asked, looking him dead in the eyes. He was not my damn daddy. I could do whatever the hell I wanted to do.

I promise you it looked like he turned into the devil right before my eyes. Before I could blink, he was already on my side of the table, and I was lying on the floor next to my chair that had tipped back from the force of the slap. The side of my face stung like a million bees had attacked me, and I knew for sure there would be a mark on my face from where his hand had landed.

"Or," he said, breathing heavily as he stood over me, "you will learn the hard way what will happen to you if you don't do what I say. Now get your stupid ass off the floor and finish this plate. Don't waste my damn food."

I'd never been so scared in my life. I stayed on that floor long after he left, and I did as I was told and ate everything on my plate before cleaning up the mess I made from cooking. I still didn't quit school regardless of how much we fought. He had to slap on me many times before the semester ended, and I still managed to graduate at the top of my class. The beatings were going to be worth it because I was determined to be the best at it. I had plans to open a restaurant, and I wouldn't need him anymore after that.

Shortly after my son was born, I met Monica. She was like a breath of fresh air that I didn't know I needed. I hired her to do my son's newborn baby pics after she came highly recommended by a mutual friend. I was shocked that she agreed to do it since her roster was full of celebrities, but she agreed, stating that sometimes she just wanted to capture the beautiful things in life. We did the shoot in her gorgeous home in a studio that she had set up in a back room. She was so patient with my baby and really knew how to work the props that she had set up for him. You could tell that she loved what she did, and I couldn't wait to see all of the photos when they were done. I just sat in the corner silently and watched her create magic with the magic I had brought into the world.

After the photoshoot was done, she laid my son down in the Pack 'n Play, and she offered me a light lunch while we went over some of the photos that she had taken. The way we oohed and aahed over the photos was crazy. She did an amazing job with him, and it was so hard to pick out some that I really liked. She smelled amazing by the way, and I really didn't mind the feel of her body pressing against me periodically as we scrolled through her camera roll.

"When was the last time you took photos?" she asked as she cleared the table of the lunch that we had.

"Not since before I got pregnant. I didn't even have a maternity photoshoot."

Truth was I was too embarrassed to tell her that the reason why I didn't take pics was because I had to hide the bruises on my body. The only parts of my body that were off-limits were the middle to bottom part of my back and my stomach. He gripped me by my neck too many times to count, and slapping me around appeared to be his favorite thing. I noticed that he was inebriated more often than not, and it was just becoming a lot to deal with. I birthed my son at the hospital by myself, and he showed up three hours after he was born, asking me why he was light skinned, and smelling like a brewery.

"Follow me," she said, and I didn't hesitate as we made our way back up to her studio.

"Take off your clothes," she instructed. I stood there looking stupid as she began walking circles around me, snapping pictures.

Sometimes she got close, other times she stood back, but she never stopped clicking the button. I slowly began to remove my clothes one piece at a time until I was down to just my skin. She smiled as she took in my curves. She laid her hand lightly on my fupa, bending to kiss me there. She positioned my body on the floor, moving and stretching me all kinds of ways, never putting down the camera.

At one point, I leaned back and closed my eyes. I was on my elbows, and my legs were bent at the knees. My eyes snapped open when I felt her lips slurp my clit into her mouth. It was like an electric volt shot through my body, and honey began to pool at my opening immediately. She toggled back and forth between sucking on my clit and using her tongue to stroke me into a frenzy.

I opened my legs wider, pulling my knees up to my chest, allowing her more access to my sweet spot. Never once using her hands, she made her tongue stiff, plunging it inside of my walls, causing me to scream out. The slurping and sucking sounds she made as she hummed against my clit was like music to my ears. I hadn't been touched like this in months, and I didn't remember it being this good with my husband.

The orgasm she pulled out of me sucked every bit of energy I had left. As I lay on the floor, panting, trying to get myself together, she stood and licked her lips and then left the room. As I struggled to get myself together, I realized that there was a light blinking on her camera. Was she recording this? I quickly got myself together and met her downstairs, where I found her rocking my son and cooing at him. The sight made me smile, yet I felt a little awkward.

"So, I'll have the pics ready for you in about six days, and then you will be able to decide which ones you want blown up. I have the packet info already emailed out to you," she said as she smiled and passed my baby to me like something so intimate didn't happen between us. "Let's get together soon, okay?"

"Okay?" I responded more like a question. I left her home in a daze, feeling amazing but confused at the same time. We didn't talk again for almost three weeks, and that was when we really started to get to know each other. She would often take pics of my son and of us together. As time went on, I would let my mom watch my son so that she and I could really get it in. We were twisted like pretzels many nights and early mornings. I'd never forget that morning that she took the strawberries that were supposed to be for our waffles and stuffed them inside of me, using her tongue to pull them back out as I barely was able to keep my body on the edge of the kitchen table. Monica was like a breath of the freshest air I'd ever breathed, and I didn't want to give her up.

My husband, though. He got worse as things with her got better. She was livid that night I showed up bloody and bruised, icing my body for hours as she vowed to kill his ass. I would've let her, but I didn't want my son to not have a father. This went on for over a year until that one night when everything changed. He came home drunk, but even more than I could ever remember. He was accusing me of fucking one of the partners at his firm, but it was really Monica the entire time. I had plans to meet up with her, and I guessed since I never showed up at her house, she showed up at mine.

It happened so fast I couldn't even really understand what was going on. I remember being down on the floor as he stomped and kicked me, and then I felt the warmth of his blood splatter all over my body. The room just went quiet, and I didn't even recall hearing the shots. I remembered Monica putting the gun in my hand and mouthing something that I couldn't hear before she ran from the house. The next thing I knew, there were cops all over the place, and when I looked up, Marcus, my husband, was dead. Shortly after that, I was behind bars. It was all a blur, and Monica said that she had me.

Three years later I was still in this bitch, but I had to hold on to hope. *She will get me out of here. I have to believe that she will.* I wouldn't be able to live with anything else.

Chapter Twenty-one

James

I had been standing outside of Monica's house for at least twenty minutes, several times resisting the urge to hop in my car and stay away forever. Hating to admit that I may be slipping again, I called the hospital just as I had for the past three weeks, checking with the nurses to see if she was okay, not wanting to talk to her directly. Fabricating my relationship to Monica so that I could find out information on her, information only privileged to family, I kept tabs on her progression, the entire time telling the nurses that I was her brother from out of town.

Upon finding out that she was discharged, I took off from work early to check in on her and find out if she was still carrying the baby because I didn't have the heart to ask the nurse about it. Stopping to get soup and juice for her, I stood outside, peering up at her windows, the sun relentless on my skin. Finally taking a deep breath to boost my courage, I went up and knocked on the door, announcing my arrival at her home.

On the other side of the door, I could hear Monica racing down the steps. My heart beat just as quickly as her footsteps on the hardwood floor. Waiting in anticipation for her to open the door felt like an eternity. My voice came out weak and soft when she asked who was on the other side.

Monica paused before opening the door. Maybe I was just the person she was looking for. I was preparing for her to read me the riot act for abandoning her the way I did. When she pulled the door open, I all but jumped back, gasping out loud at the woman standing before me.

Cheeks and eyes sunken in and bones showing under the once-tight shirt she was wearing, Monica looked like she had been binging on coke for the past couple of weeks. Gone were the sexy smile and mischievous eyes. Standing before me was a woman I didn't recognize as a million questions flooded in my head at once.

"Are you going to stand there and stare at me, or are you coming in?" she quizzed, sounding frustrated that I caught her looking her worst. Monica always looked her best, even at her worst, so this was a rare occurrence.

As I stepped through the open door, memories of that night flashed before my eyes, causing me to sway a little as I thought about the blood and the circumstances under which it came. Daring a glance in that area, I saw that the once-bloodied sofa was replaced with a soft butter leather sectional, showing no signs of the gory scene from a couple of weeks ago.

Following Monica into the kitchen, I set down the contents in my hand, taking a seat before my face became acquainted with the floor. I breathed heavily, trying to control the lightheaded feeling I was having. Monica leaned against the sink, taking it all in, not even offering me a glass of water to ease my anxiety.

"So, James," Monica said while examining her nails, "what brought you to this side of town? I thought maybe your fingers had been broken or you had amnesia."

"It wasn't like that," I began, deciding against telling her that I had checked on her every day while she was in the hospital. "I had to keep things tight at home. Maintain balance with my own family. You know how it is."

"No, I don't know how it is! As you can plainly see, I am the only occupant under this roof. Or have we forgotten already?" Monica stated sarcastically, causing me to get on the defensive.

"Look, I didn't come here for all that."

"Then what are you here for? To see if I'm still pregnant with your child?"

I didn't want to just bust out and ask her the obvious, even though she had hit the nail right on the head. I was trying to be a gentleman about the situation and was determined to do just that no matter how hard Monica made it to be.

"Monica, you need to slow the fuck down," I said, all of a sudden feeling strong and taking Monica by surprise. "I heard you were out of the hospital, and I came to see if you were okay. I bought you some stuff so you wouldn't have to leave the house because I was concerned. I know you're not used to people caring about your well-being, but the sarcastic bullshit I can do without."

"I just know you've lost your mind!" Monica said, stepping away from the kitchen sink and toward me like she was two seconds from pouncing on me and ripping my heart out of my chest with her bare hands.

"You know what, Monica?" I said, backing away from the table and making my way to the front door. "This shit is for the birds. I don't want or need the drama!"

As I walked to the door, my one step about four of Monica's, I could hear her playing catch-up behind me. Regretting turning my back to her, I hoped she wasn't running up on me with a knife or something. Monica had major screws loose, and I didn't feel like having to explain it to Jazz later. I was supposed to be at work anyway.

"James, wait," Monica said as she came up behind me.

"What?" I said, still facing the door with my hand on the knob. I just wanted to know if I was going to be a father again. Anything else was irrelevant.

"I lost the baby. I don't know how happy that makes you, but it damn near killed me. That's all I had to keep you near my heart, the only thing I could call mine. Someone to finally love me," Monica said through her tears. She didn't want me per se, but she knew that a child would give her unconditional love regardless of whether I was around. At least that was what I got from her last statement.

"All you would have done is cause problems. I don't need another kid right now, and even if you had kept it, we still wouldn't have been together."

"Who said it's you I want, James?" Monica said before catching herself.

"Then who do you want, Monica? I don't think you even know."

Without continuing the conversation, I opened the door. The brightness of the sun blurred my vision for a few seconds as my eyes adjusted to the light. Monica stood in the doorway watching me walk away, and I didn't really feel any remorse. She looked a horrible mess, and that was the only reason I resisted her, but that wouldn't be for long. She'd bounced back many times, so surely this time wouldn't be any different.

Chapter Twenty-two

Monica

It took me five months to pull it together. Pulling up to the news station, I let the pimple-faced adolescent park my convertible after retrieving the picnic basket from the back seat. It was a nice fall day in the City of Brotherly Love. A slight October chill could be felt on my bare skin under the trench coat I wore, making me wish for a second that I had worn more than a thong and a garter belt. Placing my free arm across my chest, I pressed down against my erect nipples as I made my way into the building from the parking garage.

It had been a while since I'd seen James. The little scene at my house during his last visit played repeatedly in my mind as I worked at getting my appearance back to what it used to be. My once-sagging breasts were back to their perky selves, sitting at attention as they brushed against the underside of my soft pink trench coat.

My hair was braided up in micro braids, set on straws with a flower on the side, giving me a carefree summer look even at this time of year. My thigh-high boots peeked out of my trench coat every time I took a step across the marble lobby of the Urban News Network. Every eye was on me as I walked like a high fashion model, confidence dripping off of me with lots left to spare.

When I reached the desk, the security guard was speechless as he sat looking in awe at the beauty in front of him. His erection was damn near about to break his zipper, and I took this opportunity to get upstairs to James's office hopefully without him knowing I was even in the building. Bending over to talk to the guard, my breasts in full view, I took control quickly before the woman I knew normally sat at the desk came back from her break.

"I need you to do me a favor," I said to the flashlight cop in a tone only he could hear. "I'm visiting my husband in the engineering department, and I don't want him to know I'm here. Is it possible for me to get a key to his office so I can surprise him when he walks in? His name is James Cinque. What was his office number again? I always get confused."

The guard couldn't answer. His tongue was caught in his throat. When I touched the side of his face, the front of his pants immediately showed a wide circle forming from his ejaculation. Passing me the keys with the office number on the tag, he couldn't take his eyes off me as I kissed him on the cheek, leaving my Passion Fruit Revlon mouth print on the side of his face. I walked slowly away from him, letting him take all of me in as I boarded the elevator, opening my coat for him as the door was closing, giving him a frontal view of what he would never have.

The elevator took me to the eighteenth floor quickly. I stepped off the elevator, thankful that no one got on as I came up. Finding James's office without a problem, I drew the blinds shut tightly so that no one could look in. After I set up my flameless candles and picnic lunch, I stretched out on the leather sofa in my outfit, awaiting his arrival.

James, not paying attention to the darkness in his locked office, opened the door, finally looking up at the scene. Noticing me mostly naked on his sofa, he closed the door abruptly, being sure to put both locks on.

"What are you doing here?" James asked, taking in my smooth body stretched out before him. Gone was the skeletal me who was nothing more than a bag of bones the last time he saw me. What lay before him was a curvaceous ebony sister, thick in all the right places. This Monica was ten times better than the Monica before my skeletal state, my body radiating heat that he could feel from his spot at the door.

"Well," I said as I opened my legs for him to see the crotchless thong I was wearing, the candlelight bouncing off my pierced clit, "it's been a while since the last time I saw you, and I wanted to remind you of what you were missing."

Getting up off the couch, I looked to make sure the mini camera was on. I had placed it beside the picture of him and Jasmine he had hanging from the wall. Walking up to James, I began unbuttoning his shirt, kissing him on the neck in the process.

"Monica, what are you doing?" James came back, trying to get some control over the situation. His manhood standing at attention gave away his real thoughts.

"I'm reminding you of what you've been missing."

Sliding down to waist level, I unzipped his pants and pulled out his thickness, marveling at the evenness of his skin tone. Circling the head with the tip of my tongue first, I took just the head in. James leaned against the door for support.

"Monica, we can't do this," James said weakly as the effects of the brain job he was receiving took effect. "I'm at work."

"Then that means you'll be quiet, huh?" I replied between kisses as I swallowed James up, his seed dripping from the sides of my mouth showing his excitement.

I pushed James over to the couch. He sat down with a thud, and I stood over him, holding him by his tie. Squatting down on his length, I moved slow and then fast, contracting my muscles around his shaft, causing him to explode inside of me almost immediately. Raw Monica felt amazing to everyone who got to try me.

Me being a pro, I kept him inside of me, working my muscles until he was stiff again, bouncing up and down on him like I was auditioning for a rap video. James held on to my waist as he sucked hard on my nipples, adding to my pleasure. He reached between my legs and softly tugged on my clit piercing until I threw my head back in pleasure. We climaxed together, evidence of our session all over his stomach and pubic area.

I got up, bending over in front of him to remove all of the juices from his penis with my mouth, causing him to explode in the back of my throat one final time. The entire time, my pussy dripping his seed was at eye level for him.

Allowing James to catch his breath, I stepped over to his desk, retrieving the chilled bottle of Moët I had brought for our meal. Pouring the clear liquid into two flutes, I offered one to James, opting to remain standing in front of him. He didn't even bother to adjust his clothes, downing the champagne like it was spring water.

Finally, he dared a look at me, and his length rose to the occasion again at the sight of me. Once again, he didn't use protection. He made this too easy. Turning my back to him, I straddled James again. With his head leaned back against the sofa, he just enjoyed the ride, deciding to worry about the consequences later.

"James," I moaned softly. My body movement slowed down as my orgasm approached. "Can I cum, *papi?*"

Instead of responding, James pumped back harder, causing me to almost fall off of him. Motioning for me to stand up, he stayed inside of me as he bent me over his desk, recklessly driving into me, trying to hurt me purposefully. I was staring at the photo of him and his family the entire time, in my mind replacing James's image with my own.

"Monica," James said as he banged my back out like a madman, "make this your last time coming to my office. It's over. You hear me?" I took too long answering, so James drove into me harder, my breasts bouncing against the side of the desk.

"I said do you hear me?"

"Yes, I hear you. Please, you're hurting me," I came back, still surprised at James. He had never fucked me with so much intensity, and for once I couldn't handle it.

Instead of stopping, James continued his barrage against my swollen cave, holding me up as my knees tried to buckle under me. Hitting it hard, he didn't pull out until he was about to explode, doing so all over my braids and back. Stepping away from my now-crumpled form on the floor, he stepped back into his clothes, afterward taking a sandwich from the basket.

"Have my office back to normal by the time I get back," James threw over his shoulder as he gathered both sets of keys and made his way to the employee shower room at the end of the hall.

I sat for a moment longer, gathering the feeling back into my legs. First popping in a menstrual cup so that the semen wouldn't all drip out, I made sure it was secure before disconnecting the camera and checking to make sure I had clear footage of what took place. I put what little clothes I had back on and straightened the office back up, leaving a sandwich and soft drink on his desk before exiting and taking the evidence of everything else with me.

On my way out the door, I noticed Jasmine at the front desk, talking to the old white lady who should have been there when I came in. Not wanting to be noticed, I walked quickly toward the side exit, tipping the still-smiling guard on the way out and then the valet boy as he pulled up in my convertible.

Screeching out of the parking garage, I sped all the way home, leaving the basket in the car as I raced to my room so that I could do a headstand on my bed for better results. This may have been my last chance at getting pregnant, and I didn't want any problems making it happen.

Chapter Twenty-three

Monica

Walking up to the county jail took forever. The short walk from the car to the menacing gates seemed like an eternity as the sun beat down on my head. On the inside I felt like I deserved the torture because I knew it could have easily been my stupid ass behind those four stone walls, calling this place home for many years. I tried to harden my heart as I approached the desk, but my soul wouldn't allow it.

This visit wasn't like the many times I'd visited my baby sister because she had committed some petty crime. This was a matter of life and death and the well-being of a 3-year-old who didn't understand his mother's predicament. This was reality, coming face-to-face with the real. My legs willed me to leave. To take the chance and haul ass back to my car and jet up out if this lot and let Tanya figure this shit out on her own. That would just be too fucked up even for me, and my guilt made me stay.

Approaching the desk slowly, I took in the rough faces of the security guards both male and female, but on some it was hard to tell the difference. These chicks looked like straight dudes in the face, but I just chalked it up to them being a product of their environment. While waiting my turn, I observed the impatient girlfriends, baby mommas, and family members suffering in the sweltering waiting area in order to see their loved ones. This was some bullshit, and it was crazy how we all had to suffer.

Women were in jeans so tight I was sure they would have a yeast infection by the end of the visit. They sat and conversed with other females they recognized from their weekly visits to the pen. They had formed friendships among one another. Belly shirts and extravagant weaves, with too much skin showing to be appropriate for visiting an inmate. I wondered how long they had to wait for their male counterparts to come from the prison down the street. Although I had never been to the female holding facility, I knew the men were housed on a separate unit.

"Who you here for?" the slightly overweight guard barked from behind the podium. I looked into her bulldog-like face, almost about to vomit on the paperwork that sat in front of her from the stench of her breath. The only reason I knew it was a woman was from the tone of her voice and the fact that she had breasts. If the woman had been flat chested, it would have been hard to tell.

"I'm here to see Tanya Walker," I responded as another whiff of the guard's foul breath made me take a step back.

The guard didn't seem to notice as she searched the books to make sure I was on the visiting list for Tanya. Searching my purse for the identification Tanya said I would need to get in, I placed it on the desk while the guard called over to the holding block to have Tanya come down. I checked my attitude as the guard looked over my ID and then set it on the desk as if it weren't handed to her. I wouldn't show my anger. I drove too far to be turned away, and I would deal with the guard when I got back out.

Taking my seat after, I put my belongings in a locker and turned my $20 bill into coins so that we could have something to eat. I sat patiently waiting to be called to the back. The woman sitting next to me was doing a horrible job trying to keep her baby quiet, and my annoyance was super evident on my face. She looked like she was ready to cry her damn self, so I gave her some grace because this was a horrible place to be in for both the convicted and the free.

Her skirt was so short you could see her dingy panties underneath, her outfit broadcasting legs so white from ash you could write your name on them. I laughed to myself as I remembered a joke from my childhood about a woman looking like she worked in a flour factory.

When the guard called the name out for the woman's jailbird boyfriend, she hurriedly got her stuff together so that she could get up front, her body smelling like a combination of piss and cheap perfume. I placed a finger under my nose discreetly so as not to embarrass the woman as she struggled with the baby and a diaper bag on her way up. I was lost in my own thoughts for a second, trying to steady my nerves as I fought to keep my legs from carrying me up out of there. It had been almost three years since I'd laid eyes on Tanya, and I hoped I could handle being that close to her again.

The commotion not too far from me broke into my thoughts as I witnessed two women up front having a shouting match and the guards doing nothing to stop it. Being nosy, I eased a little closer so that I could hear what the drama was about. When I got up there, the woman who had been sitting next to me and another equally as tacky woman were having a debate about who was going inside.

Come to find out both of the women were there to see the same guy, and what made it even more interesting was they were cousins. The woman sitting next to me had his child, who only looked to be a few months old, and the one she was arguing with looked to be about seven months pregnant. The pregnant female knew her cousin had a baby by him, but that didn't stop her from testing the waters before he got locked down the last time. Damn, I wished I had some popcorn because this was getting good!

The guards sat back in amusement as the ladies went on and on about who should get to see him. After several minutes of nonstop bickering, I thought the women were going to come to blows as the one holding the child sat her baby down on a nearby chair as if the infant could hold itself up.

After seeing that, the guards decided to finally break it up, telling both the women to leave for causing a disturbance in the waiting area. The women were still going at it as they walked out the door, the pregnant one going toward the bus depot, and the other going toward the parking lot.

"Family for Ms. Tanya Walker!" the manly looking female guard called out, getting everyone's attention. Holding my change purse tightly in my hand, I walked up to the front, following the guard who was escorting me to the back.

Halfway down the hall, we came to another waiting area, where I was fingerprinted and checked for contraband. The bulldog-looking guard came back and told me to step out of my shoes and clothes so that I could be searched for anything illegal that the detectors hadn't picked up.

"You want me to take my clothes off?" I asked the guard, surprised by her request. When did visitors start getting strip-searched? Had I known I would be going through all this, I wouldn't have made the trip.

"All of them so I can see those pretty titties," she came back with a dirty look on her face like she wanted to eat me alive right there.

"Where is that in the rule book? I was never told about a strip search," I came back angrily, refusing to take any article of clothing off. I didn't know the law like that, but I knew I had some rights.

"Leave the girl alone, Tommy," a guard said from behind her. "Miss, put your purse in the tray and walk through the detector, please."

Thankful for the interruption, I was more determined to deal with the guard when I came out as I took one last look at the guard to etch her face into my memory. Somehow, I would get the info needed from one of the visitors or guards before I left. She would have a nice little surprise waiting for her once she left work. Stink-mouth–ass bitch!

Entering the room, I spotted Tanya immediately. From across the room, I could see her sad expression as she sat at the table with her arms folded in front of her, waiting for me to come over. She didn't stand when I approached the table, and I had a little salt on my shoulders because I was waiting to give Tanya a hug. She wasn't happy to see me like I had witnessed with the other inmates and their loved ones, but then again, why would she be? She was doing a bid for me, and I had left her stranded for the last three years. I wouldn't fuck with me if I were her either. I took the seat across from her, and we said nothing as we studied each other.

Prison was not going well for Tanya. I don't know that it "went well" for anyone, but you could see the toll it was taking on her physically. Her once-long jet-black hair that flowed past her shoulders in a stylish wrap was now braided into cornrows straight back off her face, making her face look tight and raw. Although her skin was still clear, she now sported a small, jagged scar above her right eyebrow, no doubt from a fistfight behind these walls. Her acrylic nails that always had a fresh French manicure were now bitten way down, and her pretty, pedicured feet were sporting Timberland boots. She definitely looked like what she had been through, and it was all my fault. I felt like shit.

I resisted the urge to cry as I sat looking at my former lover, regretting having her in this horrible place, but not the circumstances she was there for. Had I not murdered Marcus, he would have surely murdered Tanya, putting her six feet under instead of in these human cages.

"When am I getting out of here?" Tanya spoke, skipping the pleasantries and getting right to the point, catching me off guard. Surprised by the bass in her voice, I leaned back in my seat to get a good look at Tanya. I had not expected our visit to go like this. Tanya was usually soft-spoken, unlike the angry woman sitting in front of me now.

"Well, I talked to the judge yesterday, and he's working on your paperwork now," I said in a calm voice, not liking the direction our conversation was taking.

"Do what you do best. I just need to get out of here."

"What the hell is that supposed to mean?" I said, my temper rising quickly.

"It means," Tanya began in a slow, deliberate voice, "that I don't care if you have to fuck him, suck his dick, and take back shots from all of his judge friends in the same night. I want out of this hellhole. I want to be with my son," Tanya responded, trying to control her tears. She said she wasn't going to cry, and she was determined to hold it down.

"Well, Tanya, I'm doing the best that I can, and—"

"Fuck the best, Monica!" Tanya came back, almost knocking the chair back. "Do you know what it's like to be in here? Imagine someone telling you when you're allowed to take a shit. You have to share showers with a million other motherfuckers on a daily basis. Your fragile ass wouldn't last an hour in here. I want out! Get me out of this hellhole!"

I was speechless because she was right. I did not look good in orange. That was the first problem right there. Jail was not for me. There was no way I'd be okay with people telling me when to come and go. I felt like shit that I put her in this situation.

"Every morning like clockwork, they wake us up at the crack of dawn to eat some unrecognizable shit," she began with a faraway look in her eyes. "Try sharing a shower with a million other bitches. You can't even take a shit in peace because you have to constantly watch your back. Imagine not being able to afford simple shit like fucking pads when your period is on. Everything about this is an ongoing horrible nightmare.

"And you can't even fucking cry. You know why? Because the minute you break, somebody gonna try to break you in half. Being fresh meat is a horrible experience. I don't think I've gotten into this many fights in my entire life. You see this?" she asked, pointing at the scar right over her left eyebrow. It was small, but it was there. "I got that from a bitch who was mad about me looking like her sister." She laughed in an unfunny way. My mouth was open as she spoke, and I literally had nothing to contribute to the conversation.

Tanya began telling me how it was to have someone tell you when and how to make every move. How privacy was nonexistent as you showered, went to the bathroom, and lived your life in front of 5,000 other inmates. How she had to fight the women off in the beginning because she was what they considered "fresh meat."

She drilled into my head all the nights that she lay in her cell and cried because she could no longer go as she pleased. How she would never see her son's smiling face. She told me about her fear of her son forgetting who she was because he was only a couple of months old when she was put away.

All the birthdays she missed and her child's first steps. She told me of the pain she was in when she miscarried her second week in jail because she had gotten into a fight with one of the other inmates, and she didn't know she was pregnant. It tore her up carrying around a secret inside of her because she thought I would come back for her, and I had left her hanging in there to rot, not giving a damn what happened to her next.

I shed tears as I listened to Tanya's story, thanking God on the inside that I didn't have to go through such torture. I was a crazy bitch, but not half as crazy as I thought. Tanya was right. I'd be lucky to get through three minutes in here, let alone three whole years. They would have eaten my ass up on the inside, and not in the way I liked it. If I didn't know before, I definitely knew now that being behind bars and being taken away from your family was some serious shit, and I had to do what I could to get Tanya out.

"Tanya, I know sorry isn't enough, and I will see the judge again in the morning so that we can speed up the process. I'll do what I can to get you out of here."

"Monica, I loved you, and you don't know how it hurt for you to do what you did to me. I'm willing to let bygones be bygones. Just get me out of here."

"Tanya, I will. I will."

We embraced for what felt like an eternity as we calmed our wildly beating hearts. We spent the rest of the visit catching up and making amends as we ate snacks from the vending machines.

Before I left, one of the visitors from the waiting room approached me. She had peeped the altercation between me and the female guard and shared her disdain for her. On the way out, she showed me where the guard's car was parked, and we both slashed all four tires, getting into our respective vehicles only after the woman poured a bag of sugar into the tank of the beaten-down Honda. She had already planned on messing the car up anyway because the guard had given her a hard time on her last visit, and after seeing what she did to me, she thought I would want my revenge too.

"That dog-faced, shit-smelling-breath-ass ho. I hope this bitch never starts again." The fly sista in yellow smiled at our handiwork, afterward spitting at the car as if would cause more damage.

"Will they know it's us?" I asked, assuming that the lots had video surveillance. I didn't want to get locked up for destruction of property fucking with this car.

"I had the lines cut last week. They slow asses haven't even noticed yet." She smiled as we began to walk away.

We exchanged numbers, both of us seeing that we had a lot in common, from the way we dressed to the vehicles we drove. Hers was a canary yellow, and mine was hot pink. As if the world needed two women like me. We exchanged brief hugs before getting into our respective vehicles and driving away. When I got to the stoplight, I took one last look at her card before putting it into the glove compartment.

"'Shaneka Montgomery, World Class Photographer.' Who would have thought?" I responded as I sped off before the light could turn yellow, ignoring the thirty-seven calls I'd received from Sheila since that morning. I had to go talk to the judge, and tomorrow would be too late.

Chapter Twenty-four

Monica

Breaking record speed, I pulled up to the judge's hide-away, searching for my key in the glove compartment before I exited the vehicle. Calling the judge before I got there to make sure he would show his face, I popped my trunk and grabbed my duffel bag with tapes of him with several women just in case I needed some extra reinforcements.

Upon entry into the small house that his wife knew nothing about, I frowned my face at the dusty room, opting to set my bag in a corner where I could retrieve it later. Taking the liberty of lighting the vanilla candles I had strategically placed around the living area the last time I was here, I opened a few windows to let in some fresh air to the otherwise-stale environment. From the amount of dust on the sheets I had placed over the furniture, I could tell no one had been here in months.

Carefully removing the dust covers so it could look like home, I placed them in the washing machine located in the shed kitchen so they could be ready to be put back once we left. Stomach growling a little, I instantly regretted not stopping for groceries. I grabbed one of the menus off the counter to order something to eat.

I turned the television on to occupy myself while I straightened up things here and there until the food arrived. A few minutes later, I heard a key being inserted into the door, and the judge's face appeared soon after. Not bothering to greet him, I turned back to my task of channel surfing, deciding on *Wheel of Fortune* and checking my watch to see how much longer I had to wait to eat.

Judge Stenton was a handsome man, not looking anywhere near his 50-something years. The little patches of gray at his temples showed signs of age, but the judge in full form looked good enough to eat. A silver fox for sure. Standing at least six feet five inches, the judge had to bend slightly to clear the entrance of almost any room he entered. Not quite light skinned, but not really caramel, he fell somewhere in between a golden glow and sunset, turning heads wherever he went.

The fact that he worked out five days a week certainly helped, and his use of weights and scheduled morning power walks showed in his legs and upper body. Judge Stenton was well put together, and many women were killing themselves for the chance to have one night with him. How he and I hooked up was not that much of a mystery, but what kept us together was a sin.

Ignoring me completely, the judge walked past me and up the stairs to put away his clothing in the master bedroom. Placing condoms in the drawer next to the nightstand on his side of the bed, he disrobed in front of the mirror so that he could check out his body in the process. Satisfied with his appearance, he jumped into the shower in no rush to find out why he was summoned by me. He was sure I wanted a favor as usual, and he wanted to be right when it came time for me to serve him for it. He knew all too well what I was capable of, and his length grew just thinking about it. I knew his routine like I knew my own, and I knew to be expected to perform like never before.

Resisting the urge to satisfy himself in the shower, deciding I would surely do a better job, he washed quickly and wrapped a towel around his waist before going downstairs to see what I was doing. From the stairs, he could see me now engrossed in *Jeopardy!* and snacking on vegetarian shish kebabs. Walking up to me, he placed his lips on the butterfly tattoo on my neck, surprisingly getting no reaction. Continuing his journey, he reached around to caress my breasts when I stood up as if he weren't even touching me and took my plate into the kitchen.

Confused at first, he stood there looking at me as I walked away. Walking behind me, he caught up to me bending over in front of the refrigerator as I retrieved ice cubes from the bottom of the freezer. When I stood up, his erection was pressed against my back, his full length very impressive. When I turned around, he tried to kiss my lips, but I turned my head, his mouth landing on my cheek.

"What's up with you? Why the cold shoulder?" Judge Stenton asked as I squeezed from between him and the icebox, making my way back into the living room.

"I'm not here for that. We need to talk," I said from my spot on the couch, turning the television off, waiting for the judge to join me.

All hopes dashed of getting at least some head before we got into anything serious, the judge dragged his body over to the couch, plopping down on the cushion across from me, his once very full erection down to nothing. Taking a good look at me for the first time since he came in, he saw the sadness in my eyes.

"What's on your mind?" the judge began as he straightened the towel around his midsection, suddenly self-conscious of the way he was dressed.

"I need you to work a miracle," I began without hesitation. I didn't have time to be bullshittin' with him. I needed him to be on the same page I was. This felt like my last chance to do something right in life, and I didn't want to mess this up.

"A miracle like what? You already know what it's hittin' for," the judge came back, letting me know what I needed to do without actually saying it.

"It's for a friend," I began, choosing to ignore his underlying message. "I need you to get her out of jail."

"What she in for? Murder?" the judge asked jokingly, not realizing how close to the truth he was.

"Yeah. She's in for the murder of her husband. It's been about three years now."

Not knowing what to say, and shocked that his joke was actually a serious matter, the judge sat with a numb look on his face, not knowing how he was supposed to react. After all, he was only joking, and on the inside, he hoped I was too.

"Well, what . . . what happened?" the judge asked, his facial expression showing that he was hesitant to know the details.

"Her husband was abusive."

"And that's a reason to kill him? Why didn't she just leave?" he asked. He had a wife at home, and every so often he had to knock her in the head to get her to understand, but that was to be expected. He didn't see the harm in running a firm household.

"He was abusive to the point where he left bruises that took weeks to heal. Broken bones and shit like that."

"Then why didn't she leave?"

"Because I promised to save her."

"And how, pray tell, did you 'save her'?" the judge asked, trying to get to the bottom of the story.

"I killed him."

The room got silent. You could almost hear a pin drop on the carpet as we dared to take the next breath. One was shocked by what was said, and the other was shocked for saying it.

"And who is your friend?" the judge asked, not really wanting to know.

"You should know. You sentenced her," I stated sadly as I waited for him to search his memory for recognition.

"The Walker case?"

"Exactly."

The judge looked at me for a long time, not knowing what to make of me. He knew I was a freak and pleased him in every form imaginable, but he had no idea he was dealing with a possible murderer. Sweat began to form on his creased forehead. He tried to rationalize as a million questions swam through his head.

"So, you were the one who emptied the clip into her husband's face? Why did you do it? How do you know Mrs. Walker?"

"We were lovers," I began. "She was supposed to be leaving him to be with me. I met him first through a colleague at the art gallery, and I liked him. We fucked often, and he treated me like a queen until I met his wife Tanya. It was like love at first sight. She was a little quiet and a lot timid when we first saw each other. They had just had their first child, and she was glowing from motherhood.

"It wasn't hard to talk him into getting her to have a threesome, and after that first night, she was hooked. It surprised me when she approached me the morning we were leaving the hotel, asking if we could possibly get together for a private session. I agreed, not thinking much of it, but I wondered how far she would go because my girl was a tigress in the bedroom. Anyway, we started hooking up, and she began telling me how she wasn't satisfied at home and how she wanted out. We would hang out all the time, and Marcus didn't know because we would just tell him we were out shopping when on the real we were at my house, eating each other up. Excuse my French."

I went on to tell the judge how we ended up falling in love, and how Marcus became jealous of our "friendship," not wanting to share his wife with the woman he was still sleeping with too. I was really telling him the story of James and Jasmine, but he didn't need to know that. It sounded good either way. Marcus always had a problem with alcohol, and when he did get drunk, he would beat Tanya for things she hadn't done or he thought she was doing, often leaving bruises for me to clean up. Tired of waiting, I went over to the house to lure Marcus away so that Tanya could leave, and I walked up on him beating the life from her.

I recapped for the judge how in that instant, I went back to the day my stepfather was beating my mother in his drunken state and killed her right in front of me. Not being able to distinguish reality from my past, I ran in to help Tanya before it was too late, doing to him what I wished I'd had the nerve to do to my stepfather all those years ago. Before the cops got there, I left the house with Tanya there. I left the gun with her after cleaning my fingerprints off of it, and once the cops got a hold of it, only Tanya's prints showed up.

Tanya and I had an understanding, and when it came time for her to go down for the murder, she wouldn't tell the investigators I was there, so they placed her before the Honorable Judge Stenton to receive sentencing. I left out the part about me falling for Jasmine and abandoning Tanya for the last two and a half years, figuring that was info he didn't need to help her out. I did include the fact that one of the detectives took the gun out of evidence for me after the trial was over, and I sold it on the street. I refused to give him the detective's name.

"So what exactly do you want me to do?" the judge asked, not really knowing what to make of the situation. After all, he had been having sex with a murderer, and now I wanted his help to get my naive friend out of prison. He was probably hoping that I wouldn't turn on him if he declined.

"I need you to get her out. That gun has a lot of bodies on it by now, I'm sure. Just arrest the guy I sold it to, pin the gun to that murder, and set her free. It's simple."

"It's not that easy. We have to catch him in the act of a sale with a large amount of product on him, and—"

"I can set that up for you. To make it sweet, I can get him busted right at his house where he keeps everything. You ain't said nothing but a word."

"Who is the guy?"

"Rico. I know you've been trying to get him for years. I can help you."

"How soon can you do it?" the judge asked, becoming excited about catching a known felon he wouldn't otherwise be able to touch. The police department had been trying to get him for years, and putting him away would surely get him a seat on a higher court. His eyes looked like dollar signs when he turned back to me.

"Set it up for this weekend," he said. "I need to make a few calls."

"That can happen, but I need to know that I have your word on this. She's in jail for a crime she didn't commit, and her son needs her."

"You take care of me like you been doin', and I'll take care of you. My word is my bond, and you know that already. I need to make a few calls. Be naked and ready by the time I get upstairs."

I went upstairs to prepare for the judge, hoping I was doing the right thing. While I bathed, I could hear the judge on the phone, making connections to bring down Rico and get Tanya out of jail. Making sure my diaphragm was in properly, I lay back on the bed, waiting for the judge to join me.

A half hour later, he came into the room full of excitement, me not knowing if his energy came from the case or from my naked body as he pounded into me with an intensity I never felt before. I was thankful that I didn't have to tell him to put a condom on as I watched him put on two for extra safety. I spent the sex session thinking of a way to hook up with Rico so that we could set the plan in motion. This had to work, and I was ready to do whatever it took to succeed. Rico couldn't resist me, and by the morning, I was ready to get rolling on bringing him in and getting Tanya out.

Chapter Twenty-five

Monica

"Wassup, ma. Long time no see."

Rico spotted me jogging through Fairmount Park about a week after my talk with the judge. I had put the word out that I was looking for him, and as sure as gossip spreads, he found me. Not that Rico was a jogger, but drug addicts communed near the park, so that was the best place to catch him at.

"Hey, Rico, how you been?" I asked as I stopped to catch my breath from the mile-long sprint I was engaged in. If things were going to work, I had to be absolutely irresistible, and my body had to be tight. I was thick in all the right places, just the way he liked it, but I had to keep my waistline right and tight.

"I been good, ma. I hear you been trying to find me. Are you finally giving in and becoming mine?" Rico joked as we took a seat on a nearby bench so that we could talk.

"Stop playin' with me. You know you don't want me like that," I responded, blushing, my acting skills in full gear.

"Ma, I been trying to get at you since I first laid eyes on you almost five years ago. You just never wanted to give me any play," Rico came back, getting comfortable on the bench but at the same time watching his back just in case the cops chose that day to take him down.

The cops had wanted Enrique Casarez, or Rico to everyone who knew him, for years now. They could never catch him with anything major to hold him, and everything he owned was in his mother's name, so his papers were legit. Although he lived in the Mount Airy section of Philly, he stayed on the west side where he got his hustle on and made his name famous.

Rico had West Philly on lock. Just about every block was covered with workers making his money, and he knew if he were ever caught, that would be one for the books. He stayed clean, never carrying too much money or product on him just in case he did get pulled over by some hatin'-ass cop. They hated how he was able to floss right in front of them, and they couldn't do anything because half of the police force on his side was on his payroll, and the other half who weren't wished they were. It was like stealing among thieves, and nobody wanted to be the snitch.

"So, word has it that you been tryin' to find me. What's that about?" Rico quizzed, looking me in the eyes. His mother taught him when he was young that when you want the truth, look into a person's eyes when you ask a question. The eyes tell you what you want to know, but I wasn't the average storyteller, and his little trick wouldn't work here.

"Well, I needed your assistance in getting some protection. You know I stay by myself, and there has been someone lurking around the neighborhood, and I want to be prepared just in case he decides my house is his lucky pick one night," I said with a sincere look on my face like I might really be afraid.

"Why didn't you go to the guy you got your first burner from? The one you asked me to get rid of that night," Rico asked, still trying to make sure I wasn't up to any bullshit. As pretty as I was, he knew I had to have some sneaky ways about me, and he didn't want to find out the wrong way.

"He's locked up. The cops caught him for drug possession and arson. He had like ten guns in his trunk when he got pulled over and way too much coke for him to be smoking it himself."

"I see, and you don't know anyone else to get some heat from?"

"No one I can trust, and I knew you would take care of me," I replied, hoping my story worked.

"If you let me, I would treat you like the queen you are," Rico said, sizing me up. He had been trying to get me for a while and needed someone in his corner he could trust with everything he owned. I was already established, so he knew I wouldn't be on no gold-digging type mission. I would be loyal to him.

As it was known, Rico was large, but he was a good investor. He started selling drugs when he was only 19, making a way to put food on the table because his father wasn't about shit. Although he had graduated from high school, he wasn't making the kind of money needed to maintain a household with two other children in it. Burger King wasn't paying that kind of money.

Working for a known kingpin, Johnny Constanza, Rico was paid weekly to run packages and was also given his own cut to hustle for extra pocket money for being loyal to his provider. Being business conscious, Rico put away a portion of his money every time he got paid until he had enough to purchase his own package.

Seeing that he was about making a come-up, he was put on to the same connect Johnny had so that he could do his thing. Rico knew it was only a matter of time before Johnny went down, and he wanted to be put on before it was too late. Soon after that, the man he worked for was snatched off the street, giving Rico full opportunity to blow up, and it didn't take long. He scooped the city up and made major bread off the walking dead.

"Rico, it's not that easy," I replied, happy that he played right into my trap. It was easier than I thought, and I was bursting at the seams with anticipation. All I had to do was find out how his operation worked, and then I could end all this madness.

Keeping in mind the time frame the judge gave me to make this work and knowing they were on twenty-four-hour surveillance, I agreed to let him take me to dinner later that night so that we could discuss the possibility of a future together. Rico walked me to my car and, after making sure I was safely inside, made his way to his Jeep, looking over his shoulder to make sure the Feds weren't on his neck.

On the way back to my house, I called the judge to inform him that the plan was set in motion. Even though the judge and I had a sexual relationship, we were actually kind of close—friends, if you will, and I knew that if anyone could help Tanya out, it would be him. Most people sent up for murder got consecutive life sentences or were sentenced to death. The judge, although he still put Tanya away, wasn't nearly as harsh as he could have been. Friends with benefits were good to have, and I made sure the judge was always taken care of.

Over the next three weeks, Rico spoiled me, happy that he finally found someone to hold him down. Trusting me with his very life, he put me on to how his operation ran and told me enough to satisfy my curiosity so that I wouldn't feel like I had to sneak behind his back. He couldn't honestly tell me everything. He wasn't a fool, but he wanted me to know that there was definitely a level of trust there on my behalf.

Good pussy will do that to you, and Rico found himself getting more relaxed around me and not worrying about the Feds as much. He was slipping up in a major way, exactly how I had planned it.

"Rico, instead of having your money in your house, did you ever think about hiding it somewhere else? I mean, just in case the Feds did come here. You could lose everything. Maybe you should put it in a Swiss bank account or something not traceable."

Me and Rico had just finished round two of lovemaking, and I was wrapped in his arms like he would never let me go. For the first time in Rico's life, he was at peace, and it felt good. He was able to be himself around me, not having to lock everything down before I got there. He left bags of money out, not concerned that any would be missing because in his mind, his money wasn't any of my concern.

"I ain't putting my money in no bank. You can't trust those cats," Rico replied, pulling me farther into his embrace. His manhood was awakening slowly but surely, preparing for round three. At that moment, he didn't want to talk about money. He wanted me bent over the side of the bed with my ass in the air.

"Okay, I understand your apprehension, but I'm just saying, baby, that if you at least purchased a safe, you could keep it in my house. Only you and me would know the combination, and if you were ever raided, I could pay your lawyer with no problem. At least do that for the time being until you figure something else out. It would be a much safer option for you."

As I hit on a nerve, Rico contemplated the scenario I laid before him, not sure what he should do.

"Let me sleep on it, ma, okay?"

"Okay, baby. I'm just looking out for you, you know."

"I know, boo. Now turn over so I can get in there," he replied, referring to my wetness.

By the time I got done turning him out, we were dressed and at Home Depot that night, purchasing a safe to take to my house. By morning, the safe was stored in my living room closet, and Rico deposited a little over $1 million in $10 and $20 increments into the safe. I made sure to keep the combination in a safe place, and after I made love to him in front of my fireplace, we enjoyed breakfast and made a trip to the mall on him.

All this time Rico was buying me little odds and ends, from clothes to jewelry. I would put it up in the hall closet for Tanya. I wanted her to be set when she got home and not have to want for anything. Rico trusted me completely, and on the days he gave me his credit cards, I purchased gift cards and clothes for Tanya's son, telling Rico they were for my baby sister. Not really knowing my family, he went along with it, finding no reason not to trust his favorite girl. After all, I would never lie to him.

Time was winding down, and I had just about everything set up for the bust. Rico gave me a key to his home in Mount Airy and a key to the apartment he rented in West Philly where he did business. I made sure that he separated his money in amounts of $10,000, giving him the excuse that it would be easier for him to keep track of. Rico didn't know that he was dividing the money up for the cops who were in on taking him down. Love will make you do crazy things, and his whole demeanor was in chill mode because he felt that I had his back. With me by his side, nothing could go wrong.

Chapter Twenty-six

Monica

"Monica, girl, wha'chu tryin'a do to me?" Rico moaned as I rode on top of him. He still couldn't believe how he had lucked out and got me. He had been trying to get with me for the longest, but nothing he said or did worked. I didn't date drug boys. Not when there were people in much higher places with much more money. Drug dealers were so bottom of the totem pole to me. I just didn't have the energy needed to slum it with them.

"Turning you out, boo. Ain't that what you wanted?" I responded as I contracted my walls around his shaft, making it virtually impossible for him to speak. I didn't expect him to answer as I continued to work my magic on top of him. I made sure to double up on the protection with Rico because I didn't want any mistakes this time.

This might be the only chance I had left, and when the test came up positive, I knew I had to do whatever was necessary to hold on to this baby. James really wasn't fucking with me like that anymore, and I had to be prepared to swoop in when the time was right. I had to be only a few weeks pregnant since I was sure it happened at the news station, and I took the liberty of scheduling an appointment to my ob-gyn so that I wouldn't have a repeat of the last pregnancy.

Today would be the day. I had Rico spending mad cash on me, and I was doing what I could to get him to take me to his place. The Feds had been watching our every move from day one. They were going to put us in separate cars when they raided the place, but once they drove off, I would be set free. The plan was to bust in on us having sex so that he wouldn't have any guns on him.

My body shook from anticipation. I couldn't believe that I was actually going this far and possibly putting myself in danger of being murdered, but I had to do it. Tanya would be set free upon his capture, and I would be walking away with a nice stash because I convinced him that it was safer to hide his money in my house so that if he were to ever get busted, they wouldn't have everything he worked for. I would be walking away with a little over $1 million, enough to set up wonderful living arrangements for Tanya when she came home.

I didn't want Tanya back, but I figured the least I could do was provide her a lavish place to call home. Hell, she for damn sure ain't want my ass back either, but I owed this to her, and it was only right for me to set her up lovely. The house I planned to purchase was from a guy I knew in real estate who owed me a favor, and he cut me a nice deal on a three-bedroom home in the Overbrook area of Philadelphia. It would be perfect for Tanya and her son and not too far from the other gift that I had for her.

Looking at the clock across the room, I saw that I only had about ten minutes before we were busted, and I made sure he wasn't going to cum until then. I had given the judge a key to Rico's place so that they could get him without breaking the door down. The judge was concerned about me being nude at the time of arrest, but I assured him it was perfectly okay. After all, half the police force had already seen me in the buff, so what difference did it make now? Rico was getting the death penalty, and the Feds had already set it up for him to be picked out of a lineup for the murder by some guy they had paid off.

It didn't matter that the guy didn't even know Marcus. They just needed someone to say Rico killed him. They had a jury ready to go made up of officers on the squad and all, and even the lawyer he appointed was in on it because they were all walking away with a nice amount of cash in their pockets. Rico's money had money, so there wouldn't be any problems dishing out the dough. Judge Stanton would be presiding over the case, and Rico was getting the death penalty by lethal injection as soon as he came in. Everybody would be eating for years off this one and couldn't wait.

I maxed out all of his credit cards in the last couple of days by paying off my house and car note and had him purchase a cotton candy pink Ford Explorer in my name for the winter months, paid in full at the dealership. Rico was blinded by all the attention I was showing him and pretty much did what I said. There was no way this shit should be this easy with him, but Rico was as soft as Q-Tips cotton. I was surprised more chicks weren't getting from him like this. He gave up the bread too easily, but what was the catch? I couldn't quite put my finger on it, but at this point, it didn't even matter. This entire scenario was about to be a wrap.

At exactly two o'clock in the morning, the Feds started entering the house while Rico and I were in the room, getting it on. I had the radio on as planned so that Rico couldn't hear the front door open. I turned the lights off in the hallway so that when they opened the door, it wouldn't shine into the apartment. After the building was properly surrounded and they were in the house, the plan went into action. I pulled him into me, making him explode just as the Feds kicked open the door, catching him off guard. They literally snatched him out of the pussy and caught him completely off guard. His nut was barely out good. I played my part as I screamed and tried to cover up my body. Placing Rico in handcuffs, they let me put pants and shoes on him as I cried fake tears, asking the Feds what was going on.

They took Rico down the steps and put him in the car, and I wasn't too far behind with the handcuffs loosely placed around my wrists for appearances. Rico went off when he saw me being placed in the car next to his. He was trying to tell the cops I had nothing to do with it, but no one was listening to him. As they pulled off, he twisted into the seat, screaming for me at the top of his lungs. After he was good and gone, I hopped in my car and took my ass home. My job was done. I just had to wait for them to get through all of the technicalities before letting Tanya out, but the judge promised me that it wouldn't take long. For the first time ever, I felt like I'd done a good thing, and that should take the place for most of the bad that I had done.

As I cleaned myself up and prepared for bed, a small smile spread across my face as I palmed my flat stomach, ready for a new beginning. Jasmine was going to be mine. She just didn't know it yet.

Chapter Twenty-seven

Rico

I wasn't allowed to make my first phone call for almost two weeks after I was put in placement, which was completely against the law, but those crooked-ass cops wasn't worried about that. My thoughts stayed on Monica, constantly wondering if she was okay. I didn't know if she was brought in, but in the back of my mind, something kept nagging at me. I didn't want to think it because I was truly in love with her, but something smelled like a setup. I just couldn't quite put my finger on it. The thought stayed on my mind well after I went to sleep, causing me to toss and turn at the thought of my love betraying me. What reason would she have to set me up? I had the means to give her a life that she could never imagine. I thought we were vibing, but maybe not. Or maybe I was just overthinking this shit because I had way too much time on my hands.

When I woke up the next morning, I went through the motions of washing and getting dressed, but Monica was still on my mind. The way things went down was just way too coincidental. I would have never gotten caught ass naked like that.

The thoughts stayed on my mind, damn near driving me crazy by lunchtime. When the guards came by to check their cells after lunch for count, I noticed the female guard from the day before. She was always giving me flirtatious looks, and I wondered to myself if she could get me at least one call.

"Excuse me, miss lady," I called to the guard as she walked by. She was sexy as hell, but I couldn't really appreciate it as I tried to make sense of my current situation. The guard smiled at me, looking like she was relieved that I finally noticed her. She had been walking past my cell every day since I was brought to the facility, probably wondering when I would notice her. Yeah, she knew it was against the rules to engage in any contact, sexual or otherwise, with the inmates, but I was the shit. I was sure she could definitely hold it down for me. I had a reputation for being the man everyone wanted to get next to, and I felt like now was the best time ever to shoot my shot. All of the fools behind bars wanted to fuck, and those who absolutely refused to give in to the urges of their cellmates fucked on the prison guards who would allow it. It was common practice, and they all knew not to say a word.

"You talking to me?" she asked as she flirted openly with me, giving me a beautiful smile. She was pretty, thick as fuck, and filled her uniform out perfectly. She really could pull any dude she wanted, but some dumb ass on the street more than likely knocked her confidence down to dust long before now. I saw this and immediately took advantage of it.

"Yeah, I had something to ask you," I flirted back as I got up from the hard mattress, flexing my muscles for her viewing pleasure. She leaned against the bars after she looked around to make sure none of her coworkers were around. One of her colleagues had just gotten fired for getting caught having sex with one of the prisoners, and she was not trying to go down like that. I had overheard a few other guards gossiping about it, and she looked like she definitely wanted to keep this job.

"I was wondering if you could help me get a phone call," I said as I talked close to her ear so that no one around us could hear our conversation. I breathed softly down the side of her neck before catching her earlobe between my teeth, making the guard's panties wet instantly. I knew if I got caught, I would be sent to the hole, but I was willing to chance it.

"What's in it for me?" the guard asked as she thought of ways to make it happen. She was sure she could get her cell phone, or someone else's for that matter.

"What you want? There's only so much I can do in my situation, you know?" I said as I passed the back of my hand over her tight-fitting uniform shirt, lingering around her nipples before making my way to her neck.

"Let me see what I can do, but you prepare for some me-and-you time once it's done," the guard said before walking away, neglecting to check the rest of the cells so that she could put her plan in motion.

Almost two hours went by before the guard came back. She opened my cell door and handcuffed me before leading me to the back of the building, using the cuffs to keep up appearances. Her captain was on vacation, so while everyone was out in the yard and in the recreation room, she made use of the office while no one would be able to see her.

"You can use the captain's phone, but make it quick," the guard said quietly as she locked the door behind her, keeping the lights off so no one would know we were in there. "You have to be as quiet as possible, though."

I was already dialing my right-hand man, paying the silly-ass guard no attention. I knew I would have to twist her back out, but I had to get this phone call before she got scared on me. My partner's phone rang five times before he picked up, each ring sounding longer than the last. I was trying to make it quick, and so was the guard as she stepped between my legs to untie the strings on my pants.

"Yo, it's me, man," I said into the phone, trying to control my breathing as the guard pulled my dick out of my pants and began to perform orally on me. I leaned back in the chair, making it easier for her as I continued my phone conversation. She was giving me some super sloppy head, and I could hardly get my thoughts out. Every time my tip hit her tonsils and she gagged, I had to clench to hold my nut back. I needed to hang in there long enough to at least figure out what the word on the street was.

"Rico, my nigga. Don't worry, baby, I got your lawyer handling everything," he said into the phone, glad to hear from his friend. He didn't know what to do and didn't want to make any noise the night I got caught. He was just turning the corner to go to my place when he saw the law parked outside. Watching everything from across the street, he didn't leave until he saw them put me into the squad car. He heard from the grapevine, not knowing that if he had stayed a little longer, he would have seen them let Monica go, but he didn't tell me that because he didn't have the full story.

"Good looking, man. I really appreciate it. Now, this is what I need you to do. . . ." I continued to tell my partner about the way things went down and my suspicions of Monica. My partner agreed that it sounded like a setup and told me he would keep his eyes open.

In the meantime, the guard went from giving me head to riding me with her back facing me. Ending the call, I held the guard by her hips and thrust back as hard as I could until I finally exploded. Knowing I had just made a huge mistake, I pulled my pants back on, not able to look the guard in the face. I wiped my fingerprints off the phone, and she straightened everything up. We made our way back to my cell quickly, and I lay down on the cot so that I could gather my thoughts. Shit just got heated, and I was not in the mood.

Word traveled fast on the streets, and when my partner went to my apartment and saw everything missing, he knew for sure I was got. Moving fast, he passed word to another partner on my team who had family in the same jail I was being held in. He updated his family member on everything, giving him strict orders to only talk to me about what he heard.

I was due to see the judge in a matter of weeks, but I felt like I was betrayed because I still hadn't heard anything yet. I stayed to myself, not really coming out of my cell except to eat. I was afraid of going down but didn't exactly want to do the time I knew I would be facing. I had been careful not to get caught all this time, making my beliefs that Monica had set me up seem more believable. Philippe was the connect between me and the street, and I had been trying to run into him but hadn't had any luck. He knew I was about to be sentenced, but for some reason, we had a hard time crossing paths. It was cool. I'd bide my time until I couldn't. I was going to end this on my terms, and there was no other way around it.

Chapter Twenty-eight

C.O. Miller

One night, after a poker game, Philippe had one of the prison guards bring a letter over to me, explaining to pass it off to Rico. I wasn't concerned about my coworker knowing because she fucked on Phillippe every chance she got. Her secrets were safe with me and vice versa. I tucked the note into my back pocket, promising I would take it to him before I was off duty. The captain was back, and I didn't want to make it obvious that Rico and I had a thing, or they would assign me to another station or fire me if they found out he got some of this good pussy. I was a little paranoid, but I knew how to play it cool and just had to wait it out.

A couple of hours later, while everyone was in the cafeteria, I noticed that I didn't see Rico in the chow line. He wasn't a fan of prison food, but he typically tried to get some nourishment so that his strength wouldn't be depleted. I was going to slide the letter to him in there on the low while no one was really paying attention. He never showed up, so I decided to go up to his cell block to pass the letter on. When I reached his block, it just seemed a little too quiet for me. Even when most of the population was in the dining hall, you could still sometimes hear something, a hum from a radio or a conversation from anyone who may have skipped this meal. Something wasn't right, and I couldn't quite put my finger on it as I made my way past the empty cells. Rounding the corner to Rico's cell, I almost fell out at the sight of his dead body hung from the ceiling, slowly swaying back and forth, his head in an awkward position.

Screaming uncontrollably over the radio, I called for backup as I struggled with the key, unsuccessful at getting the bars opened. My coworkers had to help me as I slid down the wall to the floor, not believing my eyes. He was dead. How did this happen?

"Sis, you okay?" my coworker who passed me the note asked me on the low, not wanting anyone to hear our conversation. She didn't know all the details, but she knew that I had let Rico hit that one time. She was the one who gave me the idea to take him to the captain's office to make the call. I was crushed and speechless. I was hoping to play my cards right just in case he had a chance to get out and we could work something out.

Everyone was put on lockdown as guards swarmed his cell, everyone crowding the bars of their own cells as Rico's dead body was wheeled through the corridor. I didn't know what to do, absolutely forgetting about the letter in my pocket. I was going to reveal to him that I was pregnant that very evening, but he had hung himself before I got the chance.

I was an entire mess for the rest of my shift, not knowing what to really say. I was called to the captain's office after all of the commotion died down, and it was daunting trying to hold it together when all I wanted to do was cry.

"How did he end up left alone?" the captain quizzed as he wrote his report.

"I'm not really sure. My shift had just started at chow time. I was taking count of the inmates on my roster and noticed a few inmates missing. I came up to do a sweep after securing the bond in the dining area, and when I got up to the block, that's when I found him," I said in a monotone voice that even sounded foreign to me. My lungs felt tight in my chest as the vision of his limp body swaying in the small space came to mind again. The thought was unbearable, but I had to hold it together.

"I have you out on ten days' recuperation. No matter how many times I see a dead inmate, it's still pretty taxing. Be sure to make an appointment with the therapist, and we will see you in a few weeks," he responded, looking at me with sympathetic eyes and then looking back down at his paper. I thanked him, then made a hasty exit to get out of the building so that I could breathe.

Sitting in my car, trying to stop my body from shaking so that I could get home safely, I was searching my pockets for my phone when the note fell out. I had totally forgotten about it and opened it immediately to see why it was so important. My mouth hung wide open as I read about this woman named Monica and how she had gotten Rico locked up in here on false charges. I knew he wouldn't have been happy to find this out, but none of this would be in vain. I knew a few people who knew Rico's people. Whoever this bitch was had better watch her damn back. She took my unborn child's father away. She had to pay for this. There was no other way around it.

Chapter Twenty-nine

Monica

When morning came about a month out from the day Rico was taken in, I was up at the prison in the office where Tanya would be released. After about two hours' worth of paperwork and fingerprinting, we were ready to go. When I saw her approaching, I stood up, ready to receive a hug. Tanya acted like she didn't even see me as she walked past me and pushed the button to call the elevator. I was hurt and confused by Tanya's actions, but I walked with Tanya to the car quietly, not really knowing what to say.

We drove for a couple of blocks before I could say anything to her, not knowing what to expect from Tanya.

"Do you want to stop for a bite to eat?" I asked, hoping Tanya would lighten up a little.

"I just want to see my son," Tanya replied, not taking her eyes off the road. I was sure she was glad to finally be out of that hellhole she called home for the past few years and just wanted to see her family. They didn't know she was getting out, and it would be a pleasant surprise.

The night before Tanya's release, I had Rico's apartment cleaned out, giving all of the furniture and clothing to Goodwill. The money he kept in the three safes he had in his house went to the law, each taking their share of the pie. I pawned all of the jewels after taking the diamonds I wanted for myself, adding another $500,000 to the money I already had.

Before taking Tanya to her son, I decided to show her the house and the car I had purchased for her. Pulling up to the single home, I got out of the car and walked around to let Tanya out. Tanya just sat there looking at me and not budging.

"Monica, this doesn't look like my mother's house. I haven't been gone that long to not recognize it," Tanya said from the seat with a frown on her face.

"I know that, Tanya. This is your house, for you and your son."

Stepping out of the car, Tanya took a good look at the peach and white house with the black 2004 Acura sitting in the driveway. Walking slowly up to the house, she noticed a key taped to the mailbox of her new home. Looking back at me, she opened the door, not knowing what to expect. Upon entry, Tanya saw that the house was fully furnished, and very tastefully, I might add. It looked nothing like her old home that she had lost once she was incarcerated, and she was glad because she had no desire to go back there. Every room from top to bottom was decorated, and I had turned the back bedroom into an office for Tanya, complete with a computer and printing system. I would show Tanya the restaurant I purchased for her the following week.

Getting back into the car, Tanya still had nothing to say, but at least she had a smile on her face. Dropping her off at her mom's, I decided not to stay for the reunion. I was pretty sure I wasn't welcome there.

Once I got home, I took a bag of money from the safe before I went upstairs, setting it by my bed as I ran a bath. After cleansing my body, I lay down in the middle of the bed, not knowing what to do with myself.

Tears came from nowhere as I reached for the bag of money. I took a handful and threw it up in the air, and the money slowly floated in the air, landing on my wet skin and around me on the bed. I rolled around on the money until it stuck all over my body while I cried for reasons I didn't even know. Finally falling asleep, I felt a little peace for getting Tanya out, and I wondered what I was going to do about my and Jasmine's situation. The Cinques weren't fucking with me like that either, but that had never stopped me in the past. I'd be popping up over there to shake things up sooner than they were ready for.

Chapter Thirty

James

"James, you already wore that shirt this week. Why can't you just wear a different one? What's wrong with the one you got on?" Jasmine asked me, tired of the entire disagreement. We had been arguing about that damn shirt all morning, and I didn't want to hear any more about it.

"I don't want to wear another one. I want that one. I told you I had a meeting today, and that's my lucky shirt. Every account we've ever landed at TUNN, I was wearing that shirt," I replied while adjusting my tie in the mirror.

I had since put on a different top, but my irritation at the situation hadn't lessened any. I didn't really care about the shirt. I was just picking a fight with Jazz so I would have a reason to not come straight home. I was meeting up with Monica to discuss "business" and didn't want Jazz to know my whereabouts.

"Well, I don't know what the hell you want me to do then, James. I apologized for not getting the shirt cleaned. What else do you want?"

"I want you out of my presence. The sight of you is sickening me," I replied, still looking in the mirror. I knew I had gone there and was waiting for Jasmine's reaction.

Jasmine had to step back for a minute to register what she had just heard. I had never turned from the mirror, and that pissed her off even more. Before I knew what happened she had taken her shoe off and aimed it toward me, the heel hitting the back of my head with a dull thud. Before I could grab the back of my head, she was already on the other side of the room. She was swinging and kicking like a madwoman, and I could barely get her off me.

"I know you've lost your damn mind!" Jasmine yelled into my face as I caressed the knot on the back of my head. "I don't know who you thought I was, but if you ever mistake me for one of those flunky bitches at your job again, shit will get ugly real fast."

Walking away, she grabbed her blazer from the bed and put her shoe back on before grabbing her briefcase. I was still shocked by her reaction. I was expecting her to snap, but not like that, and I would never admit that it scared me a little bit. Jasmine wasn't the physical type, but her reaction just went to show you never really know a person no matter how long you've been with them.

"Oh, and by the way," Jasmine said before exiting the room, "the five minutes you gave me last night sickened me. Get it together because I'm tired of being a damn actress. I went to school to study law, not to fake orgasms with your trifling ass."

She took a good shot, and that thing hit hard. I didn't get a chance to respond as she exited the room. Watching her from the room window, I saw her get into her Jeep, and I realized after she had pulled off that she didn't have any kids with her. Racing down the stairs, I stopped at the kitchen entrance and saw my angels sitting at the table, eating breakfast while watching cartoons on the thirteen-inch color television.

"Now she knows damn well I don't have time to take these kids to school," I complained as I raced upstairs to gather my stuff up, hoping God would spare me a traffic jam so that I wouldn't be late for my meeting.

Once I got the kids settled in the car, I searched for my cell phone, almost sideswiping a school bus as I zoomed through my neighborhood well past the speed limit. Dialing Jasmine's number, I waited until voicemail picked up before hanging up and dialing again. It took three calls before she answered the line.

"What, James?" Jasmine said, still obviously irritated.

"Why would you leave the kids with me knowing I was already running late?" I barked into the phone, getting even more frustrated by the snail's pace traffic movement.

"You should have thought about that before you changed your shirt four times," Jasmine responded nonchalantly, knowing it would get under my skin even more.

"How many times I changed my shirt is beside the point! You knew I had something to do this morning." I glanced at the clock on the dashboard and the sea of cars in front of me, the scene making me angrier by the second.

"I do that every morning, so deal with it!"

Jasmine just hung up. I, hating not having the last word, dialed her number right back, waiting for her to answer.

"Don't you hang up—" Before I could finish the sentence Jasmine had already fed me the dial tone. Moving to call one more time, I looked up to see my children's school up the block and decided to call after I got them situated. I didn't like arguing in front of the kids and was upset that they had seen me angry with their mother.

After walking the kids to their respective classrooms and giving each a hug and $5 because I felt guilty about arguing in front of them, I jumped back in my car, racing toward the expressway. My eyes just happened to catch the reading on the gas gauge, the red arrow not that far from the E. Not wanting to be any later than I already was but not sure if I would make it to the city on what little gas I had, I reluctantly pulled into the gas station, calling my boss before I got out of the car.

Fidgeting around for my wallet as I apologized repeatedly to my boss, I almost lost it as I remembered leaving my wallet on the kitchen table. Having given my last $10 to my kids, I thought I would go crazy as I searched frantically for a credit card, knowing I wouldn't find one in the car. Not knowing what to do, the first person I thought to call was Monica as I rested my head on the steering wheel in an attempt to calm down. Calling Jasmine instead, I waited for her to answer her phone as I rationalized what to do next.

"What, James?" Jasmine talked into the phone, sounding like she wasn't in the mood for my shit.

"I need you to come give me gas money. I left my wallet in the house and gave the money I had to the kids."

"And I care because of what?" Jasmine came back, not giving a damn what was going on.

"Jazz, come on with the bullshit. I'm not working with a lot of gas here. What's in the tank won't get me to work," I said with desperation creeping into my voice.

"You better take a cab, My trial starts in a few minutes."

"I just said—"

Jasmine hung up.

Not knowing what to do, I began dialing Monica's number. Before I could finish dialing, I looked up just in time to see Monica roll into the gas station at the pump next to mine. Silently thanking God for looking out, I rushed over to Monica, explaining the situation I was in. She didn't hesitate to pass over her gas card. I promised to make it up to her later while I filled up the tank. Not having time to talk, I gave her a kiss on the cheek and hopped in my car, arriving just as the presentation for the new business was beginning. I made it by the skin of my teeth. I knew I would hear it later, but by the time I sealed the deal and had the newest client sign on the dotted line, all of that would be forgotten. Jasmine was going to hear from me later because this was some bullshit, but I refused to let that throw me off of my square. Fuck her for now. I had bigger fish to fry.

Chapter Thirty-one

Sheila

Snapping her cell phone closed, Jasmine signaled me to meet her in her office so that we could talk. I grabbed a pencil and paper after getting her a cup of coffee fixed just the way she liked it. The temp they had in my place just couldn't seem to get it right no matter how many times I told her how she liked it. That was one of Jasmine's biggest complaints when I got back. I stepped into her office, and she held up one finger, indicating she would be with me after she finished her call. While listening, she graciously took the cup of steaming liquid, silently thanking me for the beverage. I occupied myself by drawing little knife and bullet wounds on a sketch of Monica as I waited for her to end her call. Ten minutes later, she hung up, finally able to talk to me.

"So, Sheila, how have you been? I didn't know you were coming back into the office today," she said as she searched her briefcase for the files I had placed inside.

I was glad to be back. Not that the secretary she had wasn't doing her job, but it's smoother when you have someone who already knows what to do and you don't have to constantly direct their every movement. I was like her left brain and always knew what she needed, sometimes even before she did.

It had been a while since I had been to work, and my
first week felt kind of awkward. Now that I knew everyone's secrets, it was harder to look at her in the face every
day and not have the urge to tell her what was really
going on. I wondered if she knew that Monica and I were
still sleeping together. The thought alone tightened my
chest a little, but I kept it moving. Monica could be very
aggressive when she wanted something, and I wouldn't
be surprised if she had her claws in Jasmine still. She had
James sprung in these streets, and I hated to keep that
secret from Jasmine. Monica was always on edge, but I
chalked it up as her not knowing how to express herself
properly.

Sitting in Jasmine's office, waiting to take notation for
a court-ordered child support document, I kept my fake
smile in place while she told me all about how things
were going with her and James.

I wish this chick would come the fuck on. I was waiting
to hear from Monica and was already developing an
attitude because she hadn't returned my call yet. It was
already lunchtime, and I had called Monica's cell phone
at least seven times since eight that morning.

"So, what do you think I should do?" Jasmine asked me
in the midst of her correcting notes for the document I
would be typing up.

"I'm not sure," I responded, partly because I hadn't
heard a word Jasmine had said.

"Well, do you think I should go with the sexy cream
dress or the magenta pantsuit? I look good in either one,
but . . ." Jasmine continued, unaware that I was once
again paying her no mind.

"I think you should go with the cream, but why all the
trouble?" I asked, trying to jump back into the conversation I had missed. I wanted everything cool so that when
I put my plan into action, everything would work to my
benefit.

"Because we said some hurtful things to each other this morning, and I really want our marriage to work. This on-again/off-again relationship is not working for me. I need something more solid," Jasmine said as she briefly listed the latest events that had transpired in her life. She wanted things to be how they were when she and James first got married, but she didn't have the slightest idea on how to get there again.

"Maybe do something that shows that you're trying to work it out. An 'I'm sorry even though it's your fault' gift."

"Please explain." Jasmine laughed as she gathered her papers on her desk. This had to be good, and she gave me her undivided attention.

"Well, what was the argument about?" I asked, again to get all of what I missed when I was ignoring her.

"I forgot to get his lucky shirt cleaned for his business meeting today. He wears it every time he signs a deal," Jasmine said, recapping her morning.

"Okay, since he already decided to wear a different shirt, as a gesture of kindness, add two more shirts to his wardrobe. Men in James's position can never have too many button-down shirts with him having to wear suits all the time. What's his favorite sport?"

"Basketball," Jasmine said, wondering what I was getting at.

"Buy him two tickets for tomorrow night's game and make reservations for dinner at his favorite restaurant. After all that, break him off real nice and put him to sleep. He'll be fine in the morning."

"That sounds good, but when will I find time to do all that? I have to be to the courthouse in twenty minutes, and—"

"Look, I'll go get the shirts and tickets during my lunchtime. Start tonight by making him dinner to see if it'll soften him up a little."

"That may just work. Will four hundred dollars do?" Jasmine asked while searching her pocketbook for a debit card so she could use the machine in the lobby.

"Sure. I'll go over to Businessmen, Inc. and see what they have on sale. Maybe I can find ties to match, too, and I can order tickets over the phone for the game and pick them up before I come back. I have connections, so I can probably get him courtside seats," I said while gathering my paperwork from the desk. I planned to spend the afternoon shopping at Jasmine's expense and would be walking out the door right next to her.

"That'll work. How fast can you have it done? I'll be back in the office by four."

"Are you extending my lunch break?" I wanted to know so that I could cover my ass if something went down.

"Yeah, take as long as you need. Just have it by the time I get back."

"I will, don't worry. Now get going. I have some calls to make."

Taking my seat as Jasmine raced out of the office, I sat down to call Monica one more time before leaving. This not answering the phone thing was making me mad, especially since I found out that Tanya was out of jail. I was under the assumption that Monica and Tanya were together and that was why Monica wasn't answering her phone, and it pissed me off. I should have been thankful someone else finally had her attention, but we needed closure sooner rather than later, and I just wanted to get it over with.

Chapter Thirty-two

Monica

I hadn't heard from Tanya since the opening of the restaurant I had purchased for her. I was too busy trying to get pregnant again by James so that I could put my plan into action, and Tanya was the furthest thing from my mind. The pregnancy test I took already confirmed the obvious, but I wanted to be extra sure this time. It just so happened that I was about to call Sheila when my phone began to ring, and it was her.

"Just the person I wanted to hear from. What's good with you?" I said into the phone like everything was cool. I wanted Sheila to come over to my house when James got there so that we could have the threesome and it wouldn't be so obvious that I was trying to get pregnant by him again. There was no way James could resist both of us at the same time, and he was so damn stupid at this point that it was just easier to remove him from the equation once this was done. Jasmine wouldn't want him after this. I was sure of it.

"I've been calling you all week. Why haven't you returned my calls?" Sheila responded, heated because of my nonchalant attitude. Sheila was probably tired of playing cat and mouse with me and Jasmine, but I couldn't care less. She would be getting dismissed right along with James when this was all done and over with.

I wanted to end this nonsense as soon as possible so I could move on with my life.

"I've been extra busy, sweetie. I'm sure you understand, and I am so glad you called."

"Why are you glad, Monica?" Sheila wanted to know. She sounded so frustrated with me, and I had to hold in my laugh because I didn't want to really piss her off. Sheila liked to disappear, and I didn't need that right now.

"James is coming here later. We can do what we talked about."

"Well, I have a better idea," Sheila said, sure of her plan.

"What can be better than what I came up with? We both know who the mastermind is on this team, Sheila."

"If it were you, you would have Jazz by now, right?" Sheila stated boldly as she listened to the silence on the other end. "That's what I thought. Now this is what we're gonna do. . . ."

Sheila told me about the incident this morning and how Jazz planned to make it up to him. I shared what James told me at the gas station, and I told Sheila how I got him to agree to come over there and the episode at the news station. I didn't tell Sheila I was pregnant because I didn't want to jinx it this time, but I did want them to meet up later.

"It would be better if we did it at their house, Monica. What woman wouldn't freak over that?"

"Yeah, but what if she snapped on all of us? That would defeat the purpose," I said, not too sure if Sheila's plan would work.

"Look, trust me. When she comes back to the office, she'll do some paperwork for about an hour, and it will take her an hour to get home from the city. We could already be there. Just have James take you to his house when he comes there and let him know that you know for sure Jazz is working late."

"How will I get him to go there? He doesn't want his wife to know he's cheating, idiot."

"It's simple," Sheila said, checking her attitude before she snapped on me. "Tell him you're fumigating your house or something. You know he has no money from this morning's incident, so suggest that you go over there. Give him some head in the car or something, and he'll do it. Believe me, he'll do it."

"And what if he doesn't?" I asked, for the first time doubting myself.

"It'll work. You know how to get shit done."

"What time should we be at the house?"

"We should be in the house getting it in by six. She'll be there no later than six fifteen, maybe six twenty. I'll meet you there. After y'all go in, I'll knock on the door like I'm looking for Jazz. If you can, try to keep the door unlocked so that I can come in without him actually answering the door. Y'all should already be having sex. I'll just join in."

"Sounds flawless. Talk to you later."

"Monica, one more thing. I need you to call your man at the ticket office. I need two courtside seats for the married couple for tomorrow night."

"Done, anything else?"

"What's James's favorite food?"

"Caribbean. We always order from this place called A Taste of the Islands that's near their house."

"Okay, that sounds perfect," Sheila responded as her mind raced from one thought to the next as she put her plan in order.

"Anything else?" I replied, ready to get off the phone. For some reason I was a little nervous about how this evening's events would end up, and I wanted to get my heart together so that I would be ready for James when he arrived.

"Don't be late."

I had to give it to Sheila. She showed out with this one! I mean, what woman wouldn't be pissed off at her husband for having sex in her house? I was Jasmine's weak spot, so once she calmed down, because surely she would be pissed, I could get next to her again with no problem. Once I revealed the pregnancy and the plans I had for our future, we would be set. This was going to be so good!

I ran up the steps to get prepared for later today. I was excited about what was to come. I was finally getting my girl!

Chapter Thirty-three

Sheila

After we hung up, I went on my shopping spree, getting James's shirts and ordering dinner for Jasmine so that all she had to do was pick it up later, which would buy me a few more minutes until her arrival at home. After getting an outfit for myself, because why not, I made my way back to the office just in time to see Jasmine enter the building. I came up behind her, and we caught the elevator together as I explained my plans to her.

"So, all you have to do is pick up the food from A Taste of the Islands on the way home. I put the order in and paid for it earlier. I told them you would be there by six to get it so that they can make it fresh closer to the time you would be arriving."

"A Taste of the Islands? But that's all the way on the other side of town," Jasmine complained as she inspected the shirts that I picked out. Satisfied with the selection, she took a peek at the tickets for the game, impressed by the courtside seats. James would love it.

"Yeah, but it's closer to your house, so the food won't get cold before you get home. You and I know there ain't no heating up Caribbean food once it's gotten cold."

"Yeah, you have a point there. What did you order?" Jazz replied while starting her paperwork. By the time she finished noting her files, she would go get the food and be home in time to put the kids to sleep and spend the night making up with her husband.

"All of James's favorites with beef patties and fruit punch on the side. I also got a bottle of mango rum just in case you decided to get creative with the fruit punch . . . if you know what I mean," I responded like I put a lot of work into it.

"Thanks, Sheila. I really appreciate this. You're leaving, right?"

"Yeah, I have to go pick up my boy. See you Monday?"

"See you Monday."

I got my purse and stuck what few personal items I had at the office inside of it because I knew that would be my last day after what would be popping off that evening. I knew I would miss working for Jazz, but this was the only way I could see getting Monica off my back.

Calling Monica once I got into the car, I let her know everything was a go as I dashed across town to get my son and take him to my mother's house so I could get to Jazz's house in time. Everything had to go as planned or shit could backfire in everyone's face.

Chapter Thirty-four

James

Not wanting to take my children anywhere near Monica, I sighed as I came to a stop in front of her house. I'd made plans to be with Monica, forgetting that I had to pick my babies up from school. I knew Monica would have a fit, but I hoped she would stay cool in front of my children. They were sleeping in the back seat, and I hoped they would stay that way until I pulled away from Monica's door. I knew kids had a tendency to repeat what they saw and heard, and I didn't want Jazz to know I was anywhere near Monica. Ringing the bell, I stood outside the door with a sad look on my face, hoping Monica would understand my situation.

"Hey, sweetie. I missed you," Monica replied while trying to wrap her arms around my neck. I stopped her advances and stepped back, taking a look into my car to see if Jalil and Jaden were still sleeping.

"I can't stay. I forgot I had to pick my kids up from school. Can I make it up to you tomorrow?"

"I'm leaving town in the morning. Why can't we do it tonight?" Monica asked, crossing her arms over her chest and pouting.

"I just told you why. Why can't I see you when you get back?"

"Because I want you now. I can follow you to the house and come in after you put the kids to bed. Come on, James, I need you today."

"What if Jazz comes home and catches us? Then what?"

"Have we ever gotten caught before?" Monica asked, getting impatient with the situation.

"No, but now could be the time."

"James, come on with the bullshit. We doing this or what?"

"Look, just follow me and wait until I tell you to come in."

Monica said nothing, just reached behind the door for her keys and locked the door as I made my way to my car. Following me to my house, Monica found a parking space a few houses down while I pulled up into the garage and got the kids into the house.

A half hour later, I motioned from my bedroom window for Monica to come into the house. Monica found me in the kitchen standing by the sink, drinking a soda. She said nothing as she walked up to me, taking the bottle from my hand and setting it on the counter. Walking me around to the other side of the table, Monica began to undress me as she sat me in the chair by the entrance with my back to the door. That was the dumbest shit I ever did, because had I been facing the right way, I would have seen Sheila slip in. They say hindsight is twenty-twenty, but on that day, I couldn't see a damn thing clearly.

"Monica, we have to be quick. I don't know—"

She placed her fingers on my lips, simultaneously ushering me to the chair. I was just trying to get this over and done with so that I could go on with my life. This was my last time . . . for real this time.

I took it upon myself to strip the rest of the way so that we could get it done and over with. The last thing I wanted was for Jazz to walk in and catch us in the kitchen having sex. She would go off for sure. I had left condoms upstairs, but it didn't matter at this point because Monica was already undressed and riding me like the true rodeo queen she was.

I melted instantly as her walls contracted around my shaft, almost causing me to ejaculate prematurely. My kids being in the house only crossed my mind once before I stepped up to the plate. I didn't lock them in the room because if something happened, I wanted them to be able to get out, and normally when they were asleep, it was for the entire night. I figured I would do Monica and get her out of the house before anything serious jumped off, and I would have enough time to clean up and get a meal in their bellies, and we could watch a movie until Jazz came in.

Taking her nipples into my mouth, I closed my eyes and enjoyed the taste and feel of her wrapped around my body. I didn't hear the door open. Just out here slipping! Monica turned and started riding me with her back to me as Sheila neared the kitchen.

"What's going on in here?" Sheila asked as she made her way around the table. I didn't know what to do because even though we were caught, Monica never stopped riding.

"Sheila, you know what it is," Monica said as she leaned back into me so she could take me in deeper. "Care to join us?"

I was at a loss for words as Sheila stood there con-templating whether she was going to be a part of this threesome. Looking at her watch, she knew Jasmine would be pulling up in a matter of minutes, and she was deciding if she should duck out to keep her name clear or go with the plan.

The look Monica gave her helped make her decision as she undressed and climbed up on the table, positioning herself so that Monica could feast. All of her nervousness subsided as Monica devoured her, her legs wrapped around her head and her hands gripping the table's edge. I was so into it I didn't even hear the front door open, and that's when my life changed forever.

Revelation . . .

Chapter Thirty-five

Jasmine

No matter how much you think you are in control of a situation, you can never prepare yourself for the unimaginable. Even the most detailed person can be shocked into speechlessness. I don't even think a word exists to describe what I saw when I walked into my house. James and I had been going at it for what seemed like an eternity. Just that morning, we had an argument before I left about some damn shirt that he said he asked me to get dry-cleaned. I was looking at him like what the hell? He had a closet full of shit that still had the tags on it and he was complaining about a shirt that he already had on that week? Give me a break.

As the day went by, my anger lessened, and I decided I would be the adult and apologize. On the way home, I stopped and picked up a bottle of Red Door, his favorite cologne. I topped it off with a bottle of mango rum Sheila got for me so we could make frozen drinks, and two new shirts to make up for forgetting to put his other shirt in the cleaners. He had picked up the kids on the way home, so I stopped to get my feet done and a Brazilian wax just in case some wild lovemaking popped off after the kids were sleeping. Sheila told me I had to pick up the food by six, and my home was only fifteen minutes away from there, so I had a little time on my hands. I called the restaurant at five thirty to make sure my food was being prepared, and I arrived just as they were bagging it up.

I had Sheila pick up two tickets to the Sixers game, and they were some good seats. He would be chillin' right behind the bench, watching the game up close and personal. If any sweat dripped off one of the player's armpits, he would be able to see it from his viewpoint. I told her two tickets just in case he wanted to have a guys' night out. Wasn't that sweet of me?

Also, I knew that by the time I got off from work, I wouldn't have time to defrost anything to cook a decent meal, so I stopped by his favorite Caribbean soul food restaurant and picked up his favorite meal. Thanks to Sheila's help, this evening would be perfect.

So it was ten after six in the evening, and when I pulled up to the door, I saw what looked to be Monica's car parked a couple of doors down from my house. I didn't think anything of it, thinking maybe she was visiting someone else on the block, taking into consideration that I told her of my plans before I left the office. Monica's car was one you would readily recognize, so it was definitely hers. I just didn't know that she knew other people around here. You couldn't put anything past her, though. She was always on to the next victim.

After parking my car and getting all of my purchases out of the back seat, I saw Sheila's car parked in front of my neighbor's driveway. Now the hair was standing up on the back of my neck, and all of a sudden I felt like something wasn't right. I refrained from dropping the bags as I moved as quickly as possible to my front door. All of the lights downstairs were on, but the upstairs was dark as hell. There was no sign of the kids besides their backpacks sitting in the corner. I knew James was home because his car was in the driveway.

My stomach was knotting up even more as I set the bags down on the love seat. I walked toward the kitchen, and it sounded like I heard voices that were not my husband's. Hesitant at first, because I swore I was not in the mood for any more bullshit, I damn near fainted once I reached the doorway.

On my brand-new oak kitchen table, the shit that cost me almost $2,000 because James said it had "chemistry," the place where my kids and I enjoyed several meals a day, the spot where I hadn't parked my ass yet because I was trying to be a fuckin' lady . . .

The murder scene . . .

James sat in the chair, while Monica rode him with her back facing him. Sheila was sprawled out on my table like she was a dish at the Old Country Buffet, and Monica's face was so far up her ass it looked like she was touching her uterus with the tip of her tongue. James's eyes were closed, and all of them were moaning like they were at a hotel some damn where. Everything in my body came to a standstill: blood flow, heartbeat, vision, and hearing. I was stuck and couldn't move. After what felt like an eternity, I was able to take a deep breath, and my entire body was on fire.

"What the fuck is going on here?" I asked in an even tone that surprised me. My face was as red as a Crayola crayon, and my fists were balled up so tight at my sides that my fingernails cut into my palms.

I scared the shit out of all of them. James exploded inside of Monica from the shock, and when he pushed her up, I saw that he didn't have on any protection. Sheila fell off the side of the table and crawled underneath to stay away from me when she saw the expression on my face. Monica stood looking at me with a smirk on her face that I was so damn close to knocking off.

"Jasmine, what are you doing home so early?" James asked in a "damn, I done messed up" voice as he tried to cover his stiff-as-granite erection with a potholder. The fact that he was still rock hard after busting a nut made the situation worse, and it wouldn't go down as fast as James wanted it to.

"What the fuck is going on here? Where are my kids?" I asked as I tried to keep control of my breathing. I took a few more steps into the kitchen, causing everyone there to step back.

"The kids are cool, just calm down. It's not how it looks," James began in a scared voice. How could it not be how the fuck it looked? Were they not standing asshole naked, fucking all over my kitchen table set? He knew I was about to snap, and I wondered if anyone else could sense it.

"Where are my kids, James? This is my last time asking you," I said evenly as I made my way over to the drawer where I kept my butcher knives. Looked like someone was going to die this evening.

"They're upstairs. They should be sleeping," James said as he watched me pull out the two largest knives without turning my back to them. "Jasmine, just calm down and let me explain."

"You had a threesome in my kitchen with my secretary and my friend on my brand-new table, and you want me to stay calm? My fuckin' kids are in this house, and you want me to stay calm?" I was actually the calmest I'd ever been in my life.

My brain completely registered without a doubt what I had witnessed. There was no unseeing what I just saw. If you don't know anything else about people, please understand that if they *shenan* once, they will *shenan*-again. Before he could respond, I threw one of the knives at him, grazing his thigh. It landed, stuck in the wall. Monica's smirk fell off her face like a tick off a dog as I reached into the drawer to replace the knife I just threw.

"Jasmine, fall back. Why you trippin'?" James screamed out, holding his now-bleeding leg.

Instead of answering, I turned and grabbed a handful of knives and began throwing them at the trio one at a time, barely missing them like I was throwing darts at a dartboard. I wasn't going to really stab any of them, but they would feel my wrath. I just wanted to get out peacefully, knowing if I really hurt someone, the cops would be involved. I did not look good in orange.

"Jasmine, please let me explain," Sheila said from her spot behind Monica under the table. Sheila was scared as shit and feared she would be cut next, especially since she was the one who went and got all the stuff for this so-called "perfect" night. She was the brains behind the damn operation, I'd give her credit for that. She definitely had me fooled.

James tried to get under there with them, but there wasn't any room. Blood was running down his leg, forming a puddle that he slipped on as he tried to join the ladies and get out of my path. He came crashing down on the floor beside them, dick and balls all on display, still glistening from Monica's juices.

I took a good look at them all looking like they were all about to shit on themselves as they cowered under the table. I didn't even have words to say, and I didn't want to hear any excuses. Taking a look at them then around the kitchen, I suddenly felt dirty. I dropped the knives on the floor with a loud clatter, then turned and ran quickly up the steps, not stopping until I got into my children's room. Thankfully, they were still sleeping when I got there because had they witnessed any of this evening's events, I would have had to definitely cut somebody up.

I didn't pack any clothes. I just scooped my babies up and headed downstairs. When I got down there, Monica, Sheila, and James were clothed and standing in the living room, waiting for me. I said nothing as I struggled to keep my tears in, not believing these bitches would do me like this. I trusted both them hoes, and they cut me deeper than any knife ever could. Gathering my keys and my pocketbook, I juggled the twins in both arms as I finally got the door open and prepared to walk down the driveway.

"Jasmine, you just can't leave like this. Can we talk?"

I turned to look at James, then the other two. Sheila looked like she was about to pass out, and Monica wouldn't make eye contact. James looked like he was trying to make himself cry, but at that moment, any love I had left for him was nonexistent. I could feel the ice form around my heart as I turned away and made the long trek to my Jeep.

James knew he was wrong and just stood in the doorway watching me strap the kids in. Monica was in one window, and Sheila was in the other. Proud of myself for not snapping, I got in my car and pulled off. I kept my tears in check all the way to my brother's house by blasting my Tupac CD because I didn't want to hear any slow jams. I didn't want anything replacing the hate I was building up in my heart for James, the scene in the kitchen playing constantly in my head. It wasn't until I pulled up into my brother's driveway that I let my tears fall.

I was a complete mess as I told him and my sister-in-law what I had just witnessed and what I had done to them with the knives. He was ready to go over there with a nine millimeter and off all of them, and my sister-in-law wanted a piece of Monica and Sheila, but I talked them out of it. Yes, I was an amazing lawyer and could spin this any way I needed to justify murdering all of them, but at the end of the day, it just wasn't worth it. I had no business entertaining Monica from the start, and it was only a matter of time before we got here. I didn't think "here" would look like this, but here we were.

I put the kids in the guest room, and then I stretched out on the couch, contemplating what went wrong in my life. There was no way I willingly signed up for this.

Epilogue

Sheila

Back at the house, James and Monica argued as I sat on the side, taking it all in. I didn't know how I was going to face Jasmine at the office, and I knew I could never go back there. I didn't know what I was going to do about money now, and I briefly thought to take a few thousand off the card she gave me to go shopping with, since I never gave it back to her. I didn't want to go to jail for theft, so that was out. At the same time, I was glad that Jasmine found out so that Monica wouldn't have any power over her anymore.

Slipping out the back door as the argument got heated, I snuck by the window just in time to hear Monica tell James she was pregnant with his child. A loud crash came afterward, putting an extra pep in my step. My steps faltered a little as the revelation of what really happened popped in my head. Monica went about getting Jasmine the wrong way, and even if Jasmine were to take James back, Monica was carrying his seed. How were they going to work that situation out?

Shaking my head in defeat, I made my way to my car and pulled off, trying to come to grips with how I was going to survive from here on out. I wanted to talk to Jasmine, but I knew it wasn't a good time to do so. Everything seemed like a dream as I drove on the quiet streets, seemingly moving at a snail's pace. I hoped to never see Monica again, and even never would be too soon.

Monica's Epilogue

Welp, I really fucked that up, didn't I? The plan was to get the girl and destroy the boy, and I fucked around and lost them both. Now here I was looking good and stupid while carrying this man's baby. *What's wrong with me? Like, seriously?*

I almost got out of the house before James snatched me by my neck and started slinging me around his living room like a rag doll. He straight snapped on me, and that shit caught me off guard completely. I was expecting Jasmine to do more, but I promise you the lawyer in her saved our asses. Now, did I expect this bitch to start throwing knives at us like she was in target practice? Nope. And I was thankful that her aim wasn't on a hundred because we would have been done. James got cut, but Sheila and I made it out nearly unscathed.

I barely made it to my car in one piece, and once inside, I got the fuck up off the block as I saw him running out of his front door with a bat. This fool was really trying to take me up out of here, and he barely missed connecting with my back window as I sped up past him to get away. I could see his neighbors start to come out to see what all of the commotion was about. I was so damn embarrassed and pressed on the accelerator harder just in case he planned to hop in his car and follow me. I wasn't above calling the cops on his ass if he popped up at my house either. This shit just got way out of hand, and I felt so damn stupid.

It took hours for my nerves to calm down. I jumped every time I heard a car pass by my home, thinking it was James coming to finish the job. By the time night fell, I was sure that he wasn't coming, and I was able to go soak in the tub to relax my body. As I replayed the events of the day I knew, if nobody else, Sheila's ass was on my radar. How the hell did I let her play me like that? It was cool, though. I was patient. For right now, I had to focus on growing this seed, because the Cinques hadn't seen the last of me.

James's Epilogue

There's no damn way I'm this damn stupid. How in the entire fuck did I let myself get trapped like that? If it weren't for me not wanting my kids to be without a father, I'd already have the gun at my temple, pulling the trigger. What's wrong with me? This was supposed to be a fun thing. How in the hell did we get here? Jazz said she didn't want to do this, and my greedy ass just had to pressure her until she folded. Now my damn side bitch is having my baby . . . again. WTF!

Before I could control myself, I had gripped Monica so quick and started flinging her ass around the room. Sheila was able to dip before I could grab her, because there wasn't a doubt in my mind that she was next. I wanted to find somebody, anybody, to blame for this, but it was all on me. My wife should have been enough. She was enough. I just had to be on some extra shit instead of putting my focus on making us better. No one from the outside can add to your household. Please trust me on this. I was just mad I wasn't able to at least knock her fucking back window out before she got away. I had my damn neighbors looking at me all stupid, putting our damn business, or at least what they could speculate, on blast.

When I got back in the house, I could still smell Monica's essence in the air, and I was irked that my dick started to harden in response to it. She was so damn juicy it was a sin. That's how she had trapped my ass from the beginning.

Shaking the thoughts from my head, I began putting my house together, taking the broken pieces and the entire kitchen table set to the garage to put out for trash the next day. I didn't know if Jazz was ever coming back here, but I knew that table couldn't be here if she did arrive.

Taking a shower and resting on the edge of the bed, I finally just let my tears fall. I had really made a mess of this marriage, and I honestly had no clue where to start to fix it. It didn't make sense for me to call Jasmine because I knew she wouldn't answer, so I didn't. I eventually ended up falling asleep, feeling helpless and just wanting to be left alone.

Jasmine's Epilogue

Fuck James.
Fuck Monica.
Fuck Sheila.
Fuck everybody related to them (except my kids when it comes to James) and anybody who comes into contact with them for the rest of their days. They can all line up on the roof of the lowest building in the city and take the highest leap possible off of it, banging their heads in the way down, messing up their damn spines and leaving them wheelchair bound and paralyzed from the neck down for the rest of their days. Death would be too easy.

I want them to sit in this shit and think about it all day, every day. I pray they can only get one hour of sleep a day, and every time they fall asleep, they dream of me throwing knives at their stupid asses.

I hope Monica and Sheila lose their edges just in the front of their hairline and their hair keeps receding until they both look like George Jefferson clones. I hope their fucking toenails turn black with fungus that they'll never be able to cure and no amount of white nail polish will ever be able to cover it up. I hope they get a yeast infection that's so bad the shit spreads down to their fucking kneecaps and no amount of Monistat will stop the itch. I hope James only has thirty-second erections once a week for the rest of his days. I hope his nut sack swells up like grapefruits and shrinks down to the size of grapes, alternating every other day. I hope his two front teeth fall out and he can't get replacements. I hope James grows thrush on his tongue so thick he won't be able to taste his food. I hope every time he eats he gets explosive diarrhea.

Fuck them all!

I'm so damn angry I don't know what to do with myself. I knew it was a bad idea fucking with Monica, and my weak ass really fell for the okey-doke. I'm a lawyer. I graduated at the top of my class. There's no way I'm this damn stupid. And Sheila? Oh, there's a special place in hell for her. How the fuck did I let the weakest link lead me right to disaster?

Wait . . .

Oh, shit!

Was I the weakest link?

My stupid ass allowed all of this shit to happen because of a mind-blowing orgasm. Lord, I had to do better. It took me forever to get myself together that night, and I couldn't even look my kids or my family in the eyes the next morning. I tried to save face as I entertained my kids during breakfast, explaining to them why they wouldn't be in school for the rest of the week. They loved school, and I hated that I was doing this to them. I crafted some half-assed explanation in an email to their teachers so that they wouldn't be alarmed about them not being there. I needed a few days to get my head on straight and get my heart condition in order. I was hurt and feeling defeated right now, but sorrow doesn't last always, right? I was going to get my lick back on James, Monica, and Sheila. I just had to get myself together.

If I could just give you one word of advice, it would be to say no. Stand ten toes down on that shit, too. If it don't feel right, it's not. Don't be me in these streets looking stupid.

Thanks for coming to my Ted Talk.

The Aftermath

Nobody Has to Know

As Monica felt the pain of the contractions, she wondered if the pain she was enduring had been worth it. She had been in labor for ten hours now. Yup, she was getting ready to deliver the baby that she and James had conceived, and the physical pain from the contractions was almost so unbearable that she began to wonder whether getting pregnant by James in the first place had been worth it. And while she contemplated her present plight, her mind also began to drift back to the emotional pain that she had endured during her childhood and adolescent years. Monica didn't know which pain had been worse, but while the physical pain would eventually end, it seemed like she would forever be plagued by her emotional pain from years gone by. Of all times, why during labor was she thinking about her dirty old no-good uncle? She could still hear his voice as if it were yesterday.

"Monica, open this damn door! What I tell you about locking my damn doors around here?"

Monica was on the other side, fearing for her life as she hurriedly dressed before her drunken uncle broke the door down. She didn't want him to see that she was anywhere near undressed, knowing what would happen if he did. Finally zipping up her pants and tucking her shirt in tightly, she unlocked the door and opened it just as he was about to kick the door in.

"Who you got in this room, girl? Who you tryin'a hide?" Uncle Darryl asked, barging into the room and almost knocking the frail 14-year-old Monica into the wall.

She stood as far away from the bed as possible, not wanting to give him any ideas about them getting in it. She didn't know how she had ended up in this never-ending nightmare, but she knew that when she was old enough, she would leave. In her heart, she vowed that a man would never touch her once she escaped. Not like this.

"I was asleep and didn't hear the door," Monica replied in a barely audible voice, not wanting to upset her uncle any more than he already was.

"Let me find out you lying," he responded with a snarl. His lemon yellow teeth and pimple-filled face reminded Monica of a troll every time she looked at him. "Ain't nobody hittin' that but me, and as ugly as you is, won't nobody want'cha anyways. Get'cha ass downstairs and clean that kitchen. I told you I wanted that done before I came home from work."

"Okay, Uncle Darryl. I'm right behind you," Monica stated, looking around the room for something to do so that she wouldn't have to walk past him.

"I said I want it done now. Move ya ass!"

Hesitant at first, Monica moved by him as quickly as she could, almost running. She wasn't fast enough, though, because when she got past the doorway, he reached out and grabbed her pants pocket, his other hand pulling her back by her shirt collar. He reached into her shirt, fondling her formations of breasts because Lord knows she didn't have any yet. Monica, grimacing from Uncle Darryl grinding himself against her and kissing behind her ear, did everything she could to hold her tears in, hoping he wouldn't try to make her go back into the room.

"Nobody betta not be hittin' this but me. Ya hear?" he whispered into her ear as he continued to explore her underdeveloped body.

"Yes, sir," was Monica's only reply as she made her way downstairs once he released his hold on her.

For the life of her, Monica couldn't figure out what a grown man could see in her. Boys her age thought she was hideous, so she couldn't gather her thoughts on why she had to practically beat her uncle off her at least five nights a week. He would never actually penetrate, but he seemed to get off on just rubbing the head against her, and she gagged almost every time. She knew the slimy stuff he left behind was not supposed to be there, and honestly, she thought the only reason he didn't actually do it to her was because it wouldn't fit.

Monica found herself on a few nights holding a mirror between her legs so that she could look at herself, wondering what he saw different. There was barely any hair there, and to her, it didn't look appealing, but that didn't seem to keep his mouth off it. From her sex education classes, she knew what he was doing was wrong, but who could she tell? Uncle Darryl had threatened to kill her if anyone found out, and her 14-year-old mind believed it, so she just took the abuse, hoping he would just die one day or opt to leave her alone.

She didn't know what to do about the red bumps that hurt like hell when she went to pee, but she knew she had to do something soon because she couldn't take the itching and burning anymore.

Starting to cry, Monica wished her mom were still alive. She was killed at the hands of her lover, and Monica wished she had the strength that night to help her mother out. Her feet seemed to be made of lead, like they were superglued to the floor as she watched her stepfather beat her mother until she was no longer breathing.

When the cops came, this after she had the courage to reach for the phone by the end table, her sister, the baby of the family, was taken to go live with their Aunt Joyce over in West Philly. Her brother, the middle child, was taken to their grandparents' house, and Monica was stuck with drunk-ass Uncle Darryl. She didn't know if she was going to make it out alive but knew that once she did, every man from here on out would pay dearly for what she went through. She thought it was over when her mom passed away. At least then she wouldn't have to worry about her sister's dad trying to sneak into the room late at night and their mom acting like she didn't know. It seemed now that she jumped from out of the frying pan and into a big-ass fire because Uncle Darryl was bold with his shit, and the fight was no longer easy. Uncle Darryl would pay when the time was right. He and every man after him would get what they deserved.